To mum & dad
For the life to live the adventure

About the author

Mark Johnson is a journalist, writer and broadcaster,
born in the beachside town of Kirkcaldy in Fife.
He left Scotland in the mid-1980s, aged twenty, and
made his way south to study English at the University of
London.
He has worked for award-winning news organisations
such as the BBC, Bloomberg TV and Dow Jones
Newswires.
He spent three years living in Dubai and has extensively
travelled the world for work and pleasure.
He now lives between London and New Aquitaine in
France, travelling often by Eurostar and TGV.
He longs for the day when he doesn't have to change
trains to get to the south-west.
Changing Trains is his first novel.

Other books:
The Expat Commuter

1

MARK JOHNSON

CHANGING TRAINS

First published in 2018
ISBN: 9781983982002

"All these frontiers…such a horrible nuisance"

Mr Norris Changes Trains,
Christopher Isherwood

Chapters

1. A guy on a train

I've always loved travelling. Today I'm taking my regular journey from the UK to the Continent for the weekend. The journey starts by taxi - Finsbury Square to St Pancras International.

I love the familiar buildings of my adopted home city, especially in the Square Mile, where I work. Their shapes have earned them odd nicknames like The Gherkin, The Heron, Cheese Grater and just across the river, The Shard. I've watched them go up. I feel part of the fabric of London. I've been here for decades. It's not where I was born, but it's become home. I treasure its internationality, if that's a word. The capital of capital cities. There's nowhere in the world that beats it. But London's not the entire world and it is important to get out often and appreciate other places.

It's a warm and balmy Friday afternoon in July. I pay the driver and stop in the heat of the afternoon sun for one last cigarette before checking-in for the Eurostar to Poitiers, in the south west of France. It'll be another four hours at least before I can have a smoke.

"Have you got a light, please?" I'm always forgetting or losing my lighters. A fellow smoker obliges. We smile briefly as he cups his hands towards my face, pulling on his lighter, a strangely intimate moment with a complete stranger.

The station's busy as I line up to pass through the security scanners. They check everything these days. It's been years since the terror attacks of 9-11 in New York, but travel has been forever changed by this single dreadful moment. Now, millions of innocent travellers continue to suffer the necessary yet undignified security scans at international border points, the only real lasting legacy of the age of terror upon the world.

Of course the killing continues. Only this morning, in the newsroom, we reported 56 dead in an attack on a mosque in southern Iraq. Will the terror never end?

Here in London, we've suffered too. Our intelligence agencies do their best to keep us safe, and the security checks keep us all aware. But it is tedious. Remove your shoes, your belts. Put all metallic items in your bag. Take off your jacket. Laptops out please. I always find myself praying nothing slips through unnoticed.

I enter the vast waiting hall, which is filled with passengers of all sorts, off on their summer adventures. There's a group of schoolchildren heading off on a field trip, all with the same bright red mini-packs. Youthful backpackers, their noses buried in Lonely Planet guides or eyes trained on their mobile phones, lurk in corners or sprawl on the concourse floor against stuffed to the rim backpacks. Flustered mothers keep offspring in check, dads stand watchful over their luggage. Older, bewildered-looking travellers sit quiet, nervous they might miss their train. And business executives type away at corporate laptops, scrutinizing contracts, or carrying on acronym laden phone conversations with unseen colleagues.

We're all waiting for the big, high speed trains that will carry us south through the Kent countryside, under the English Channel and back home to France or off on some happy summer adventure in Europe.

I escape to the relative calm of the Business Premier lounge, a perk I've earned from regularly using the service.

My iPhone rings. It's Michelle, a neighbour in the little French village where I have a summer house.

"Hello sweetie,"- she's always cheerful and upbeat, "Just want to check-in to let you know I'll be at the station to pick you up after eight."

"Thanks gorgeous, that's great." I'm equally cheerful. Perhaps it's because I've just left behind the frenetic noise and relentless pressure of the TV newsroom, at least for the weekend. Don't get me wrong, I love it really; especially when there's a big, breaking story. And it's a real team effort to get the job done. When it works, it's very satisfying. If you're drained by the end of the shift, you know it's been a good day.

"There's a bunch of us heading to 'Basque' for supper.

Will you be up for joining us?"

Basque is one of my favourite restaurants in the region. It's also conveniently within stumbling distance of the old French house I own.

"Love to."

"Great. Weather's fab by the way. Enjoy your trip."

The doors to the platform for the Bordeaux-bound train eventually open and we all make our way up the travelator to platform five, where our train is waiting to speed us away from our normal lives. Platform five is my personal favourite as it runs parallel to Searcy's, the longest Champagne bar in Europe. There's an array of intimate bench seats from which you can savour the best fizz while taking in the grandeur of the restored station and watching the Continental trains come and go. Even in winter it's the perfect stopping off point, because the bar has a cosy secret - customers are kept warm by hot air which is pumped-up from beneath the bench seats.

I make this journey every month, more sometimes, and I always stop to take in the grand vista of the main concourse at St Pancras. I wonder if the other passengers fully take in the awesome splendour of this cathedral-like shrine to the art of rail travel. Perhaps not, in the rush to get settled into their assigned seats? It's just a train station after all. Yet the magnificence of St Pancras, a once discarded relic of the golden age of British rail travel, now lovingly restored and re-energised for the modern Continental traveller, deserves more than a passing glance?

I work hard and have few outgoings, so I allow myself the treat of travelling in business class these days. It's not something I could ever afford when I was younger, so I appreciate it all the more now that I can. Plus, it's a four-and-a-bit hour journey to my stop in the south-west of France. I want to be comfortable and I like the civilised service that Eurostar offers. Dining at your seat on a train as it travels across beautiful landscapes through different countries is one of my guilty pleasures. More so, with a glass of champagne in your hand. There's a kind of unspoken rule about travelling in business class, which requires one to talk in hushed tones, to respect the quiet ambiance of the cabin. It's always calm, which allows one time to relax, daydream or sleep – why not?

I settle into my seat at the end of the carriage. It's a club-style four-seat configuration by the window, but the other three seats around me remain empty. I give a little inward cheer for this small but welcome bonus, which means I can stretch out more, relax more, and don't have to involve myself in conversation with other passengers.

I watch my fellow travellers file down the platform. The schoolchildren march along in a straggly, informal line, monitored by tense teachers. Business executives, scurry along with more purpose, still on their phones, doubtless updating on the success or otherwise of their London meetings. The elderly couples, heading off on yet more pension funded travel breaks, shuffle along the platform, and the backpackers, young and carefree, expectant, hungry for adventure, mingle with the throng.

I'm closer to the pensioners in age now, and I wonder for a moment if people my age will be able to travel so much on our meagre pensions, when we hit retirement. Probably not!

In the crowd I spot one slim young guy, in khaki shorts and a blue t-shirt, with what looks like a new grey-blue pack on his back. He's ambling along the platform, checking the numbers on the train for his carriage. I decide it must be his first trip abroad alone. He's on a gap year, or perhaps undecided yet about college. Whatever, I hope he's about to head off on a wonderful summer adventure. The dark blue sleeping bag and plastic water-flask suggest he'll be moving around from place to place, I find myself attracted to him, not in the obvious way, but more for his air of youthful freedom. I wonder whether I'd like to be that age again. Then, as he passes by my window he looks up, our eyes meet and we exchange a brief smile. His brown hair is cut short, in a preppy sort of style, much as mine was, when I was his age. He's handsome and fresh-faced. Life is yet to write its story upon his young features. He suddenly digs a hand into his pocket, pulls out a mobile phone and answers a call.

I'm tempted to intervene, to leap off the train and tell him to dump the phone. If he's off on an adventure, he should leave home far behind – no mobile phones. That's the point of travelling when you're young, surely? Leave home behind.

Watching him disappear along the platform, phone still clamped to his ear, I feel a twinge of nostalgia. It reminds me of my first solo trip abroad, more than 30 years ago, in a world so different from the one we live in today. Back when I, too, was a backpacker; a young, fresh-faced and handsome boy waiting for a train...

2. Sacked and packed

It was late summer 1985, but I remember it like it was yesterday. A couple of dozen people were standing on platform one at Dundee train station in Scotland, waiting for the 10.19 Intercity-125 from Aberdeen to London Kings Cross. It was a sunny morning, but the station, slightly below ground level at the east-end, was chilly and shaded. I wandered along to the opposite end, where the platform emerges at ground level and benefits from the warmth of the September morning sunshine. I removed the red back-pack from my shoulders and leant it against one of the ornate Victorian pillars that hold up the platform canopy.

The distant rumble of a heavy train gradually became louder until the long, yellow-nosed locomotive glided slowly into view and passed along the platform. I grabbed my backpack and walked back down the platform, to find the standard class coach. The young don't care about travelling in First Class - pre-occupied with a sense of adventure, it never occurs to us that how one travels may sometimes be as important as the destination.

I remember the train crossing the two-and-a-quarter-mile long Tay Railway Bridge, slowly and gracefully, before I found my seat. I looked back at the city I grew up in. 'Yeah adventure' I breathed. I had £600 (a lot of money in 1985) my father had given me to go discover Europe. It would be the first time I had ever really travelled abroad alone and I was excited, scared and full of expectation.

Maybe it's just something you notice more when you're young, but the summer seemed endless that year. Long and warm and pleasant. The perfect time for an adventure in foreign lands. I always knew I wanted to travel, and now that I was here, at the start of a long journey, I was the happiest I had ever been. The smile on my face probably lasted the entire eight hour trip to London.

I wouldn't have even been on that train at all, though, if I hadn't just thrown away my job as an accounts clerk at the Post Office headquarters in Dundee. It all came about due to the management's shock at my turning up to work one day with dyed blonde spiky hair (it was naturally dark-brown in those days).

The human resources manager was a heavy, overweight man, who perspired a lot, had a classically bad comb-over and possibly the worst breath I have ever encountered. Talk about human remains. Anyway, I was summoned to his office to be read the riot act for turning up to work with different coloured hair.

"This is a place of work young man. There are rules. Standards. What's the meaning of this?"

I told him the truth. That I and a group of friends worked as models in our spare time and this involved us appearing in local fashion shows which were organised by a local hair salon. The latest event was a show jointly produced by one of the city's top hair salons - Jack&Irving – together with design students at Dundee University's fashion and textiles faculty. We never got paid, so it was just a hobby, although we got free haircuts and occasionally we were allowed to keep the clothes we modelled.

The HR manager, wiped his bald reddened brow with a grey-white handkerchief.

"You know, if you're lucky, you could spend the next 40 years of your life working here, and retire with a decent pension. Many young boys like you would give their right arm for that kind of career. It's a job for life."

If he was trying to jolt me into bucking up my ideas, he utterly failed. The horror those words filled me with at that moment still send a shiver up my spine today. Forty years? Forty long, tedious, boring years? I sat there staring at him. I knew that one needed an occupation. One needed to work. To earn a living of some sort. But listening to him sum up the rest of my life in this way made me anxious. I saw it more as some kind of dreadful life-sentence for the crime of being young, than any sort of lucky break.

"We won't take any silly nonsense like this here

young man. It's against the rules. If we let this go it'll be nose piercings and God only knows what else next. Look at you!" Across the desk I could smell his acrid breath.

"Now I want you to go away and change that ridiculous head of hair, and have a really good think about what I just said."

It took all my strength to resist the urge to point out his own dreadful appearance. His vain attempt at covering his baldness with a truly grotesque comb-over was absurd almost in the theatrical sense.

I had to battle the laughter exploding from me.

Somehow I managed to keep it together, composed myself and looked him in the eye. By this time a voice inside me was screaming: 'Run, run, as fast as you can – get as far away from this place as you can and never look back'.

"Thank you sir, I appreciate what you're saying, but really, it IS only a haircut, it doesn't change my skills."

"Now, you listen here useless boy..."

"I'm NOT a useless boy. I'm a young man. I'm 19. I work hard here and I'm not as impolite as you, sir. If it's not good enough for you, well, I think there's more I want to do with my life than hide out here for the next million years."

His shock was palpable and his already red face changing to a bulbous purple slightly unnerved me. I was almost expecting him to get up and take a swipe at me from behind his regulation post office grey desk.

How dare I turn down the opportunity of spending a lifetime in a drab and featureless office adding up collections of phone bill receipts.

"Right then," he said, finally, "I take it you wish to resign?"

"What? Really, over a haircut?" I replied: "Do what you like, sir."

"One month's notice. Good luck, you'll need it." We never spoke or saw each other again.

Mum and Dad were shocked when I told them. But I could see that Dad understood more than Mum. I repeated what the HR manager had said about being there for 40 years and the pension, and told them how it had made me feel that my life was already over, before it had barely began.

Dad had confided in me once that, when he was a young man, around my age, he had dreams of being an archeologist. He'd wanted to travel to Egypt and search for the as yet undiscovered grave of the lost army of Cambyses. But life got in the way of his ambitions. Back then, in his youth, in the 1950s and early sixties, I guess there was little time for dreams like those.

So, less than a week later, there I was on the first of what would be many trains across Europe. I smiled, content I no longer had to sit within the grey dullness of the Post Office accounts department, happy to have given someone else the opportunity of that job, that kind of life, that retirement.

Instead, with my new found freedom, I looked forward to crossing the English Channel and heading into what for me would be uncharted territory. I just needed to make the ferry-crossing and be in Paris by the middle of the next day in time to meet Yvonne, who was my kind of girlfriend and who had been spending the summer in France with friends.

After Edinburgh, I grew hungry. Mum had lovingly packed me off with some sandwiches, crisps and soft drinks. As I bit into the delicious ham, salad and mustard sandwich, I tasted everything I adore about my mum – the effort, the care, the softness of the bread assured me she was there with me, her eldest son, travelling into the unknown for the first time in my life. It was her way of saying: 'Go on, have a great adventure, son, but come back, safe and intact, with that smile I love so much'. I felt cherished and comforted by that on this first leg of the journey. I finished the lot before we even reached Newcastle.

The afternoon sunshine gave way to occasional clouds and rain as we pulled into York. I remember the railway museum there and seeing it again reminded me of the time uncle Joe had taken me to visit it when I was just 11 years old. We did the trip in one day - Dundee to York and back - and I was thrilled by the building so big it housed full-size trains, many from the steam age. Seeing it again now, with raindrops dripping off the building, no crowds milling around, no excited children queueing up to see these amazing machines, reminded me time passes quickly, like the train I now sat on, hurtling along its tracks. Uncle Joe died when I was in my early teens. I wondered what he'd make of this trip I was about to experience.

Back in 1985 travelling by train was a quieter affair than today. Although the famous British comedian Ernie Wise made the nation's first ever mobile phone call to a small company called Vodafone that year, the industry was still in its infancy. So listening to the seemingly pointless, half-witted, half conversations of fellow passengers on their phones was an annoyance that had not yet emerged.

Instead, passengers played cards, worked their way through magazine quiz books or disappeared inside a good novel, perhaps set in a foreign land. Others took the opportunity to chat to fellow travellers. Making new friends, exchanging stories and details of where they were heading, was all part of the art of travel. This was how one got to know people in those days. Or you could drift into a half-sleep or lean back and stare at the bustling towns and verdant greens of the passing countryside. The casual, relaxed, chilled-out ambience is not so easy to come by on a train these days. At least not in Britain.

At York more passengers boarded and a couple in their thirties took up the two seats opposite me. I was listening to a cassette on the Sony Walkman I'd received as a gift the previous Christmas. The soundtrack to Simple Minds' *Glittering Prize* was drumming through my ears, but eventually I turned the machine off. I don't know why I did that. It seemed the polite thing to do when more people were boarding. I might want to talk to them. Perhaps I also felt I needed to save the batteries.

As part of my preparations for this trip I was advised by the guy in the camping store, that a 'bumbag' would be a worthwhile purchase, just so that my passport, money, travellers cheques, youth hostel cards and so on could be safely stored in one place – and easily carried when I was out and about. I fished it out of my rucksack while the new passengers were boarding and inspected its contents.

There was the 200 French francs I had ordered at the bureau de change in Dundee. Two fifty franc notes, three twenty franc notes and four tens. The rest of the money for the trip was in American Express travellers' cheques, which my parents insisted was the safest way to travel. The French notes were lighter than the British ones I was used to, but they appeared far more exotic. As well as the French francs, on this journey I would also come to know the Spanish peseta and the Italian lira. In those days you experienced foreignness even through the money in your wallet. You felt like you really were in a foreign country, which had its own history clearly marked out in the denominations of its currency notes. The introduction of the euro in 2002, a single currency for Europe, has changed all that. I miss the old Continental money.

Having finished all Mum's food and drink, I sought out the restaurant car, but after studying the price list, decided I could only afford to buy only a cup of tea. I returned to find a couple sitting in the seats opposite. They introduced themselves as Alan and Elaine, from Barrow-in-Furness. I smiled back and returned the introduction. They explained that they were on their way to Ostende in Belgium for two weeks. They would base themselves in the beachside town and planned to visit neighbouring towns in Belgium and Holland, too.

"Where are you headed young man?" Alan asked.

"I'm Interrailing. Trying to get to Paris first, then, I don't really know. Maybe Spain, Monaco, Italy, Greece..." I trailed off.

"Well that sounds like a real adventure, doesn't it Elaine? We've been to Paris, you'll love it."

Elaine smiled and offered me a chocolate biscuit.

"Thanks very much," I was glad to have something to go with the tea. "Well, the train ticket lasts for a month and I can go pretty much anywhere in Europe. I'd like to see Spain and the Mediterranean coast. And Italy, too, but not sure if there's enough time to do that and also places like Germany and Switzerland."

We fell into a long easy conversation during which they gave animated accounts of their various travels as a young couple and I listened intently, making notes of this place or that, which I promised them I would also one day visit.

After a while, I returned to my Walkman, listening to Frankie Goes to Hollywood yelling 'Relax...', then WHAM!'s *Freedom,* which I hummed along to. Later,

The Pointer Sisters' *I'm so excited* made me feel very jolly, and, well, excited, too. I studied the cassette box, delighted to see that Madonna, Duran Duran, Spandau Ballet, Culture Club and Jimmy Somerville would all take their turn to entertain me as the train sped south.

As the sun began to wilt in the evening sky, the 'Aberdonian' train entered the dim suburbs of North London before gliding slowly into Kings Cross. We gathered our bits and pieces, exchanged addresses for postcards of my adventures across Europe. We wished each other well and they melted into the London crowd.

They were stopping at a nice hotel at Lancaster Gate before the next leg of their journey to Belgium the following day, but for me it was straight over to Victoria Station for the train to Dover and the night crossing to Calais. For a boy from Scotland, London can be a truly daunting place to arrive in alone. We don't have underground trains in Dundee, so the idea of travelling through tunnels hundreds of feet below ground was alien to me and a little unnerving that evening. So different these days, now that I'm a seasoned traveller and I know my way about. But station guards pointed me in the right direction and before long I was in Victoria Station boarding a far less salubrious train than the one from Scotland.

The service was very busy and these southern people looked different to me than those back home. Less colourful, less friendly-looking, as if they were reluctant, annoyed even, to be on this train. I didn't realise that many of them were commuters, returning home from their day jobs in the City. This was a daily event for them, a regular grind which had long since washed away the excitement of rail travel. Unable to identify with these dour commuters, I popped the headphones from my Walkman on and let Madonna's *Holiday* carry me off.

After numerous stops at small local stations, the train pulled into Dover. Most of the tired looking commuters had alighted at the stops along the way, leaving only the holidaymakers and expectant travellers, bound for the cross-Channel ferry. It was cool and dark as we all collected our bags and cases and made our way to the main port terminal building. Once there, I joined the line to pass through the Dover customs hall. This was the first of many times I would need to show my passport. I couldn't afford to buy a full ten-year one, with its impressive dark blue leathery cover. However, in those days you could buy a one-year passport for a smaller price. It was a flimsy three-leaf document, that could be easily torn. I felt slightly ashamed of it. Like I wasn't really an intrepid adventurer. But it was a sort of thrill to present it that first time. 'Yes, look, that's me in the photo. I'm off abroad on my own. So there!'.

After passport control, everyone gathered in the large departure room. Were we still officially in Britain? Of course we were still on the island, not even on the boat yet. But was the waiting area a sort of international territory where one is neither here nor there? If so, I wondered, which rules applied.

Hours later, the midnight Sealink ferry crossing got

underway. I was starting to wane, but I still made it up to the top rear deck to watch the White Cliffs of Dover – and therefore Britain – recede under a moonlit sky. "This is it", I remember thinking, as the tiredness crept through me. "It's all new from here on in."

A feeling of melancholy crept up on me. I wondered if I could face telling Yvonne that I was uncertain of my life and that I might prefer boys. She was special to me and I didn't want to hurt her. Alone on the rear deck I took a big deep breath. I had really tried to fit into being the way the world wanted me to be, but, watching my homeland disappear into the darkness, it felt time for that world to change. How would she react? Would she hate me? The tiredness took over and I turned away from the cliffs, and Britain, and went inside to find a seat and grab some shut-eye during the two-hour crossing.

* * * * *

"Bonjour monsieur, would you like somzink to drink, peer-aaps some champagne?" I'm jolted back to the present by an attractive, smiling Eurostar cabin crew hostess, standing before me in her pristine charcoal and yellow uniform, her palm upturned, pointing to the drinks trolley.

"And 'ere is your menu, sir, for ze meal, shortly." She says. Her accent is welcoming and her English excellent.

"Oui, merci, thank you. Champagne would be lovely."

We're coasting through the access tunnel outside St Pancras which takes us under the whole of London to the Kent countryside. It's the one thing I don't like about the new station. When Waterloo International was the home of Eurostar in London, the departure and arrival was a far grander affair. I loved the way the train glided gracefully past Battersea and along the river Thames, through Vauxhall and the great views of the Houses of Parliament, the London Eye and finally into Waterloo. It felt like you were arriving at the heart of a great city.

Grand though St Pancras International is, it doesn't offer the same sense of arrival or departure. The big long tunnel deprives you of wonderful views of the suburbs and the views of the heart of the city. I was on the last train to Waterloo before the service made the switch and I remember feeling sad that Waterloo International's days for now at least were over.

But soon enough, we pull into the sunny open fields of Kent. I take a sip of my champagne and settle back into my seat. I decide on the Dover sole (nothing like a sense of place) with a lemon and tarragon sauce, together with pomme noisettes and mange touts. It reminds me how different things were on that first morning in Calais after the midnight ferry crossing.

* * * * *

3 France: Spies on a train

It was damp and misty when the Sealink ferry arrived in Calais that September morning and dawn was yet to break.

Along with the other foot passengers, I disembarked and followed the signs to the waiting douanes. We were channelled to the platform for our Paris-bound train.

I'd managed to get a little sleep on the Sealink, but I was still bleary-eyed at this ungodly hour of the morning. My tummy was rumbling too. I ambled along the platform, vainly looking out for a little station café or at least a vending machine offering some nourishment for a few francs. I was out of luck.

It became lighter and through the morning haze, I spotted the rear-end of a coach reversing into view, being shunted along with all the other carriages of the train by an as yet unseen engine at the front. It was tediously slow, but finally we were all clambering aboard and finding our allotted seats for the four-hour ride to the Gare du Nord in Paris.

I headed off to the buffet car. I was famished! But, as

I walked along the narrow corridors of the SNCF train, I became distracted. There I was, my first morning in a new country! These new sights, smells, scenes all began to hit me! The carriages: far superior to anything I had seen in Britain. Even in standard class, sturdy, shiny, steel handrails all along the window of the side corridor allowed me to keep my balance as the train hurtled through the Normandy countryside. The strong glass and steel doors to the compartments swished open with ease and were so clean I almost buffed my fingerprints off them afterwards. The comfy seats, in differently coloured soft leather, reclined– even in standard class. There were pretty, patterned curtains on both sides of the compartments, providing shade and privacy from passers-by in the corridors. Why didn't we have exciting, cared-for, dignified trains like this in Britain – the birthplace of rail travel?

Wandering along those corridors was to my young mind like being in a scene from one of those European spy thrillers from the seventies, only it felt more real, more dangerous. I noticed a smartly dressed lady in one compartment, sitting alone. Her blonde hair neatly tied back, perfect makeup on her pale skin – she looked very foreign, perhaps German. I imagined she might be a secret agent, on her way to some important rendezvous in Paris. She would meet her contact in a quiet corner of a busy café just across from the Gare du Nord, where she'd be passed, surreptitiously, some top-secret document or microfilm in a small case. The exchange successfully executed, they'd wait a few moments. She'd get up alone and leave, hailing a taxi outside the café, and make her way to the Gare de Lyon and some other train back to Germany. Then her handlers would guide her beyond the Berlin Wall, to safely deliver the contents of the microfilm to a foreign Communist government, keen to learn the latest defence plans and secrets of the West.

I arrived unchallenged in the First Class section of the long train. In one compartment sat an elderly man with a short salt and pepper beard. His dark, heavy coat seemed out of place for the warm season and he looked shifty, sitting there smoking and glancing at his watch. He eyed the man in the smart pin-striped suit opposite, who, with his face buried in a copy of *Le Monde*, was unaware of these furtive attentions. A third passenger, a wiry-haired old lady, dozed in the opposite corner, her grey cardigan and dull tartan skirt the pattern of which is interrupted by the book - whose title is written in a language I cannot comprehend – resting, open, in her lap. The grey-bearded man in the corner spotted me. Startled, I moved on quickly, wondering if I'd just witnessed the early overtures of a real-life scene from *The Lady Vanishes*.

At the front end of the train, I had to acknowledge there was no buffet car. My hunger still banging on the walls of my stomach, I returned, noticing in another compartment a sole occupant. He looked British. His hair struck me as odd. He seemed too old to have such a strong, full, crop. He sat upright, stiff. One leg crossed over the other, smoke filling the compartment as he dragged on a cigarette. I noticed a tan leather suitcase on the floor beside him, with his name etched in capitals

29

next to the handle, "NORRIS'. He seemed prim, from a bygone age. Somehow sad, yet doubtless full of stories.

I stopped and looked out the window for a bit. The rooftops of houses in the passing villages were orange/red terracotta. I hadn't seen such brightly coloured tiles before. The distinctive terracotta finish, baking in the morning sunshine, looked warm and exotic, so different from the land I grew up in. A motorway swung into view and I realised that the vehicles were being driven on the right side, as opposed to the left, as back in Britain. My senses were slowly absorbing all these foreign differences. But having noticed this major variance in the road networks of the UK and the Continent, I was then surprised to see that the very train I was travelling on was on the left side of the mainline track – the same side that British trains use While I mused over this, 'Mr Norris' emerged from his cabin, closing the door behind him. He stood for a moment, then started towards me. When he passed me he made an awkward struggle of it, pressing against me, apologising and grunting slightly.

"Bloody nuisance, these trains, eh?" He uttered, rolling his eyes upwards. When he disappeared into the toilet at the end of the carriage I sensed his head momentarily popping from behind the door, looking back at me. I kept looking straight out the window, thinking 'no way, old man'.

Later, I too had to use one of the toilets in the first class carriages. The sheer size of the convenience was luxurious. Almost a cabin in itself, I thought – BR passengers could only dream of such space for their ablutions.

Finally, I reached my compartment and closing the glass door, threw myself into one of the seats by the far window to enjoy the gentle cool of the air conditioning. A figure was now sitting in the opposite corner by the door, a woman I imagined to be in her early thirties.

"Pardon," I said to her, "Anglais?" My French was not great back then, but I knew some of the basics. I'd started out doing well at French in school, but they lost me at the point where all the irregular verbs came in. Now I had only a spattering of words to get by on, I wished I'd stuck with it.

She smiled a jocular affirmation: "Yes, I am."

"Oh great. Do you know if there's any food on the train? I've gone right to the end and can't find any buffet carriage."

"Mmm, it's probably because it's the first train from Calais to Paris. Too early for them. I think you may have to wait."

My heart sank.

"I've got some fruit, would you like an apple?"

I smiled back and nodded gratefully.

"Thanks, I feel so stupid. I should've brought more supplies, but I ate all the stuff mum made for me yesterday Didn't think to get more."

"Here," she said handing me a perfectly green and

31

tasty looking Granny Smith. "And I've got some tea too."

She pulled a decent-sized flask from her travel bag.

"Hold this," she said, as she fished out two little plastic cups, then gently slid the large expensive looking duffle-weekender to one side with her foot.

While I crunched my way through the apple, she put down the sheets of paper she had been leafing through earlier, took a sip of her tea and looked at me.

"Where are you going?" she asked. Then: "Are you meeting up with friends?"

She wanted to know how long I would be travelling for? Where was I from? What did I do for work? I happily answered all her questions. It was a small price to pay to satisfy my hunger.

By the time we were hurtling past Lille, it was my turn to interrogate her. I discovered she was a foreign correspondent for Reuters. That explained all the questions. She could see I was impressed. I told her this was a career I would maybe like to follow one day and started asking her how one became a journalist. Were there any positions for someone like me at Reuters? (I'd need a job once I returned from my European travels). What are the main qualities required? Why was she on a train at such an early hour? Was she by any chance on the trail of some dangerous spies who'd stolen some of our top military secrets?

"Because if you are," I said lowering my voice to a

near whisper, "there are a few people on this train I could point out to you as possible suspects straight away."

She laughed. "Nothing so exciting or glamorous, I'm afraid. I'm a maritime reporter. But I'm sure the whole train is full of foreign agents." She winked at me.

"I'm going to Paris to try to arrange an interview with Jean-Louis Michel. Do you know who he is?"

I didn't have a clue.

"He's a French oceanographer and part of a team that has just found the wreck of the Titanic."

"Wow, the Titanic? That's amazing – they've really found it?"

Another adventure in another age. A big one which ended in terrible tragedy. You never know when you set off on a voyage or journey quite how it will end. Most of us travel without incident, but none of us do so without some kind of risk. I looked out of the window, thinking of all those poor souls who suffered on that fateful liner. There is danger in every adventure. This could not be denied. There, but for the grace of God, go I.

She gave me a soft and understanding smile.

"You're thinking about all those adventurous people on the Titanic, aren't you?

I nodded. She brushed away the length of wavy copper hair that had fallen across her face and took a long intake of breath.

"That's good. We haven't forgotten them either. That's why we're interested in the story. It could happen to any of us."

"So I'm off to spend some time in Paris to do all the research and report back. I'll be interviewing some of his colleagues. And hoping to interview the man himself"

"Good luck. I hope you find out all about it, so you can tell the world." I finished off my apple and listened to the intrepid Reuters reporter tell me about some of the other stories she'd worked on recently. Every now and then I would ask a question of her.

"So how did they know it was gardener?"

"Who was responsible for that?

"What's going to happen next?"

Looking back, she must have thought I was so naïve. The truth is, I was.

Soon we were coasting past the sunlit suburbs of northern Paris. I looked out at the neighbourhood houses, which eventually gave way to taller, slim tenements, with their long windows and petite balconettes. Double decker commuter trains ran alongside us or sped passed in the opposite direction. Rows and rows of electric cables busied the skyline and the siding walls were covered in graffiti. It was more industrial than I had expected. When the train slowed to enter the Gare du Nord terminus, Janet wished me well and promised I would have many adventures.

"Just keep an eye out for those spies though" she said,

winking, "Britain needs you."

* * * * *

"Monsieur, vous faites un choix?" The Eurostar attendant is smiling over at me from the lunch trolley.

"The fish please."

"And some wine with your meal?" She asks, flipping into English for my benefit. A white Bordeaux I think. How comfortable and looked after I am. The sun is shining and we'll enter the Chunnel in a few moments. I tuck into the salad starter and then the sole.

Across the aisle, a woman is trying to work on her laptop while negotiating a place for her lunch tray. Her mobile phone jingles a horrible ringtone and she struggles to answer it, among the other tasks she is trying to complete. The stewardess assists by moving her laptop further back on the table, her helpful but silent way of saying 'stop all this multitasking and take time out for your lunch, madame'.

"Yes? Yeah, hi, sorry, bit busy here, and I think we're about to enter the Tunnel, so I may lose you..."

"Please do," I whisper to myself.

"Yep, got the mail, meeting arranged for 5.30. I'll head straight there soon as we get into Paris..."

Suddenly, daylight is extinguished and the sounds around us change as the train glides effortlessly into the Channel Tunnel. The passenger looks at her phone, sighs and puts it down and picks up her fork at last.

* * * * *

4. City of love

No one forgets their first visit to Paris. I stepped down from the train and walked along the platform at Gare du Nord to the main concourse. It was a warm, sunny, Saturday morning in September 1985, I was in my day-old travelling clothes with rucksack on my back and a big smile across my face. It is a memory that will stay with me forever.

Everything was new, foreign, exciting. I was buzzing, thrilled with the new and the undiscovered. Until this moment my world had been a small place; the neighbourhood; provincial life; a short walk to school, a bland bus ride into town for work. A place where most public spaces were quiet on weeknights, where the shops closed on Sundays. Even the post office closed for the half-day on Wednesdays. But that morning I witnessed a whole new world.

The sounds of the station filled my ears. A series of unfamiliar musical notes preceded a voice on the station tannoy system. All I could understand was 'mesdames et messieurs', then something about 'Rotterdam'. Whistles blew on different platforms and people around me were speaking French and many strange languages. Occasionally I heard familiar English voices, and others with American accents. This, I thought, is the world. This is it. I have found where I am, and where I want to be.

The air was intoxicating, a heady mix of coffee, perfume and tobacco blending with the smell of trains that all train stations have. Every time a French lady passed by, I inhaled a delicious new fragrance. My mother is a lifelong devotee of "White Linen" by Estée Lauder, and the occasional whiff of that gave me a chance to bathe in some warm familiarity in this oh so foreign setting. Tobacco flavours I'd never known took precedence over the sweet perfumes and the coffee. They hung in the air like a stagnant mist, but I loved it. I still had some of the cigarettes I'd left Scotland with, but I wandered over to the little kiosk in the middle of the station concourse and bought a packet of Gauloises. It was my first contact with French culture..

"Un paquet de Gauloises s'il vous plaît," I mumbled to the vendor in embarrassed 'O' level French pointing with one hand.

Yvonne and I had agreed the best place to meet: under the grand Arc de Triomphe at the top of the Champs Elysées. So I headed out of what looked like the front exit to the station. The warm September sunshine hit me and I smiled, taking in the scene outside the faded grandeur of the Gare du Nord's main facade. Taxis came and went, picking up and setting down. The place was teeming with people coming and going in every direction, while across the street, the 'Bar du Nord' was filled with customers, both travellers and locals, drinking coffees, or little glasses of spirits – a late morning tipple, why not? I walked around looking at everything and everyone at once. All my senses were being assaulted. The smell of sweet sugar drifted past from a vendor selling what looked like warm nuts; freshly brewed coffee announced itself every time I passed a café. The occasional, slightly unpleasant, odour of piss wafted out from an alleyway here and there. Patisserie windows dazzled with fantastical displays of desserts of every colour, and the sight and smell of freshly made baguettes and croissants from the boulangeries wrapped me in a nourishing blanket. I'd only seen images like this in films or read about them in books, but now I was in the scene, part of it, with the added bonus of being able to smell it all, too. These were real Parisians, real Europeans, going about their business in one of the world's most fabled cities. It may have been an ancient wonder but Paris was as fresh and new as anything my young eyes had ever experienced.

I stopped a policeman and asked for directions to the Arc de Triomphe. He stared at me with a puzzled look upon his face.

"Mais jeune homme, il est très loin. Marches-tu? Pourquoi ne pas prendre le Métro?"

I didn't understand a word. So I gestured with my arms to the various streets and raised my eyebrows. "This way? Or that way?"

"Ok - c'est comme ça tout droit. Continuez comme ça. Bon courage monsieur."

'Continuez comme ça'. Keep going that way.

"Continuez comme ça, okay, cool thanks. Merci."

I set off.

The streets around the Gare du Nord were vibrant and bustling. It wasn't what I'd call a rich area, but it was grand, nonetheless. The tenement apartment blocks, were, to my ignorant eye, fantastic creations, with large windows leading to petite balconies with small steel railings from which the residents could casually lean out on to watch the passing street life below.

On the third floor of one apartment block, I spied a woman of African origin hanging out her 'smalls' on the tiny washing line she had connected to the little railings, between the two balconies of her apartment. She looked up and down the street, briefly catching my eye. I smiled up at her, but she didn't return the sentiment. Further along the street, a French guy, probably only a couple of years older than I, was leaning against the frame of his apartment window on the fifth floor, casually smoking a cigarette. He was topless and his body was slim, muscled and tanned. He looked chilled out basking in the warm sunshine.

It turned out to be a five-kilometre trek to the Arc de Triomphe. Along the way, I passed street signs from the folklore of Paris culture known throughout the world. One, pointing left, indicated I was near the "Folies

Bergère", then another, the "Boulevard Haussmann", which I knew from the Grace Jones song "I've seen that face before", and which I had in my travel music. The "Statue de Jeanne d'Arc", and countless street names I somehow knew, like the "Saint-Lazare","Rue Laffitte", and, as I drew closer to my rendezvous point, the "Champs Elysées".

Boulevard Haussmann eventually became the Avenue de Friedland and then the massive structure that is the Arc de Triomphe began to come into view - my first truly famous French sight! With renewed energy, I marched on, increasingly struck by the sheer size of the arch the closer I got.

Once I had reached the edge of the Place de l'Étoile it became clear that actually getting to the arch presented a problem. Surrounding the island is a wide circular road where cars, buses, lorries and motorbikes jostle for space in a seemingly random, highly dangerous game of automotive Russian roulette. I stood for ten minutes trying to figure out how to cross this wide road with endless traffic coming on and off from all directions. It was chaos. I was sure an accident was inevitable at any moment. But somehow the vehicles managed to avoid smashing into each other. In the end, I decided to gird my loins, found a momentary gap in the mayhem and made a dash for it. It wasn't the smartest move. I got across two lanes before cars appeared from nowhere to my left and came screeching to a halt. I managed to get a metre or so further before almost being squashed between a car and a bus. Then a whole row of cars on the inner lanes appeared to stop for me. I ran for my life, not noticing that they were actually giving way to other cars coming onto the massive roundabout from behind me. Suddenly, I did notice the real reason they had all stopped. So, whilst I couldn't understand why they would want to let yet more vehicles to come onto the already chaotic merry go round, I darted for the safety barrier on the arch island and hurtled myself, backpack and all, over it. It was petrifying!

Exhausted, I dumped my heavy bag and leaned against one of the decorative, stone monoliths of the arch. 'Whew!'

As I recovered from this near death experience at the hands of Paris motorists, I noticed that my Levi jeans had become a little heavy after almost two days of travelling in them. I really wanted to change into some fresh clothes. I could also do with a shower and hoped Yvonne would arrive soon to take me to the youth hostel.

Whilst lingering around the arch, I became conscious that I was being eyed up by some shifty-looking people hovering around the popular tourist attraction. I wasn't too bothered, but something in my gut told me they weren't just curious about my pale skin, my different 'look', my unusual clothes – my otherness. In Scotland, if one stares too long at someone, they make a beeline for you and ask you what the hell you think you're looking at, usually only after they've head-butted you and drawn blood. Here on the arch, though, they were begging for money and circled around other tourists as well. I ignored them.

I lit a cigarette and pushed a puff of smoke out into the warm air, and, as it dispersed, I caught my first glimpse of Yvonne's long blonde hair. I heaved a sigh of relief. From the shadows appeared her slim body, in a short black skirt and a mariner-style, striped t-shirt. We had met when I was on a visit to London two years before. She had a new, confident, sexy stride - it was impressive. Usually, I like beauty, style, grace and confidence, but I felt a twinge of dread, knowing that I needed to tell her something that might taint that confidence. She was also warm and honest, intelligent, fun and happy. In Paris she seemed to have become more alive, more free – was it because her parents were not around? Was it Paris? Could this great city of love instantly transform us into more exotic versions of our usual selves? I hoped so. She strode towards me, like a top model on a Paris catwalk. It was a picture, so I banished my doubts for now.

We ran the last few steps; I grabbed her up in a swirling hug that said 'you're gorgeous and you're mine'. It was the perfect way for lovers to meet in Paris. We kissed a long kiss on that island.

Eventually, she pulled her face back and smiled, confidently. "Hey cool guy, you made it. How are you?"

"Great thanks, kiss me again". I like kisses. I like them a lot and I wanted more from her. And I wanted to completely bury any trace of my earlier thoughts.

She smiled an easy laugh and cheekily snatched my

43

sunglasses from my face, saying "I'll carry these darling, they look heavy AND very now. Are you alright with the rest?"

"Yes gorgeous."

Hand in hand we moved off into the dazzling afternoon sun, hand in hand. She suggested we walk for a bit, "because Paris is a city you walk in". My tiredness was gone for now, overtaken by the rush of seeing Yvonne and being in a fantastic new world, the backpack suddenly weighing almost nothing on my young lean body.

As we wandered down the Champs Elysées, I told Yvonne about my walk from the Gare du Nord.

"What? You've walked all the way from the station? Why didn't you take the Metro?"

There was a Metro? I shrugged and we laughed. Yvonne started her commentary on Paris.

"Where you arrived at the Gare du Nord is the tenth arrondissement, it's a bit edgy. There are a lot of immigrants from North Africa who live there. I love the colours and the smells of that area."

"It looked great to me," I said, not entirely sure what she meant by 'arrondissement'.

"Yeah, but you don't want to head up here after sundown, it's a bit weird and can be dangerous. I've heard so many stories of people being robbed and mugged up there." She told me about a couple of American backpackers from the hostel she was staying at who had got into trouble with drug dealers around there after trying to score marijuana.

"One of the guys was stabbed, and they cut his face open from the edge of his lips all the way up each side of his face."

It was a gruesome tale, not one I really wanted to hear, having just arrived in my first foreign city.

We carried on, meandering through central Paris as Yvonne went on about the arrondissements.

I still had no idea what an arrondissement was, so I stared sideways at her, a 'what are you talking about' look on my face.

"Oh come on, you. Did you do any kind of reading up like I suggested?"

As I followed her, I realised I was now totally lost, disoriented, at the mercy of Paris. And I didn't care. I was a sponge, soaking up every second of this new culture. The beautifully organised tree-lined Elysées, with its wide pavements and rows of large fronted shops; the cars, mopeds and buses darting along the roads, were a dream to behold for an idle spectator like me.

The buildings, the streets and the people left me not knowing where to look next. It was exhilarating! I was changing from local boy to global citizen. I was filled with the sense of where I had come from and how small that place back home now seemed in the grand scheme of things. And this was only Paris, day one.

To be fair, my home town has a rich history of its

own. It was a key centre in the development of the industrial age. Dundee rapidly grew into a Mecca for spinning flax shipped in from India into canvas, which was then packed off to America - talk about being a global city. It's also home to *Discovery*, the ship that Captain Scott sailed to the North Pole. And it was once known as the home of the three J's – jute, journalism and jam. But all that faded away as Paris took hold of my senses, gripping my imagination with every step.

"We're in the Marais now," Yvonne said. "This is the centre of all the fun. Loads of great bars and cafés. All the beautiful people of Paris hang out in this area."

She didn't need to tell me. Everywhere I looked, there were stunning, exotic, classic, edgy, divine and just plain drop dead gorgeous examples of humankind going about their business. Everyone seemed to have their 'look' perfected. It was like someone had taken the September issue of Vogue magazine and sprinkled it over the Marais. I was ignorant of Paris Fashion Week, the high point of the global fashion calendar, gearing up at the very moment I'd arrived. The girls around the Marais were almost uniformly slim, with petite waistlines and carefree faces. On this warm day, most were in shorts and sexy little tight tops that showed off their midriffs. Many of the guys were also in shorts – cut-off denim being the favourite 'this season' and flip-flops. I'd never owned a pair of flip-flops.

Yvonne took me off the main road and into the side streets of the Marais on our way to the hostel in St Paul. I slowed my pace to take in even more. People were sitting outside cafés in the sunshine just watching all the other beautiful people coming and going. As we passed many of them glanced at Yvonne and I. Some smiled, others offered blank expressions, some even winked. Yvonne laughed and we both lapped it up. I found myself adopting a permanent smile – it was hard not to feel good there. Others wandered along, looking in shop windows, stopping occasionally to greet other beauties they knew with the three-way cheek kiss. Some gathered in little groups, chatting – and everyone seemed to have sunglasses. It struck me, in this most fashionable of cities, eye-wear was the only essential item. You simply dare not be seen without shades. I understood then why Yvonne had snatched mine earlier.

I was in awe. I wanted to be one of them. I was absorbing all their behaviours and mannerisms and couldn't wait to put them into practice, to dump the rucksack at the hostel and dive into this life.

"We're coming down here tonight for dinner," Yvonne said as if reading my mind."

"Can we just stop for a coffee now?" I suggested. "I'm sure we must be near the hostel, and I really need a nap, but I just want to sit and watch all this for a while."

"Oh God, sorry, you must be exhausted. I'm not thinking, but we're almost there."

I smiled and kissed her.

"And I know a great café just around the corner, and it's not far from the MIJE, we can go there once you've settled in."

I had no idea what a 'MIJE' was, but I was happy we'd be stopping soon.

A minute later we arrived on the long, elegant boulevard that is the Rue de Rivoli. After the busy and fashionably cool but slightly claustrophobic intimacy of the Marais, the Rivoli was big time grandeur. Flanked at one end by the majestic Place de la Concorde and at the other by the Hôtel de Ville, the Rue de Rivoli immediately became (and remains) my favourite street in the City of Love.

One of the longest streets in the city, it's a stone's throw from the River Seine. It boasts row after row of typical big French stores, such as the Galleries Lafayette, Printemps and - for some reason I couldn't fathom - a C&A. And as you walk along the Rivoli, you soon discover that it also happens to be the front door address of the world famous Musee du Louvre - home to the world's most famous artwork, Leonardo Da Vinci's Mona Lisa.

As Yvonne and I turned the corner that Saturday morning, from the little Marais street onto the wide Rue de Rivoli, I stopped in my tracks to look up and down, mouth agape. Never in my life had I seen architectural grandeur on this scale. The buildings stood to attention, garrisoned almost, with perfect symmetry, I was impressed. Until that morning my only journey abroad had been a trip to Belgium and Holland with my Aunt Peggy and Uncle Joe when I was ten. Even my first memories of the grand architecture of London, when I visited as a 15-year-old, paled in comparison to Paris.

My sister had taken a summer job in the accounts department at the Truman Brewery in Brick Lane in London when I was fifteen. Her boyfriend and I made the trip to London to visit her, and he acted as my chaperone since I was a minor. I think it was as much a pain for him as it was for me!

We did all the sights. Our first stop was Buckingham Palace, where we stood around wondering if the Queen was in. Big Ben, which made me think of the film *The Thirty Nine Steps.* Along the river we debated, ignorantly, about how they erected Cleopatra's Needle. We had chips on Piccadilly Circus, and joked about throwing chips at the prime minister in Downing Street. We took the tube to Bank and the 'Square Mile' (being so close to Brick Lane). I remember thinking London was a very big place, where powerful (and often scary) people like the prime minister and the Queen lived. "How does one make it here?" I wondered. Who knew then that I would later come to call London home?

But that first day in Paris was different. I wasn't being chaperoned. Paris felt less stuffy than London. Less authoritative, Paris appeared to flirt and tantalise among all its grandeur. I stood there in the hot sun, on that impressive street corner on the Rivoli and felt the wave of life wash over me.

"Oi, c'mon, stop daydreaming – it IS a beautiful city – but it's not really all that different from London,"

Yvonne said. Being a Londoner herself, I should have expected that from her. Nothing more than capital-envy I thought. I looked around and said: "No, it is different. It's miles more exciting."

A few minutes later we turned off the Rivoli, up a small and quiet side street, and arrived at the MIJE, (pronounced 'meej-e'). The building was a grand former aristocratic residence. A normal sized door was set into one half of a pair of giant fortified wooden entrance gates. This led onto a beautiful cobbled courtyard filled with vibrant plants in large pots and an assortment of café style tables and chairs.

The building was in pristine condition, with high sandstone coloured walls flanking a delightful, bright courtyard. The windows of the guest rooms above were typically long as I had seen earlier on the Rivoli, festooned with white linen drapes that swayed back and forth lazily in the summer breeze. Les Maisons Internationales de la Jeunesse et des Étudiants (MIJE) was, I later discovered, set up in 1958 by a group including a former minister, teachers and journalists. The organisation grew over the years to three such hostels for young travellers right in the heart of Le Marais.

Yvonne knocked on the reception door to the left of the courtyard. A middle-aged French man opened it.

"Bonjour, Réné, mon copain, il est arrivé, vous avez un lit pour lui?" I was impressed by Yvonne's confident French. There was a choice of accommodation in the MIJE, but as we were young and poor and preferred to spend our money on adventure, we opted for the cheapest. Yvonne had already been there a week with her old school friend, Suzi. They shared a dormitory room with four other girls, in the female wing. She suggested I took a similar type of room, sharing with other males in the west wing. We didn't really care that we weren't sharing together. This was Paris, we could kiss and frolic anywhere in the city. I have to admit, the convenience of this arrangement was not lost on me.

We agreed I'd check in, unpack and shower. I wanted a nap too as I hadn't slept for 24 hours. I noticed only three of the six beds were taken. There was no-one else in the room, but rucksacks and clothing were scattered on the beds. Socks and underwear were bundled under the bed nearest the door, so I decided against settling in that area. There were three sets of bunk beds, all the upper ones taken so I chose the lower bunk nearest the window,– at least I would have a view of the courtyard below. I was curious to know who the other occupants were. "Most likely out there now, enjoying all the wonder and history of the city," I said to myself.

I dropped my rucksack on the floor, pushed it with my foot under the bed, stashed my money belt under the pillow, stripped to my underwear and collapsed onto the mattress, falling instantly into a deep and welcome sleep.

5. Des amis

The sound of the dormitory door closing woke me up. A handsome young boy, about my age, was standing by the door, with nothing but a towel wrapped around his waist.

"Sorry, I didn't mean to wake you, the door's a bit stiff," he said.

I mumbled a hello and rubbed my eyes. "Do you know what time it is?"

"About 5.30, you were out cold when I came back. I'm Jeff."

"Hi, I'm Sam. I've done a lot of travelling over the last two days. I was pretty exhausted when I got here. Where are you from?"

"Oxford, you?" He crossed the room, shook my hand, then strode over to his bunk, dropped his towel on the bed and took his toothbrush from the sink in the corner by the door. He was slim and defined, and muscular, and carried on chatting with me, standing there completely naked, brushing his teeth.

I tried to avert my eyes, but was fascinated by his confident manner, handsome face and taut figure. I found myself being aroused by his presence and hoped that I wasn't making my gaze too obvious. Now and then I'd glance away, at the ceiling, the window, the floor, but then back again to his slightly hairy legs, his perfectly formed buttocks, the long slender line of his back. I was moved. I wanted to touch his skin, run my fingers down his back, kiss his elegant neck.

Instead, I rolled onto my back, stretched my arms out and grabbed hold of the slats of the bunk overhead. Deflection. I told him I was from the east coast of Scotland; it was my first time Interrailing; that I'd just arrived from London; anything that would help calm the fire in my loins.

"It's my first time travelling on my own. I'm here with my girlfriend for a few days" - (did I have to say that?) – "then I'm going to head off on my own, probably down to Spain. Yeah, Spain. I really want to see Spain."

"Cool, Spain's great. I've been twice. You have to see Barcelona. It's the best. This is my third time in Europe, so if you need any tips, just ask."

He was a couple of years older, in his final year of studying for a Bachelor's degree in History and European Languages at Durham. He too was travelling alone, but had met up with college friends and some new friends they'd met in Paris.

Still naked, he towel dried his floppy brown hair and fished out a pair of pants from the travel-worn rucksack next to his bunk. I liked his carefree nature, and that confidence. I'd never considered it before, but those were all things I hadn't yet really discovered in myself. Why was this? I wondered. Perhaps it was something that came from time spent at university. Or maybe because I didn't really know how others saw me. Or was it something else? This was all so new to me. There was so much I needed, so much I wanted, to learn. I do know that I didn't think twice about why I felt aroused by this handsome guy. Yes, I was embarrassed, but it felt good. I felt happy, exotic and alive.

There was a knock at the door and Yvonne came bounding in across the room, launching herself merrily on top of me. Luckily, I managed to pull the bed covers into a scrunch around my loins just before she landed.

"Hey sleepy, feeling rested?" she said, kissing my forehead.

"Yeah, much better, thanks." I said, easing her off. "Yvonne, this is Jeff." They started talking about all the things I must see and do in Paris.

Yvonne ordered me into the shower.

"We'll wait for you downstairs in the courtyard. Don't be long" she said, kissing me again.

I got up and dug out the beach towel mum had packed into my rucksack. I noticed out of the corner of my eye Jeff looking me up and down. Now, just as I had done with him earlier, he would regularly look away, but then back again, glancing furtively. Keeping my underwear on, I shuffled awkwardly towards the door. He leapt up, darted across the room and grabbed my arm. He smiled, while keeping a grip of me. He looked into my eyes, surely a moment longer than necessary. I stared at his hand on my arm, feeling him, feeling me. Breathless, I said nothing and just looked back at him.

"Don't use the first shower, it only has cold water."

I stood there, possibly a bit longer than necessary, still processing his words. I was tingling at the touch of his hand on my skin. Maybe a cold shower is just what I need right now, I thought.

"Right. Okay, thanks."

When I returned to the dorm, Jeff was ready to head out.

"Okay, Sam," he said with a jovial smile, "I hope you and your 'girlfriend' have a good evening. We'll be in the café du Commerce in the Marais if you guys wanna join us later."

"Sure, I'll tell Yvonne, because I have no idea where I am right now."

"Ha, don't worry, you'll find yourself, mister." He smiled a big wide toothy grin and left.

Find myself? If only he knew. A few weeks ago, I had a boring job in an accounts office, no idea what I would do next in life and no real plan to achieve it. Now, here I was, on a journey into a new world, in a strange and wondrous foreign city, chatting to a handsome naked guy in a hotel room on a hot summer's day.

I dried off and got dressed. Through the big open window I could see the girls waiting in the courtyard. Jeff passed them saying 'hi' and smiling. I felt great. Everything was brilliant. Life was brilliant. I hadn't been in Paris more than a few hours but already I could feel my world changing. My sense of self was in flux, and I liked it. No, I loved it. The late afternoon air was balmy, so I pulled on a pair of denim shorts and a t-shirt, and threw on my sneakers. The excitement of heading out to the streets of Paris for my first night abroad was intoxicating, and minutes later I was rushing downstairs to join Yvonne and Suzi.

"Okay," Suzi said, cheerily. "Let's go do Paris..."

We headed out of the little side street and straight onto the Rue de Rivoli. Fresh from my sleep and shower, I was ready to discover this city, and it didn't disappoint. The late afternoon sunshine bathed the Rivoli in a dream like haze. Little cars, taxis and mopeds jostled, veering around each other on the streets, horns beeping. Everything sounded different, more exciting than back home. As we ambled along the street, countless Parisian women, in little single dresses of all colours, glowed through their comfy attire as they passed us by. This must be what they mean by 'chic', But what struck me most about the Rivoli was the sheer number of cafés and bars with huge numbers of seats and tables outside. In Scotland, because of the climate I guess, al fresco café society didn't exist back then. At the Hotel de Ville end of the Rue de Rivoli, there seemed an impossible amount of cafés where the entire world was invited to take a seat and enjoy the lavish grandeur of the municipal architecture, and of course the passing people. Or perhaps the array of cafés were simply there to serve the government employees who worked at the town hall.

Yvonne and Suzi were getting into the spirit of Paris life. Barely had we walked 500 metres when Suzi piped up that it would be great to stop for a quick Noisette?

"A what?" I asked.

"It's a little hit of coffee," Yvonne explained. "Oui, bonne idée, Suzi. Which café?"

Suzi decided on 'Café Maroc' where we took three seats in a line, which Yvonne explained was so we could 'people watch', while we drank our cafés. "Never sit with your back to the Rivoli," Yvonne said with the affected campness of a grande dame. "It's an insult to the architecture, to Paris, to its people." I looked at Suzi and all three of us fell about laughing. Doubtless, Napoleon Bonaparte would be pleased with the way the Rivoli is used today. He built this thoroughfare to pierce the heart of Paris with a wide boulevard that would allow him to see any invading armies or civil uprisings before they got too close. But, it also afforded twentieth century invaders with backpacks great views of the palaces, as one wandered along towards the grand Tuileries gardens. Suzi and Yvonne pointed out beautiful people as they passed by, commenting on this woman's figure and gorgeous outfit, or that guy's physique and great hair. I can honestly say it only takes about an hour to 'become Parisian', or at least an expert in what is chic and what isn't. Although I perhaps didn't make the grade in my back-packer couture of denim shorts and white t-shirt, I consoled myself that perhaps my youthfulness excused me. As Suzi said, "Youth is beauty and just can't be bought at any store in Paris."

Earlier, on the train from Calais, Madonna's Material Girl had filled my ears. I wished I'd brought my Walkman out with me that evening. Looking at the people coming and going on the Rivoli and the Marais, it seemed the perfect song for this city.

I don't recall where we ate that night. Being young and on a budget, it didn't matter, for we were hungry not for food, but for experience. It was probably just a tiny little café, not in the fashionable Marais district, but nearby. We'd have ordered a salad or burger each, and shared the plates. Later we'd head to other cafés to hang out with other young travellers. I mentioned Jeff's earlier suggestion and the girls seemed keen to get to know our fellow guest and his friends properly, so at around 9pm we went in search of the little Café du Commerce in the Marais.

We arrived to find Jeff chatting to one other guy.

"Hey Sam, Yvonne, you made it. Sit down. Kai, this is our new roommate at the MIJE."

"Hello, Kai," I introduced Yvonne and Suzi. "Have you had a good evening?"

"Pas mal, as they say," Jeff replied, explaining that the other friends he was meeting had gone on to a club.

"Perhaps we will also go there later, yah" Kai added, "and also you, if you like." Kai was from Hamburg in Germany and was studying medicine at the city's main university. At 26 he was a bit older than the rest of us, but he explained it takes at least seven years to qualify as a doctor in Germany.

When he went to get in a round of drinks for us all, Suzi and Yvonne started weighing up his sex appeal. Great skin, strong white teeth, gorgeous eyes and a lovely accent. He returned with five demi-pression beers on a tray, raised a glass and said 'Prost!' to all of us. We raised our glasses and returned the German salutation. Suzi flirted with him with him while playing gently with her own long jet black hair. She told him she and Yvonne were also about to start medical training at Cambridge University.

"So what's your plan for tomorrow?" Jeff asked us. I said we were going to be typical tourists. Yvonne wanted to show me all the historic sites.

"But you also need to see the Pompidou Centre." I didn't know what this was, so he explained that it was the largest museum of modern art in Europe, and it also turned the world of architecture upside down.

"It's amazing. It has its guts on the outside. Looks pretty hideous at first, to be honest, but it's amazing to see it plonked there in the middle of all these old buildings." Jeff added.

Yvonne chirped in that we would definitely see it as it was only round the corner. She showed off her knowledge to Jeff, disclosing it was truly a pan-European effort involving architects and engineers from Italy, Britain and Ireland.

More beers came and we all chatted animatedly about Paris, the city's premier place in the world, the lesser known sights, how to say things the way the locals did, what not to eat, all the sorts of things happy, carefree young people can think of to talk about when they meet new friends. Yvonne insisted it would be perfect to live in Paris all the time; Jeff critiqued the latest films–insisting *Back to the Future* was fun, but flawed. Kai wanted to know if any of us had gone to the Live Aid concert at Wembley earlier in the year, allowing Yvonne and Suzi to talk excitedly about attending the music event of the century.

"The rest of you couldn't imagine what it felt like to be in that crowd on that historic day," Declared Suzi.

After more beers, the conversation turned serious. Suzi and Jeff debated the political situation in Europe and how it was weakening the overall structure of the European Union; Kai warned the threat would come from the Middle East.

"It's Palestine we should be really angry and worried about," he announced. "Israel is bang out of order with the way it treats the Palestinian people. It's just going to get worse, and we'll all be caught in the crossfire".

Kai's prediction turned out to be right, because later that year, a militant Palestinian group called the Abu Nidal Organisation would hijack an EgyptAir flight which was later stormed by Egyptian commandos killing 60 people. The same militant group would open fire in the main airports of Rome and Vienna, killing 18 and wounding 120 citizens. And just a month after this wonderful, warm and welcoming night in the Marais, four heavily armed Palestinian terrorists would hijack the *Achille Lauro* cruise ship in the Mediterranean Sea.

The world always seems to have been a safer, freer place in the past. The truth is, as we enjoyed that comfortable, carefree night out in Paris, the same battles that are going on today were already being murderously played out. Terror is nothing new.

"Oh don't let him hijack the evening with politics," Jeff interjected, breaking Kai's flow. "Let's talk about sex, instead". We all stopped and looked at Jeff, shaking our heads in feigned shock and disbelief.

"What?" Suzi said, "is that really the most important thing to you?"

"Hey, just trying to lighten the chat. Anyways, sex is as valid a subject as any other. And it kills a hell of a lot less people...I'm for love, not war." We all groaned.

"Okay Jeff, so what about sex?" I said. For some reason I was strangely keen to stray into this potentially dangerous territory. Perhaps it was the effect of the beers, maybe I was hoping he'd reveal more of himself, like what made him so comfortable being naked in front of other people, or other guys, at least.

It turned into a game. How much money would be

enough to sleep with a much older, really ugly person? What would you never do in bed? Who was your worst experience? How often is enough for sex? Do girls think about it as much as boys?

"I'm sure we don't," said Suzi.

"I'm sure we do," Yvonne piped up.

"So, have any of us ever done it with someone of the same sex." Jeff uttered the question I'd been itching to ask him. Embarrassingly, he and everyone else was looking directly at me. I laughed weakly and looked around at them. At Yvonne. At Jeff.

I wanted to say: "Yes. I was 16, on a trip to Blackpool. Don't remember it too well, we were a bit drunk."

Yvonne's face would redden slightly, she must have known I was like this and had been long before we met. Even though I had never confided in her.

"Go on, details man..." Jeff would say, goading for more, but I would just play it down.

"Well. It was all a bit unexpected and drunken. I was on holiday with two schoolmates and we all shared a room in the guesthouse we had booked. They were best mates, and had agreed to share one of the double beds. I had the other one, by the window, to myself. So there was this other guy on the train, who got thrown off at Preston, that's a station not too far from Blackpool. I think it was because he was quite drunk. Anyways, we met him in a pub later that night in Blackpool. He'd found his own way to town, but he couldn't remember where he was staying, so he asked if he could crash at our bed and breakfast. He shared my bed and after a while we started to edge closer to each other, each pretending to be restlessly asleep. But after a bit, we were both quite hard and in the darkness gently, quietly, but breathlessly, getting it on with each other.. To this day I'm sure the two in the other bed heard the whole thing."

"So what happened in the morning?" Kai would ask.

"Oh, we never spoke about it. It was as if it never happened. I think we just went to the Pleasure Beach."

"Sounds like you'd already been." Suzi would joke as she took a sip of her beer.

That's what I found myself wanting to say. But I didn't say that.

"Nope. Never had that kind of experience."

It would have been a story too far, I thought. I tried to cover my embarrassment with a confident laugh. Everyone turned back to Jeff, who asked:.

"What about you girls?"

They looked at each other and fell about laughing.

"Oh man, I bet you'd love to know. But that ain't ever gonna happen," Suzi said, wagging a finger ostentatiously.

Both Kai and Jeff relayed mild tales of schoolboy

group masturbation, but Kai insisted he was definitely into girls. He sidled up close to Suzi.

"I don't define myself as straight or gay," Jeff added, "we should all be open to life."

We finished our drinks and decided it was too late to go to the club with their other friends. We wandered along the Rue de Rivoli, back to our hotel and said our goodnights.

Yvonne and I lingered in the courtyard, on a bench beneath the dining room's ornate windows.

"Jeff is such an idiot," she said to me. "I'm sure he's bi." I wasn't sure how to reply. This seemed like dangerous territory.

"I don't know," I said. "I just like people. I really like you. But how can we know what we are yet?"

"Well, I know."

"Cool. Lucky you"

I smiled and pulled her towards me. We embraced in a long passionate kiss. I still had feelings for her, but I knew, and I think she knew too, that it wasn't going to go any further than kissing. Not here, not now at least. Looking back, I should have said something. But I was too afraid to ruin the moment.

When I got to my room, the lights were out. Kai, Jeff and our other unknown room-mate were all in their beds. As I undressed in the semi-darkness, I thought I could feel Jeff's eyes on me. As I lay down and pulled the covers over me, I looked over and caught his face, dimly lit by the courtyard lamps outside, looking straight across at me. I looked back. He smiled softly, then turned away and went to sleep.

* * * * *

The train emerges from the Channel Tunnel into sunlit French countryside and take another sip of my Bordeaux. The crew come round with tea and coffee.

"Tea please," I say placing my cup on the little tray offered by the steward.

"Du lait et du sucre, monsieur?"

"Du sucre oui, et citron, s'il vous plaît." I prefer lemon... The handsome young steward fills the cup and places it on the table. Mobile phones in the carriage ring and beep with messages received while we were all 'sous la Manche'.

Everyone inspects their mobile phones to ensure they're once again reconnected to the world of work, friends and family. I look out at the French countryside and return to my thoughts of that first journey to the Continent, discovering Europe and very much disconnected from my home life.

* * * * *

6. Bon courage

I woke up the next morning to the sound of voices in the MIJE courtyard. Raising myself on one elbow, I cocked my ear to confirm Jeff's voice, chatting downstairs. I noticed all his things were gone, including his rucksack. He'd told us he and Kai were catching a train to Nantes, in northwest France, in the morning. As I lay back on my pillow, something rustled. Stuffed underneath was a small postcard of the Pompidou Centre and on the back a message from Jeff.

"It was great to meet you. 'None but the brave deserve the fair'. Travel well. Au revoir, J".

I knew the line. It's from John Dryden's poem Alexander's Feast. I felt my pulse race and smiled. Nothing happened here, I thought. Yet something did happen. I looked at the note again, now alive, exhilarated. The world was tantalising, revealing new things, visually, sensually, emotionally. Every part of me was alert and keen to be washed over with new experiences. I got up and, still in my underwear, stood at the window, looking down into the courtyard, smiling. Jeff came out of the reception room on the right-hand side of the great big entrance doors and pulled on his big rucksack. As he reached the smaller access door, he turned for a second, looked up and smiled fondly. Then he was gone.

A moment later, Yvonne emerged into the courtyard and waved up to me, smiling her beautiful smile. I wanted, in that moment, to be the man she wanted me to be, but I knew right there and then I would never have a future with her, or any other girl. I looked at her beautiful, open, carefree face and her slender body, crossing the sun-dappled courtyard. Sadness welled up inside me as I accepted there would be no lasting 'us' between Yvonne and I.

Throughout my life I have known many guys who, unsure of their sexuality, or perhaps guilt-ridden by it, have chosen to take a girlfriend to keep up the facade of their heterosexuality. I've never judged them for this, but my inner self, my Christian education and my own conscience could never allow me to alter the course of a girl's life, to make her act as an unwitting cover to mask my own fear of being different, simply to appease a world that was intolerant of diversity. In 1985 it was still a crime for me, aged 19, to be a homosexual. The age of consent would remain at 21 in Scotland until 2001.

Tears welled in my eyes. Yvonne didn't know it then, but I was saving her life.

"Come on mister," she yelled. "Get ready, we've got a lot of sightseeing today." I grabbed my towel and headed for the shower.

It doesn't matter what they teach you at school about the world, there is nothing like seeing it for yourself. Paris is home to at least one man-made wonder of the world, the Eiffel Tower, but the entire city consists of endless other wonders. The Musée du Louvre is a breathtaking spectacle from the outside, but when you enter it, you find a labyrinth of world art. You just cannot 'do' in one visit. Da Vinci's Mona Lisa may be the star attraction, but this beautiful museum houses some 35,000 works of art. I couldn't help thinking when Yvonne first took me there that it reeked of aristocracy, even now, two hundred years after La Revolution. Situated on the Right Bank of the first arrondissement, dead in the centre of Paris, the Louvre serves as a permanent reminder of France's regal past. This, I thought at the time, is something they could never deny.

It was mid afternoon by the time we left the Louvre and walked through the Jardin des Tuileries to the Place de la Concorde. This, was like a driver's nursery slope for the Arc de Triomphe, as we tried to cross it on our way to the long amble up the Champs Elysées. And although we had marched down it on the day I arrived in Paris, tired and hungry after my long trip from Scotland, walking this huge boulevard now, free of baggage and able to fully appreciate the long symmetrical lines all the way up to the arch, was inspiring.

"Why don't we have great big statements like this in Britain?" I asked Yvonne.

"Because we're not French! And excuse me, but in London we have The Mall"

"Yeah, but..." I replied

Not only is the avenue itself a sight to behold, but when you reach the end it is crowned with the impressive and improbably huge Arc de Triomphe. situated on the Place Charles de Gaulle or Place de l'Étoile. At 50 metres high and 45 metres wide, the arch represents all that France is proud of. The names of all the generals who fought in all the wars are inscribed there, and the tomb of the unknown solider lies beneath it. We'd simply used it as a rendezvous point the previous day, so now Yvonne and I spent a long time studying the iconic artistry of the arch, which depicts young naked French boys pitted against bearded Germanic warriors in full metal battle dress. If you look closely at the statues and buildings of a city, you see the story of it's former citizens written in its stone.

We caught the Metro from Charles de Gaulle Étoile station to Châtelet, so we could 'squeeze in' Notre Dame. When I couldn't go another second without a Coca-Cola, we stopped en route from Châtelet station to the Cathedrale. In those days, as now, a can of Coke seemed inordinately expensive. It was almost as if it was priced as a luxury item by the French when everyone in the world surely ought to be able to savour the king of soft drinks without feeling done over. I'm certain the can of Coke Yvonne and I shared that day cost more than a beer.

After we'd jostled with the crowds and filed reverently along the aisles of the religious, gothic masterpiece, we exited the old cathedral and walked back to the hostel.

En route back to the Marais that evening, Suzi insisted we sit on the Rue de Rivoli for our first drink of the evening, which would allow us to once again play the people-watching game.

Later, we found a little restaurant in a side street off the Marais that offered baguette sandwiches and frites for a few affordable francs. This deal was boosted by the fact a pichet of red wine was thrown in for free.

We retired to the MIJE earlier that night, tired out from walking. I had the dorm to myself. I moved around the room naked, trying the confidence Jeff had displayed when I first arrived. It wasn't quite the same.

The next day, Yvonne suggested we view Paris from the banks of the winding river that runs through the city. The Seine was a minute's walk from the MIJE and we trekked along the left bank as far as the Tour Eiffel. We headed to the base and stood beneath it at the very centre.

"We have to kiss here," I said. Swept up in the moment, I took Yvonne's hands in mine. "It's probably the most powerful place in the world."

She laughed and hugged and kissed me.

We spent half an hour under the tower – unable to afford the expensive entry price to go up inside it and unwilling to wait in the endless queue. Youth is impatient, after all.

Clouds arrived and the late afternoon air was muggy

as we ambled back along the banks of the Seine to the MIJE.

This was my last day in Paris. I had an overnight train to catch for Portbou on the Franco-Spanish border.

My bags were already packed and waiting in the reception storeroom – the latest check-out is always noon, always a conundrum for travellers with a late travel plan. However, the receptionist at the MIJE was friendly enough to be happy to hold on to my luggage until my night train.

I picked up my bags and Yvonne suggested we wander round to the Pompidou Centre for a last coffee before we set off for the Gare d'Austerlitz.

"Great idea, but wouldn't it be better to leave my rucksack here?" I pleaded. I was feeling the tiredness of two full days of tourism..

"No, we'll head straight to the train station from there. Come on big boy, you'll be fine." Yvonne marched off purposefully, happily. She was definitely going to make a good doctor, I remember thinking even then. Her no-nonsense 'can do' attitude would be a great asset, but at least she could have offered to carry one of my bags.

We turned off the bustling streets of the Marais and into Beaubourg and a large open square along one side of which sat one of the ugliest buildings I had seen in Paris.

"Let's grab a coffee there," Yvonne suggested, pointing towards the small bar directly opposite the

71

French monstrous carbuncle.

"Is that it?" I asked

"Yep," Yvonne replied, "What do you think?"

"I don't know. It looks really out of place, like a wart on the face of Paris. But it's kind of funky too, Jeff was right – it's like its guts are on the outside". We argued about the architectural merits of the Pompidou for the next half hour.

Yvonne said she loved the building because it was so different. It was also, she insisted, a 'biological' construction, with all its arteries and intestines on the exterior, which, she said, makes it easier to operate on when things go wrong.

I don't know if I cared for it. It seemed too obvious. It did strike me as very different, but I wasn't sure if this was really the right place for it. Paris is full of ancient, grand architecture. So much, I thought, that this effort to etch a touch of modernity onto its face, had somehow failed.

Yvonne mentioned Suzi was indifferent. "She says if you don't like it, don't look at it. Either way, it's just one building. Plenty of other things to look at."

On the way to the Metro, Yvonne insisted on stopping at a little shop for a baguette, some ham, cheese, tomato and a small half bottle of cheap red wine – I think it was a claret.

"I'll make you a sandwich for the journey because the buffet car will be too expensive."

I was grateful for her forward thinking, which not only saved money but also made sure I didn't go hungry. I was just like most other 19-year-old boys back then – I rarely thought ahead, rarely planned. I only considered food when the hunger was actually upon me. She also bought an apple "for dessert", she beamed. On the Metro, she took a cheap little knife from her pocket and started assembling my sandwich. She said she'd 'borrowed' the knife from the dining room at the MIJE.

We took the Metro to Gare d'Austerlitz. The evening air had turned cool and it felt good to be heading south, where it would, I hoped, still be warm.

A rush of excitement hit me as we entered the station. The thought of travelling further south into new adventures was irresistible. Back then, Austerlitz was one of the key stations in Paris serving the south west of France, including major cities such as Bordeaux and Toulouse. And it was the gateway to Spain. Soon, Austerlitz would become a less important station, relegated by the impressive new concrete monstrosity that is the Gare Montparnasse, built to handle France's new age of high-speed rail travel – the Train Grande Vitesse or TGV.

I looked around at all the other travellers, waiting with their suitcases, backpacks, bags and boxes. Couples hugged goodbyes, one woman kept her three small children gathered around her, each sitting on a tiny little suitcase to await the correct platform information for their train. Office workers hung around by the café bar, sipping coffee, or enjoying discrete quarter pichets of red wine. Station guards and officials patrolled the main concourse, while gendarmes kept guard outside the station. I hadn't seen security like this before and wondered if they were on the lookout for some escaped and highly dangerous criminal or, more likely a covert spy.

My train – an overnight service to Portbou, a little town just inside the Spanish border on the coast by the Mediterranean Sea - was already standing at platform six with people boarding. Travelling from Paris to Barcelona meant crossing the border into Spain, and back then this involved changing trains at Portbou to clear Spanish customs and immigration.

"You'd better get on," Yvonne said, "if you want to get a good seat."

"Hey, there's no rush," I replied, putting my arms around her neck. "Listen, I had a great time with you. I'm sorry we didn't get more opportunity to be alone."

"Sweetie, maybe we're not meant to be," she replied. "we're so young, everything's new. I've got university soon. This has been great. I'll never forget it – Paris, with you, and the sights and the bars and the people we've met. It's been amazing. And I know you're going to have a great adventure, now go, go and have fun."

She pulled me towards her and kissed me before turning her head and placing it on my chest. I held her tightly and kissed her beautiful blonde hair. To anyone around us, we must have looked like parting lovers, which of course we were, in a way. Although we didn't get to see each other that often – she lived in London, I lived in Scotland – perhaps being in Paris together concentrated our feelings. I wished I'd done more during our time together in Paris to take on the city's aura of love – played the part, acted out the scene. Nothing is really ever as it appears.

"You'd better get on," Yvonne mumbled, wiping away tears. "God, I'm so embarrassed,'. She forced a laugh.

I climbed up the steps of voiture huit of the night train and turned around. "Don't be embarrassed. I'm the lucky one. It was great to get this time with you."

Slowly, the train pull out. The guard excused me so he could close the carriage door and I pulled down the window.

Yvonne stood there waving and smiling, as the train pulled further out of the station. I saw her wipe more tears from her face. Part of me wanted to jump off the train, run back and hug her again. But I stayed put, waving back until she and the station disappeared. I have only seen her again once, in London thirteen years later. Now a successful doctor, she was married, to a handsome American, and I was thrilled for her.

I closed the window, picked up my rucksack and made my way into the garishly lit carriage. It was too bright and the regulation blue leather seats were not terribly comfortable either. I wondered how I was going to get a decent night's sleep on those. Perhaps because of the late hour there weren't many other passengers on the train. I sat with my back to the direction of travel, so I could watch Paris melting away into the rainy night.

The guard appeared to check tickets – something they still do today. He was saying something to the other passengers that I couldn't make out. When he got to me, I finally understood. He was asking if anyone wanted to take advantage of an offer to upgrade to a couchette – a private cabin with beds and blankets – for the long overnight journey.

"Young man, eet vill be very comfortable pour vous, non?" He said, mixing in what English he knew for my benefit. "You vill need good sleep before Espagne, eh?"

I asked if I could see the couchettes first. He beckoned me to follow him through the next two carriages and unlocked one of the doors at the rear end of the sleeper coach. It boasted two rows of three seats facing each other, and with two rows of bunks above, already opened. This allowed for up to six passengers to sleep in each cabin. You could turn the lights off completely. I loved the idea of taking the 'room' but was sure it was going to be too expensive.

"Combien?" I asked the guard, "I don't have much money. Pas beaucoup de l'argent."

"Oh, c'est pas cher, monsieur. Pour vous, soixante quinze francs...er...75 francs."

I did the conversion calculation in my head..."Right, about seven pounds...mmm, not sure..."

"And there is a petit déjeuner also – café, croissant,

ou thé, si vous préfèrez."

That nailed it. While I had to watch my money, this would mean cash very well spent. I returned to the overlit seating carriage for my back-pack and headed back to the couchette for my first taste of upgrade life.

The guard took my money and settled me in – he disappeared and returned a moment later with a blanket and pillow. He folded away all the upper beds. I'm sure the money which went into his pocket, would stay there, but I didn't care. Why shouldn't he make a little on the side? Impossible in today's world with digital payments, of course, for a lowly guard to pocket a few 'tips' for himself.

He took my order for breakfast: tea, croissants and orange juice, said 'bon voyage' and left me to enjoy the private space.

I locked the door to the cabin and took from my little rucksack the sandwich and the wine Yvonne had prepared. The knife she'd 'borrowed' was wrapped alongside the sandwich and came in very handy as I had no corkscrew. I resorted to forcing the cork into the wine with the knife slowly and very carefully.

I took out my Walkman, put in a tape cassette, placed the headphones in my ears, turned off the cabin lights and sat back in the cosy darkness to watch the night go by to the sound of Simple Minds' 'Someone, Somewhere in Summertime'.

After Paris, the rain subsided, giving way to a perfect

starlit sky. As the train careered through the countryside my thoughts turned to what may lie ahead on this next step of my journey. Spain. This was going to be a whole new country for me, a whole new culture. France was new, too, but I had contacts, friends, who were able to provide the reference points. It was exciting not knowing what Spain would be like. A whole country that would present itself to me, ancient, but entirely new and fresh to this young traveller. I tucked into my tasty ham, cheese and tomato baguette, and took small sips of the tasty Claret. It was another meal, thoughtfully and lovingly prepared for me by a woman. Not my mother this time, but Yvonne. I considered this, how women seemed to always think of the details in life. How grateful I was for that; for their unconditional insistence on making sure you were looked after as you went off alone on your adventure. As I ate, the lights of villages and small towns twinkled intermittently in the distance. The music in my ears added the soundtrack to this wonderfully personal moment of my journey. Playing then, as I ate and drank, was 'That Fatal Kiss' the atmospheric and dream-like B-track to Duran Duran's 'A View to a Kill', written for the eponymous James Bond film. The piece is a slow tempo take on the theme song, arranged for the moodier scenes of the film. It was the perfect piece for that moment on the train. Slow and melancholic, but with a piercing uplift, an invitation to adventure. Its pace signals a momentary lull in the drama of the film. Now it was the track to the lull in my journey. I wanted everyone to know what that felt like. To be a young guy on a train, having new experiences and discovering new parts of the world. In the comfortable solitude and darkness of a couchette on a French train hurtling south, I was fed, enjoying the wine as I looked out into the darkness. The music added to the wonder of it all, made it a perfect lull. How lucky I was.

Eventually, I drew the curtains together, pulled the pillow and blanket over my slim body and drifted off to sleep, only the night sounds of the French railway system ringing in the distance. I wasn't sure if I should I have packed pyjamas? Who cared? I was so caught up in the excitement and beauty of all this new experience that I'd given no thought at all to what I was going to do the next morning when we arrived in Portbou.

* * * * *

The Eurostar is slicing its way through the sunny French countryside.

"Monsieur, how was your meal?" The stewardess clears away my tray.

"Very nice, thanks."

"Would you like some more tea?"

"Yes, please. With another slice of lemon if you have it".

"Of course". She smiles and offers me a sneaky second chocolate.

The long train picks up the pace as we hurtle through the French countryside. I can feel England falling away into the distance every time I make this journey. All the trials and tribulations of life and work in London ebb away as we push forward into continental Europe.

Everyone else in the carriage is relaxed by now, too. Even the annoying passenger with the mobile phone seems to have given up trying to contact her colleagues and is now gazing sleepily out of the window at the passing countryside. All is peaceful on the 1402 service to Bordeaux.

I'd love a cigarette right now, but the days of smoking coaches have long since gone. You can't even lean out the window anymore to have a shifty puff. So I settle back into my seat, remove my shoes to put my feet up on the vacant seat opposite, and take a sip of my lemon tea. Rays of afternoon sunshine bathe the carriage in a warm glow, which carries me away, again.

* * * * *

7. Iberiana

It was the lack of motion that roused me the next morning. I wondered if we had arrived in Spain already. Throwing back the blanket, I leant over and pulled open the curtains to reveal a startlingly bright sunlit morning. I stood in just my underwear and pulled open the top section of the window to get some idea of where we were.

I noticed the landscape first. I'd never been so far from home before, and I'd never seen terrain like this. The air was dry and dusty and all around was an arid, rocky landscape. No fields, just uneven rocks and dry-looking bushes strewn all over. Here and there were thick, spiky plants I'd never seen, like a cross between a cactus and a palm. Our train was stopped on a straight stretch of track in what looked like the middle of nowhere, nothing appeared to be happening. The sound purposeful footsteps came from the corridor, so I pulled open the door – still in my underwear – and asked the passing guard if we were near Portbou yet.

"Non, encore une heure peut-être – we make stopping for more water," the guard replied in Franglais.

So at least I knew where we were. I didn't really care that we were still en route. This was a train trip around Europe. There was no deadline or ultimate destination, the journey itself was the destination. I loved every minute of the experience. I lounged around in the cabin for a bit, then headed to the toilet at the end of the carriage. Yvonne had advised me to use bottled water for dental hygiene and not swallow any tap water in Spain, "especially on trains". I took care to strap the little 'bum-bag' containing all my cash, travellers' cheques and passport under my t-shirt – another security tip Yvonne had passed on to me.

Just as I emerged from the toilet, the train jolted forward and began its final slug towards Portbou. I passed the queue of other sleepy passengers that had formed outside the toilet while I was in there. They looked less rested than I felt. How many of them now wished they had taken the guard up on his offer of discounted bed for the night? In my cabin I found a small tray of tea, juice and croissants on the window side table. I was impressed! For very little money I'd travelled in relative luxury. Breakfast included - a real bonus. I finished off everything, guessing I probably wouldn't eat again until later in the day. The morning sun grew stronger and I looked out the window, transfixed by this alien, mesmerising landscape. I loved the aridness of it all. It was as if I'd journeyed onto the set of a Spaghetti Western – and the Paris express was about to pull into town.

Portbou is a tiny fishing village tucked away into the

uppermost left-hand corner of the Mediterranean. Built on a hillside at the foot of the Pyrenees, it drops right down to sea level at a very steep gradient. The inclined streets are lined with little cafés, bars, tourist shops, restaurants and guesthouses.

Back then it was a border checkpoint on the Franco-Spanish border. All trains from France terminated here for customs and immigration checks. Although the Schengen Agreement, which would remove the need for physical borders in some EU countries was signed on June 14th, 1985, just a few months before I arrived on this train, the implementation had not yet reached Portbou. Even without the border controls, at this time, France and Spain had different railway gauges, so the change was still necessary. This track border added time and inconvenience to every journey from France to Spain and vice versa. The characteristic track gauge of the Spanish railway network is 1,668 millimetres between the inner rail faces. The rest of Europe is narrower at 1,435. Those 233 millimetres had a lot to answer for. Everyone disembarked from the long, overnight French train and headed down into the little town, perhaps, like me, to take in their first taste of Spain, while we waited for the connecting train that would carry us on to Barcelona.

It was only around 9 a.m. Already the sun was hotter than anything I'd ever experienced. My pale British skin prickled in the heat as drops of sweat rolled down the small of my back. I wandered around the little town, stopping to look at postcards outside the beach shops, hoping to get a better idea of the place from the photos. The shop owners, with their captive market on account of the border and gauge controls, got to work trying to sell us items from their array of beach goods – towels, inflatable toys, sun creams, buckets and spades, sunglasses, bottled water. I'd never seen entire shops dedicated to beach life like this before. Scotland isn't exactly known for its balmy weather, and although Blackpool, where I had spent so many holidays, did have similar items, all I can remember of them was buckets and spades, 'Kiss me quick' hats and rock, the candy variety. Neither had I seen before the happy, easy enthusiasm that these vendors showed. Even if they sold nothing some days, they did have the best weather, I thought. I listened as one shop owner pointed out his 'quality' beach towels. Despite his jovial pitch, I resisted, managing to keep the few Spanish pesetas I'd exchanged in Paris for my unspent francs, firmly in my pocket. I did yield to buying a bottle of water.

Ambling around a little Spanish village under a hot morning sun takes it out of you, more so when you have a large backpack strapped to you and a mini rucksack clamped to your chest. So after a circuit of the village, I stopped at a little café/restaurant for a cup of tea.

A few tables away was a British family of five.

"Good morning, were you on the train from Paris?" I said, eager to have someone to talk to after the overnight journey.

"Mornin', aye that we were lad," the father replied.

He was a healthy if rotund man with tightly cropped brown hair. His much smaller, pretty, blonde wife smiled timidly while attending to her little blonde daughter, who I guessed was about four years old. Their two other children were sons of about six years old and they looked like twins. Like their sister, they both also sported manes of blonde hair – unmistakeably north European. I watched as the parents ate their breakfast and fussed over their happy offspring. I'll never have this, I thought.

"Where are ye off to, lad?" the wife asked, "somewhere nice I expect?"

"Oh Barcelona, then I'm not really sure. Just see what happens." I felt a surge of strength as I said this, realising for the first time that I could decide. In fact, I had to decide, no one else was going to do that for me on this trip. It felt good.

"Oh, well, that's aright for some, innit love?" said the husband, Paul.

"And you?" I was keen to know what the plan was for this fellow British couple and their kids – clearly not backpacking like I, since I could see three very large red suitcases parked by their table.

"We're off t'little place just south o' Barcelone," he said, missing off the 'a'. "Sort o' holiday camp. Great for kids, y'know."

I wondered why they hadn't just flown instead of schlepping halfway across Europe for the Spanish equivalent of what surely must be Butlin's.

"Work on railways, I do," Paul said, "get whopping great discounts on travelling all over Europe. Besides, we don't much give much for flyin' do we kids?" The whole family shook their heads in unison, clearly well-used to being asked that question - and giving that answer.

I smiled. Lucky them, able to travel all over Europe by train on a work afforded discount.

Paul's wife, Debbie, whom I guessed was, like her husband, around 30 years old, and therefore older and wiser than I, told me they had been to Spain a number of times and I should think about heading to Alicante or even as far south as Granada.

"Lucky you backpacking around Europe. We did that for honeymoon, didn't we love?" She smiled over at Paul.

"Alicante is fun, but you could spend entire month just doin' east coast o' Spain," Paul added. "Just mind yer sel in Barcelone, place is full o' bleedin' thieves 'n' pickpockets."

"Really?" I was surprised by the note of danger, which seemed at odds with the beautiful warmth, calm and gentleness of Portbou. I realised then I hadn't done much research into the places I'd visit on this journey.

"I'll watch out for that, thanks for the heads up."

The sound of our train backing into the station prompted us to ask the waitress for 'la cuenta' and we all went back to the awaiting customs officers.

The Spanish customs hall was an ugly, soulless collection of rooms, regulation green paint ageing and peeling, making it appear all the more austere. Glass mesh windows, some frosted to allow for privacy, gave a prison-like ambience. It was clearly designed to intimidate. I stood in line ahead of Paul and Debbie and their children, who took longer to get organised, what with all their luggage. As we moved slowly forward I became increasingly nervous at facing the customs officers.

When I arrived in France it was different. The French guards were waiting by the train and checked our passports as we boarded. But here, in Portbou, in Spain, in this most foreign of places, in this ugly set of rooms, the entire exercise took on an air of menace. I started to look guilty, just through sheer nerves. Sweat formed on my brow. I fidgeted and bit my nails. Irrational thoughts popped into my head, such as the realisation that anyone could have stashed drugs or some other contraband in my rucksack at any time. It could have been at the MIJE in Paris, or perhaps someone had crept into my couchette while I slept on the train and stuffed some marijuana into my bag! Why hadn't I thought to check it? The customs officers were tall and looked hard. Some smoked; they all looked distrustful. The room became hot with all the people from the overnight train. There was also a coach load of German tourists lumped in with our line of rail travellers. Overweight, middle-aged men from the German party made comments in their own language that neither I nor the guards could understand. I'm certain the guards sensed the comments were not polite because they took a painfully long time to process most of us.

Eventually, it was my turn.

"Your bag?" said the serious-looking guard, accusingly. I nodded. "Give me now," he continued, his upturned palm motioning towards him. I handed him my rucksack.

"You have drugs?"

"WHAT? No, no I don't. No drugs. I'm Catholic." What was I saying? *Where did that come from?* I muttered to myself. The question was a shock. Apart from an occasional, experimental puff of grass at secondary school, drugs were of no interest to me.

He pulled open my backpack, and slowly, carefully, almost lovingly in a weird way, started sorting through all my clothes and toiletries. I could feel the other passengers looking at me, Did I have the look of a drugs trafficker? Out of the corner of my eye, I noticed some muttering to each other. Were they saying: "I bet he's got pot in there?" The guard pulled my shoes out and fed his hand into the insteps. Nothing. Eventually, he asked for my passport, scrutinised it and asked where I was going and what I was planning to do. "Barcelona, holiday, beach," I said in a monotone. At that moment I was wishing I'd just stayed in France.

When he was finished, he pointed to my empty

rucksack and all its contents on the table and told me to repack.

"Quick, the train is leaving soon," he added, to my irritation.

My face was red, I felt relieved, sick and angry all at the same time. I repacked my rucksack haphazardly, not caring I was stuffing everything in wrong – dirty trainers rubbing against clean clothes, toilet bag at the bottom. I just wanted to get out of there and onto the train. It was a fearsome introduction to Spain.

I climbed aboard and sought a seat as far from any other travellers as I could get. Such humiliation! Even though I was vindicated, with no contraband, I still felt guilty, dirty, somehow labelled as a potential undesirable.

Paul and his wife sat in a different coach, occupied with their children. I wanted to go and reassure them I was okay, but my shame at having been interrogated kept me rooted to my corner seat.

I stared out of the window and watched the Spanish countryside go by. To the eyes of a foreigner seeing it for the first time, it was incredible. The coastal route offered splendid, tantalising glimpses of the Mediterranean Sea, tiny settlements, undisturbed beaches, until finally the azure sea was everywhere. Although I was excited and exhilarated by this new place, the scary customs experience and my tiredness left me apprehensive as to what awaited in Barcelona. No more troublesome officials perhaps, but according to my fellow travellers, the threat of thieves instead.

The harsh train from the border to Barcelona was nothing like the French service. The ride was bumpier, and the wooden seats far less comfortable than the relatively sumptuous leather upholstery of the French train. I thought about sneaking into a First Class carriage, but there didn't seem to be one. If there was, it probably wasn't much better.

After an hour I needed to pee, a dilemma for every solo voyager: Should you leave all your belongings behind and trust fellow passengers to keep a safe eye on them? Or schlep the whole lot with you? I decided money, passport, etc should stay attached to my waist in the bumbag. The risk of losing all my clothes was one thing, but passports, tickets and cash – no way.

At the end of the carriage, I found a wooden door with a scabby vent and a sign which read 'Servicios'. It sounded right. I entered to find something I'd never encountered before. I was staring at a hole in the floor and I could actually see a steel, circular, flat disc at the end of the hole flapping open and closed as the train hurtled along, revealing intermittently the rail tracks beneath us. I almost tutted and left, assuming someone had stolen the toilet seat, but then I realised that this was an altogether new kind of 'convenience' to my eyes. The hole in the floor was at the centre of a two-foot square of porcelain. In front of the hole and a little to the left and right were two raised oblongs, which I figured were footplates. This was my first experience of a squat toilet.

I was thankful I only needed to pee. The place stank and there was literally all manner of crap around the bowl. I positioned myself so my sneakers didn't touch the base. It was probably the most uncomfortable piss I've ever taken. When I turned to the sink to wash my hands – being a good Catholic boy – there was, of course, no water. I got out of there as quickly as I could, before I threw up from the stench and the flies.

Back in the comparative cleanliness of the main carriage, I spent the rest of the journey looking out of the window. Facing the direction the train was travelling in, looking left I could observe the coastline all the way to Barcelona. The Mediterranean Sea was bright blue by the shoreline. It looked unreal, almost man-made or somehow painted on. Little coves came into view every now and then. Golden sandy beaches, some inaccessible it seemed except via the railway track. The line ran so close to the coast I could almost lean out of the window and scoop up the sand and the sea. Every now and then, the views were interrupted by tunnels of varying length, through which the train snaked. Sometimes, in the dimly lit darkness of a tunnel, I could feel the train curving as it meandered through, and then all of a sudden it emerged back into the hot, bright heat of the Catalan sun.

I considered my plan of action, once we arrived in Barcelona. I would find suitable accommodation first, then take a long shower. For as long as I can remember I've always managed to find my way around new places with relative ease. I've rarely been lost, anywhere. If ever

91

I do lose my bearings, I just make my way to the centre of a place, take my bearings then find my way on from there. So that was the plan: arrive in Barcelona, find the centre, seek out a cheap hostel and take a long, welcome shower.

8. Hola Barcelona

For the last half-hour of the journey, the train crept along at a snail's pace, stopping every so often for no apparent reason. Some other passengers became agitated by our slow progress. Every now and then, an old Spanish grandma sat in the corner of the coach would let out huge sighs of frustration, half muttering something to her little husband. He just sat, resigned, as if knowing that his wife was complaining enough for both of them. The coaches were not air conditioned and since it was almost the high point of the day, the temperatures were stifling inside the old rickety coach. Everyone just wanted to get off and get on with their lives.

Finally, the long sun-baked train came to a stop beneath the monumental shaded domes of the Barcelona Estació de Franca. Built in 1929 by a Spanish architect called Pedro Muguruza, this grand station is a beautifully understated blend of the classical and the modern. Decorated in marble, crystal and bronze with art deco and modernist motifs, it is a beautiful tribute from a bygone age to the art of travel. (Shame the same couldn't be said for the country's trains.) An impressive double domed structure straddles the station and stands almost one hundred feet high and over 600 feet long. All train passengers travelling from France terminate here. It may be the end of the line, but it was the beginning of my adventure in Spain.

I couldn't help but look up as I walked along the platform to the main exit of the terminus. I imagined this is how most people react when they see this station for the first time, in the full glint and glare of the hot Spanish sun. You can't help but be taken in by the bright airiness of the station, the huge sweeping curve of the dome, the shininess of the marble walkway – in Dundee, the platform was a dark grey, dull concrete affair.

The station was busy, but not crowded. The people looked different from those I'd seen in Paris. Everyone seemed lighter, their clothes skimpier, less bothered with fashion, yet to my eyes still fashionable, merely because it was new and exotic to me. Their bodies were more tanned, they looked healthier, carefree. And everyone seemed to have dark hair, except for the occasional blonde tourist here and there. Almost everyone had sunglasses on their heads or over their eyes, and for good reason. Streaks of sunlight burst through the transparent parts of the long curved domes illuminating the entire scene. I guessed the Spanish must always wear sunglasses. All that bright sun must be hard on the eyes. I remember thinking that, back in Scotland, in those days, people taunted you for wearing sunglasses; they'd call you a poser, a showoff. But here, in this sun-drenched, warm and exotic country, sunglasses were a necessity of daily life. Pretty women ambled around casually at the end of the main concourse, waiting for the station announcements; a group of five Scandinavian backpackers were camped on the shiny marble floor, by the sandwich bar. They played cards and chatted. It seemed, from their open rucksacks and piles of books and sandwiches and drinks that they'd have a long wait for their train. Spanish men stood around smoking cigarettes, others in pairs chatted idly. Occasionally, I'd spot someone looking shifty, appearing to study the arriving passengers.

I ambled over to what looked like an information desk, situated in a corner of the station, where a relaxed looking middle-aged woman sat behind a large toughened glass frame. She was smoking a cigarette and was older than I'd figured, up close, than she had looked from a slight distance. Like a sort of faded Spanish señorita, I thought. Her bright red lipstick was dulled only by the deep suntan of her face and chest. Her lip gloss was complemented by a single red flower tucked into the left side of her auburn coloured hair. She had musky, slightly heavy eyes. Not sad eyes, though, just perhaps a little tired. Despite her obvious age, she was petite in size and wore a smart white shirt and regulation black pencil skirt. I remember thinking, she'd be a hit in Scotland, so glamorous, so exotic, even in middle age – and this is her at work.

"Buenos dias," she said in a raspy voice through the little hole in the glass. I smiled, realizing I didn't know a word of Spanish.

"Hi, centre ville?" I had learned the French word for a town centre from Yvonne and Suzi in Paris, and sadly, it was all I had to go on. "Do you speak English?"

She shook her head and said "Not many", but I got what she meant. She pointed to the map on the countertop with one hand and took a drag of her cigarette with the other. She seemed bored, like I was the millionth ignorant teenage traveller to appear at her window that day expecting her to speak a multitude of languages to cater for every nationality that might approach her little cubicle.

"Gracias señorita", I replied, not even certain if this was correct Spanish. I smiled again and moved to study the map. Proof that my education wasn't a waste of time, I could feel all those Ordinance Survey map-reading lessons in Geography 'O' level coming back. Good old Mrs Elliott. Her teaching efforts were not in vain after all. I located the north-pointing symbol, could make out the lines that made hillside contours, got the grid of the city streets and the dimensions and could see a really long, wide main street which appeared to lead all the way to the port and sea and pointed at it.

"Las Ramblas?" The señorita asked.

"Yes, yes, there".

"Take taxi," she instructed in her rough command of English, pointing with her whole right arm.

I said a bright 'Gracias' and walked off to find a taxi. As I did so, I heard her utter something indistinguishable under her breath. It sounded like 'na-na' to me, but then my Spanish was non-existent. Soon enough I would learn what she'd said was 'de nada', the Spanish equivalent of 'no worries' or 'it's nothing'.

The taxi was too expensive, so I somehow managed to figure out with the driver's help that I could hike my way down to the port by foot. Soon I was wandering along the pleasant treelined streets of Barcelona. I made sure to keep myself under the shade of the trees and buildings. The backpack seemed heavier in the heat.

All the apartments seemed so chic, almost more-so than in Paris. Tall, grand tenement buildings with imposing large, strong and heavy-looking doors lined the streets. As I drew closer to the Ramblas, the buildings became even more decorated. Coloured awnings shaded windows of the many tenement blocks that were now hotels. There was an abundance of cafés, bars and little restaurants. I thought, does everyone eat-out here? How can so many eateries exist in one city? Back home, we'd all have to eat out practically every night – and in more than one establishment – just to keep them all in business. But here the restaurants and bars seemed to serve a national pastime.

Eventually, I arrived at the top of Las Ramblas, a 1.2 kilometre-long tree-lined pedestrian mall between Barri Gòtic and El Raval, it connects Plaça Catalunya in the centre with the Christopher Columbus monument at Port Vell. I absorbed all these names within minutes, like a spy assessing a room for escape points. I wasn't sure I'd remember all the exact names, but they were now in my head somewhere. I strolled down the Ramblas wondering why they had roads on either side. I knew it was to allow vehicles access to the Ramblas, but it seemed a shame it wasn't all pedestrianised. The central mall was pedestrianised and dotted with stalls selling all manner of wares. Dark African vendors stood by their tables offering 'genuine' leather goods such as wallets and belts, purses and, rather strangely I thought, football scarves emblazoned with the names of British football teams. Manchester United, Newcastle, Tottenham Hotspur, never looked so out of place. Slim, tanned Spanish boys sold freshly squeezed orange juice and ice creams. There were portable coffee stands, and the daily newspapers and magazines, among them English papers – which didn't look out of place - like The Sun and The Daily Telegraph, as well as sweets, cigarettes, postcards and maps of the city. Not all of the vendors were able to afford an actual stall, I noticed. Instead, their treasures were neatly laid out on the shiny almost marble paving of the Ramblas. These 'budget' vendors were black, mostly men, but they were the darkest people I had ever seen. They looked African, they dressed differently from the Spanish and they looked fierce. One of them smiled as I passed by. I smiled back, which on reflection was a bad idea, because he then came after me with his great big massive white teeth and colourful robes and tried to convince me to buy a small drum. Not knowing what to say in reply, because I couldn't speak either Spanish or any African language, I waved a 'no' with both hands and quickened my pace. As I hastened away, the burly vendor let out a confident and slightly mad belly rumble of laughter. A hundred metres or so further along, I stopped by a bench, unloaded my rucksack and parked myself on the seat.

The heat of the sun was blazing. I looked around at the crazy vendors, the tall tenement buildings flanking the Ramblas, and tried to take in all the colours, smells and sounds of this new place. It was disorienting. It often happens when you're in new surroundings for the first time. I remember feeling it in Paris on the first day with Yvonne and Suzi. I couldn't figure out what was north, south, east or west, but the girls knew their way around, which made it a lot easier. Here in Barcelona, I was alone. It was dizzying, confusing. Although I had the street names and squares in my head, I was second guessing the orientation of the place. After sitting for a bit, I spotted an opening at the end of the Ramblas, sensed the port and the Mediterranean Sea must lie beyond, and so got my bearings.

I took in the place again. Barcelonians came and went, ignorant of the fact they were being watched by this idle voyager. The vendors and their stalls – not so strange on a second appraisal – continued their efforts to attract passers by. I looked up at the large trees lining the Ramblas, and the different buildings flanking the street. An elderly Spanish lady - I decide she's a grandmother - ambled past, a tiny little brown shaggy dog on a blue lead trotted alongside her. The little creature pulled its way to the lamppost just near the bench I was sat on and cocked its leg for a moment, before trotting on to its next pissing point. As they plodded off into the distance I noticed the old lady had almost exactly the same hair colouring as her pet. I wondered if that was a coordinated design. Do all Spanish women of a certain age turn to hair dye that matches their pet's coat? For her sake, I was glad she didn't own a Dalmatian.

Although it was hot, only part of the Ramblas was bathed in sunlight, one reason I supposed it was a popular place for people to gather. I sat a little longer in the shade, watching as one of the stallholders across the way, in the full sun, cranked out the awning over his stall.

I was now further south, the farthest from home I'd ever been in my life. Scotland seemed so very far away right then. The hum of life on the Ramblas enveloped me like a new stage set does an actor treading the boards for the first time. It was absorbing. Back then, I was full of curiosity, thirsty to see and feel new places. I knew I wasn't the first – or last – person to visit them. And in reality, they weren't even really so far away. But for a young working-class boy from small-town Scotland, who had never really been abroad, this was the biggest adventure.

After half an hour watching the comings and goings on the Ramblas, I decided to find a hostel. In Scotland I had bought the International Youth Hostel Association Guide Book; I leafed through the entries for Barcelona. From time to time I'd glance up and around, trying to make out the names of the street signs on the little alleys that led off from the Ramblas. As I did so, I observed a young guy, with a slim, scrawny frame in a white vest and torn jeans, approach a little old lady browsing leather purses and belts on one of the larger stalls. As she casually turned away from the stall, the man grabbed the straps of her handbag, yanked it from her and tore off up the midsection of the Ramblas. The woman gave a loud shrieking scream and started flailing her arms around.

"¡NO! ¡DETENER! ¡LADRÓN! ¡MI BOLSA!!!"

Other bystanders, hearing her desperate plea, immediately gave chase on her behalf. Instinctively, I shot to my feet, and even though he was well past me, I joined the effort to bring the scoundrel down. He was fast, but so were those of us racing after him. The thief darted, left, then right, dodging others ahead who'd clocked what was going on and attempted to block his path. Suddenly, the thief shot ninety degrees left, onto the road, narrowly missing an oncoming car, and sprinted up one of the side streets. We raced on after him – I, a policeman and three or four others all in hot pursuit. We were running flat out. The thief glanced back. We were gaining on him. When he turned his head forward again it was too late for him to avoid running head first into a large rolled-up antique rug that two workmen were carrying from an apartment block. He was catapulted backwards onto the hard road and reeled in agony.

We all stopped when we reached him, except for the policeman, who lunged on top of the thief, yanking his body over with a thud so he was now facing the ground. The thief yelled in distress. I was breathless and sweating. One of the other chasers, a stallholder I think, picked up the handbag and we all congratulated each other. A police car turned into the street, siren blaring and came to an abrupt stop. More officers jumped out and tried to corral us, but the first officer shouted something that alerted them to the fact that we were the good guys. Eventually, the victim arrived, also out of breath and the stallholder handed her back her stolen bag. She shouted through her tears about how grateful she was to us all.

"¡Gracias! ¡Gracias! ¡O Señor! ¡O mi!" Aside from 'Gracias', I didn't understand a word, but smiled and nodded anyway.

We watched as the thief was led away into the police car. He would be charged and locked up. Passing scooters beeped their approval of our actions; shoppers and shop workers clapped and whooped their support.

Then, grunting and groaning as we recovered our breath, we all walked back to the Ramblas, where a crowd had gathered. More clapping and howling cheers. People asked questions in Spanish, shook our hands and shouted what I think were words of thanks and support, but really I had no idea what they were saying. I turned back to the bench where I'd left my rucksack and felt the sickness rising in my stomach upon seeing it gone.

"Aargh! No! Not my bag too. Shit!" I started looking frantically around, twisting this way and that. Then I saw the scary looking African stallholder from earlier waving, beckoning me towards him. At his foot lay my backpack.

I bent over and clapped both hands on my knees and let out a heaving sigh of relief. Then, I threw my head back and closed my eyes, suddenly very tired, but also hugely relieved that I hadn't become the second victim of thieves on the Ramblas that day.

"Here, I keep safe for you, master". The tall African vendor summoned a huge, white toothy grin. I smiled back, and held out my hand to shake his.

"Thank you. Gracias, mucho. Thanks". My awful mix of Spanglish came gushing out as I tried to mask the embarrassment of my earlier distrust of this dark stranger. He shook his head, smiling and patted me on the back. I was excused. I realised then that one's youth can be an ally helping you through a lack of understanding of a language, one's lack of tact, lack of experience. I never knew his name, but I realised then, that however fleeting one's encounters are, the impression they leave can last a lifetime. The large, unsettling, dark, hairy African trader, with the unusually large gleaming smile, who was kind and considerate enough to look after my valuables as I ran to the aid of another, taught me the value of humanity that hot afternoon in Barcelona. I've never forgotten him.

I wandered around for what seemed like hours, taking in the avenues and port of Barcelona and was parched. On the street opposite the port, there was a little bar. In fact, it was tiny – only space for the bar counter and five or so stools – so I dropped my bags and ordered 'una cerveza', a beer. It must have been around five o'clock and there was only one other customer in the bar. Clearly, he was a regular, as he and the barman were deep in conversation. I guessed the regular was a fisherman or port worker, because he had a weather-worn face. He looked unkempt with sun-bleached, straggly hair sat upon a solid-set middle-aged body. Despite the little canopy over the outside of the bar entrance, the hot afternoon sunshine washed over us inside the bar. I climbed onto a barstool and dug into my bag for the youth hostel guide to resume my search for a suitable room.

The beer tasted delicious, cool and revitalising against the heat. I felt relaxed and happy as I leafed through the pages trying to figure out how to get to the various hostels and guest houses. Outside I could see tall palm trees across the road, blowing gently in the late summer breeze, and beyond them the distant hum of the docks. Occasionally a ship's horn would blast from somewhere beyond the port. Probably some container ship bringing exotic goods to Europe from South America, or, perhaps more likely, I thought, yet more crate loads of football scarves bearing the names of British Premier League clubs, hand made in the sweatshops of China. I stayed in the little dockside bar for around 40 minutes before traipsing off back up the Ramblas towards the little streets leading of from it that might hold the promise of a cheap hotel and a room for the night.

The great thing about travelling around Europe on an Interrail ticket was the freedom to go anywhere at any time. I cherished that new found freedom, as I moved about discovering new sights and cities. The downside, though, was that one had to put some work into finding accommodation, and affordable accommodation at that, once you'd arrived in a new place. There was no internet back then, no mobile or wi-fi to research suitable places ahead of arrival. No TripAdvisor recommendations or AirBnB. So the only solution was to wander around looking for what you hoped would be a safe, clean room at an affordable price. After three or four streets and countless enquiries at the reception desks of hostels and guest houses, I opted for a small guest house on Carrer no de la Rambla. The street was narrow, and the buildings on either side shot up five or six floors making it appear even more so from street level. It wasn't scruffy, but neither was it remarkable compared with the more prominent streets around it. Towards the top end, where it opened onto the Ramblas, there were small travel shops, a Spar supermarket, and a 'washeteria' or launderette. I spotted a couple of other backpackers on this street, which convinced me I was in the right area. Among the tiny hotels, hostels and guests houses was the Lorca Hostel, probably the cheapest on the street, and the one which fortunately had a 'single' room available.

The entrance was narrow, too, and the old, beer-bellied Spanish guy in stained black chinos and an off-white vest perched behind the small reception counter took my money upfront before pointing a hairy arm to a sign which contained the rules of staying in Spanish,

German, French and a kind of English.

'Es importante', he said without smiling.

I studied the sign – no other guests allowed in the room 'AT ANY TIME'; use your own towels; use your own toilet paper; take valuables (ie leave nothing in the room); Main door locked at 2400; Check-out 1200; No alcohol in the room (what?)

I nodded agreement and the proprietor shuffled down the small corridor to the staircase, where he handed over a small key with an unfeasibly large bakelite type fob attached (number 317), and a second key for the main entrance. He pointed upwards and showed three fingers, indicating the obvious - 3rd floor.

The room was basic. One small single bed, an ancient wardrobe, a wooden chair and a sink. The wooden floor looked original, the white walls flaked here and there and the pink curtains matched an equally pink shade over the pendant light fitting on the high ceiling. Basic, but it did have a tall window facing out into the street with a tiny iron balcony which allowed one to lean out and observe the goings on below. I put down my bags and went straight to the window to let in the warm heat of the late afternoon. The room at least had an ashtray, smoking indoors being still perfectly legal in those days, so I leaned out the window, smoked a cigarette and watched the people on the street below. Local women wandered along carrying bags of shopping; men sauntered along, carefree and idle; other backpackers strolled in and out of the other hostels in search of

rooms. I was glad my search was over. Some sat at little
tables outside the street's cafés and bars while their
friends studied guidebooks; boys on scooters disrupted
the hum of the street as they sped along the narrow
lanes, occasionally piercing the gentle hum of
neighbourhood by beeping their raspy horns. Lights
were beginning to come on in the shops and bars, and
the signs outside the various establishments took on a
gradual vibrancy as the day slowly faded. I was happy.
But I was also dirty, sweaty and tired from my journey,
so I headed down the corridor with my one and only
towel – ("You'll need this," Mum promised when she
thought to pack it). I took the bar of soap mum had also
insisted I pack and, to be on the safe side, my bumbag
containing my money, travellers' cheques, passport and
Interrail pass-book. The communal shower and toilet
was spartan but fully functioning and the hot water felt
good against my naked body. Refreshingly clean, but
still tired from all the travelling, I headed back to my
room for a nap before dinner.

It was a restless sleep at first. The early evening
sounds of a balmy Barcelona permeated my slumber.
Occasional Vespas rasping along the street punctured my
dreams, as did the strange, foreign voices of the people
down below. Soon, though, I was in a deeper state of
sleep, that place where all is quiet. Rest at last.

When I woke, it was after 10pm. I lay there in the half
darkness for a moment taking in this new room. It
occurred to me, this was the first real moment alone of
my trip so far. In Paris, the room at the MIJE was shared,

but here, now in Barcelona, it was just me. No friends nearby. No dinner dates or plans to meet friends. The small bed was just to the left of the window, which made it easy to reach out and pull on the curtain a little to get a better look at the darkened sky. The street lamps below threw a small amount of light into the room, but not much. I lit a cigarette and thought about taking myself out to find some dinner – if any place was still serving at this late hour.

Twenty minutes later I emerged onto the street in jeans and a white t-shirt. I tied a jumper around my waste figuring it may be a little chilly, but even though it was about a quarter to eleven, I needn't have bothered. I wandered along the little street, back towards the Ramblas, taking in the people at the various bars and restaurants. The Ramblas, far from winding down for the evening, was bustling with tourists and locals alike. I thought, maybe everyone had the same idea as I and slept most of the evening. Now, here we all were together heading out late for dinner. The street vendors were still there, but their stalls were now alive with lights and the stall holders were far more animated now, shouting and beckoning customers to view their wares and doing brisk business.

"You Britisher? Best prices for English. Come see madame." One vendor said to some passing tourists.

"Naranja fresco!" Another yelled from behind a beautifully arranged tower of oranges and juice making contraption. Flower stallholders were less vocal, as they tended customers buying colourful bouquets.

The night made the palm trees and other flora which lined the Ramblas more verdant and vibrant, losing the dull opacity of the daytime haze.

I wandered along the Ramblas in the direction of the sea. I hadn't noticed them earlier in the afternoon, but now it seemed like there were hundreds of restaurants lining the avenue. So hungry was I by now, that my tummy was rumbling – rumbling on the Ramblas, I joked to myself - and I could taste the saliva in my mouth. The restaurants buzzed with diners chatting and laughing, as busy waiters took orders for food and drink. I scanned the menus of the eateries along the street, my hunger growing all the time. The restaurants looked pricey for my budget, but every now and then I would come across smaller places, less romantically decorated and with no seating, but no less busy. These were tapas bars, which I'd read about in my youth hostel guidebook - a must-have experience and also very cheap. I decided on a large one on the corner of one of the streets heading off the Ramblas.

Tapas bars have to be one of the best Spanish inventions. They come with a dizzying array of choice. Instead of ordering a set meal, tapas bars offer a selection of small appetisers of different recipes, all delicious. Tapas literally means 'lid' and has its origins in the lids of jars from which simple dishes, such as olives, were once served. It had moved on to include a greater range of snack sized dishes. The menus had everything from cheese and potato balls, calamari and prawns to meatballs – called *albondigas* – and *patatas bravas*, delicious cubed chips marinated in a fragrant tomato sauce. There were Spanish omelettes, stuffed mussels, and wonderfully spiced and cooked meats called chorizo. The list seemed endless. But here in the Gaudi Tapas Bar, I knew exactly what I wanted – a plate of Croquetas de Jamon, a dish of Albondigas and a serving of Spanish Omelette. The counter was busy and my Spanish not great, but, after studying the menu for a few minutes, I decided I could pronounce all the names I needed and ordered with a combination of fake confidence and pointing with my finger at what I was trying to say.

People were drinking red or white wine with their tapas, but I was warm and decided a Coca-Cola would be the best refreshment to wash my supper down with. I paid the waiter behind the counter and he waved me to a stool by the window. I thought I might have to wait with him to take the food myself, but I somehow figured out that he was explaining that he would bring my food over when it was ready. I liked this touch. Two minutes later there he was, with all three of my dishes and chosen drink on a large single tray.

"Gracias, señor...gracias," I said, gaining a little more confidence after my ordering experience. I tucked into the deliciously cheesy ham croquetas and my hunger gave way to pure pleasure. The croquetas were exquisite, more so when I wash them down with a sip of my Coke. I noticed the other diners ate from all their dishes randomly, rather than one at a time, so I followed their lead moving onto the meatballs, cooked in mouthwatering tomato, garlic and basil sauce. I took a croqueta and dipped it into the albondigas sauce. I did the same with the Spanish omelette, which was surprisingly heavy and dense, but all the more delicious for it.

As I ate alone in the tapas bar, I noticed that most of the customers were Spanish, and mainly, but not all, men. There were small groups of three or four, work colleagues or friends, who stood around tall tables laden with the tapas plates, chatting vigorously. I tuned in to the musical tones of their words. Of course, I couldn't make out a thing they were saying, but they all appeared to be talking very fast. It was also a noisy language where expression was half the battle and words made up the rest, for they gesticulated a lot as well when they spoke. Older men gathered around one table used hand gestures towards each other as if making an emphatic point in their argument. One or other would shrug ostentatiously, whether in agreement or not with what his friend was saying, I couldn't tell. It sounded more like they were arguing. At another table, an elderly couple sat quietly, studiously working their way through a small collection of tapas. The woman, the wife I assumed, had that oddly vibrant copper coloured hair I'd noticed in other women earlier, which looked unreal. But she was graceful and sipped a small glass of white wine in between gentle nibbles of her calamari and gambas. The husband, by contrast, was almost bald, with a weather-beaten, but happy face. They sat in silence: perhaps after a lifetime together, they just had nothing more to say to each other over supper. Or they were just tired. Young couples ate standing at the main bar, laughing and talking loudly in Catalan. One woman, maybe in her late twenties, kept a tiny poodle on a tight leash as she devoured croquetas and a tomato dish. Her little poodle sniffed around the floor for titbits and scraps that fell there, straining on its lead to seize upon a stray morsel of albondigas that had fallen to the floor. It was a vibrant place to eat. We didn't have anything like this in Scotland, I remember thinking. Maybe it's because of the weather, but I wondered what our fish and chip shops would be like if the owners had ever thought of providing counters for their customers to eat their white pudding suppers or battered cod. Here in sunny Spain, food is clearly important, but it must be done socially, and often without ceremony, especially during the week. I imagined they dined in even more relaxed circumstances on the weekend when they had family members around and work was not on their minds. For the men at least!

I finished my Coke and stepped out into the night.

It must've been after midnight, but the streets were still alive and bustling with crowds. People sat outside bars at little tables, drinking and chatting. It was like everyone was on holiday, even the locals. Why couldn't it be like this back home? I thought. We're a sociable people too, surely we would take to this kind of life easily." But then I imagined standing around outside in Dundee, or any other city in Britain on a chilly September night, shivering while trying to look carefree and easy. "No thanks. This life is only to be had in places where the climate is warm and balmy most of the

112

year." I'd turn out to be wrong on that front, as the UK would become a haven for the al fresco life in the years that followed.

I trekked through the maze of streets that clung to La Ramblas. It was very late but the air still pleasant. I had never been this warm so late at night. It enveloped me and made me want to stay up, wandering around the ancient, timeless streets of Barcelona. Down one *carrer* I found many bars and cafés and decided to stop for a beer before calling it a night and shuffling back to my scruffy little hostel room. A waiter in a short-sleeved white shirt and smart dark trousers motioned me to an empty seat and table along the street and took my order. Surprisingly, when the beer came it was accompanied by a small plate of nuts, which I finished off in no time, still a little hungry after my post-supper wanderings. I sat back and took in the evening scene.

"Ello love, do you speak English?'

A girl was leaning over from her chair a couple of tables along. She was with two other girls, and dressed in a revealing short white dress, smiling.

"Yes, I'm from Scotland. How about you?"

She giggled at her two friends.

"'Aw, we're from Leeds. Scottish eh? You 'avin a good time?"

"Yes, thanks. Just arrived today. Love this city. Still getting used to it, though."

She introduced herself as 'Sheryl with an 'S".

113

"These are me pals, Sandra and Collette."

I felt my little bubble of travelling in solitude burst slightly with the arrival of English accents into my experience of Barcelona, but it wasn't a bad thing really. To be honest I was happy for the chance to chat to some people in English.

Sheryl with an 'S' was full of energy and spoke quickly. They were nurses from a hospital in Leeds, on a two week holiday. They'd been in Barcelona for four days and were heading further south to Benidorm, she said, before beckoning me over to join them at their table.

They were attractive girls. Sheryl had a sexy figure and her tight white dress contrasted with her beautiful dark skin and pretty, straightened dark hair. She had a warm personality, the most confident of the three. Sandra, a little taller, had a fuller figure and a neat short blonde bob. She wore a more restrained pair of white trousers, her tanned fair skin exposed by the striped vest she wore. Charlotte was the quietest, but no less attractive. She looked easy and comfortable in blue shorts and a white sleeveless shirt with her brown hair illuminated by the street lamps.

They chatted excitedly about their trip so far. How they liked Barcelona; how friendly the locals were – "but the waiters don't half fancy their chances," Sandra insisted.

And since I'd just arrived, Sheryl decided to take on the role of sightseeing monitor.

114

"Yev reelly gotta see the Sagrada thingy," she instructed in her warm Yorkshire accent. "What's it called again Collette, that big church we saw?"

"Sagrada Familia," Collette answered. She made an effort to utter the name in a sort of Spanish accent, which made her sound knowledgeable. It worked.

"That's it, it were gorgeous. A've never seen anythin' like it." She said I should seek out all the Gaudi buildings near the Ramblas too. "They're reelly, reelly weird lookin', but dead interestin' like."

"Okay, I'll definitely check it out tomorrow."

"So are you on yer own then?"

"Yes, I was in Paris with some friends, then headed down here on my own to see Spain."

"What ye think o' Barcelona?" Sandra asked.

"Incredible. It's sort of real and unreal at the same time; like a massive film set. Can't wait to see more of it." I told them about the events on the Ramblas that afternoon, how we'd all given chase to the handbag thief.

"Oh, what a hero, you'll be well in wit' locals then,"

We ordered more drinks and Sheryl joked about the silly things they got wrong. There was lots of hilarious laughter. I noticed after a while that Sheryl occasionally smiled at me in a certain way. She was being naturally flirtatious. I didn't really know how to respond. Well, actually I did. She was very attractive and kissable, but for reasons I was beginning to understand all too well, I wasn't really interested. So I smiled and flirted back, knowing it would go nowhere. She wasn't pushy. It was subtle and cool and fun and I respected her for that.

It must have been nearly 2.30am when we finally decided to turn in for the night, agreeing to meet the following evening for dinner at a small restaurant they knew.

9. La Sagrada Familia

I woke late the next morning, disoriented and a little the worse for wear after the late night bar encounter with the girls from Leeds. But I wanted to get going and see Barcelona. I pulled back the sheet, groggily grabbed my towel and headed for the shower.

It was hot as I stepped into the late morning sunshine, even in the shade. As the guest house didn't provide breakfast of any sort, I made for one of the small cafés on the street for some tea and a toasted ham and cheese sandwich.

People were busily going about their business and mopeds and cars passed noisily along the street as I ate breakfast and studied the little free map of central Barcelona I'd picked up at the train station the previous day. I wanted to plot a walk to the famous basilica, the Sagrada Familia. From the Ramblas I'd head up to Placa de Catalunya, then straight along to Placa de Tecuan, and then it was a march along about six blocks before turning right, then the same again and I would be at Spain's most interesting and famous Roman Catholic church. Mum would doubtless be proud. I estimated it would take about half an hour.

With the searing heat of the day beating down on Barcelona's streets, I'd done the right thing in wearing my shorts and trainers and the lightest white t-shirt I could dig out of my luggage. I took every effort to stick to the shade. Even then it was still hot, but far easier to cope with than the harsh, baking, full sun-lit side of the streets.

Eventually, I arrived at the hallowed temple. Nothing prepares you for the organic splendour of the Sagrada Familia. Back then, it still wasn't finished, and remained so decades later. As I approached the grounds around it, like all the other tourists with my head cocked and arched upwards to make out its fantasy, flute-like, pockmarked towers, I could feel a sense of movement in the tall slim edifices. It was trance-like, or rather I was transfixed by their motion. They were like lungs, breathing in the Barcelona air, these slender, protruding architectural organs.

A short and slim man sidled up to me and in very bad English asked if I'd like him to be my guide inside the bits of the church that were finished.

"Never mind the scaffolding, it's safe..." he assured.

I was tempted, but he wanted a lot of money for the experience and I couldn't do it on my budget. He turned gruff when I declined, but then soon sidled up to hustle other tourists. Not many people seemed too keen to go inside on that hot day, but plenty were milling around outside. I sat down and lit a cigarette and thought how odd to be asked to pay to go inside a church. Being brought up as a good Catholic boy – Mum had made sure I was taken on as an altar boy while at school and later I often took part in the church readings at Sunday mass – I always thought the house of God was free for all to enter.

I walked towards to a large reclining plate-stone sign outside the church, which had the whole story in English, Spanish, French and German. Construction started in 1882, but Antoni Gaudi the architect had died, in a tram accident in front of the site, before it could be completed. Little did I know then that even 103 years after construction had started, the first mass to be said in the Sagrada Familia would not take place until a quarter of a century later, in 2010, when a future pope would consecrate Gaudi's great unfinished work.

The plate also explained how the construction, on the orders of the architect had to rely on private donations only – no government hand outs allowed. Building work on the church was interrupted during the Spanish Civil War in the 1930s.

Back then, as I got closer to the building itself, the towers that were complete loomed even taller, more fantasy-like than when one first sees them from a distance. I made a circumference of the plot, hoping I might find some unnoticed quiet access passage that would allow a furtive glance inside this basilica. As I walked around to the south side of the building, the organic nature of Gaudi's work became more pronounced. I thought it the most Gothic construction I had ever seen. Even stranger, as I drifted around the site, there was this sense, as I carried on looking up, that the towers had their many eyelets trained on me and were watching my every move. More, as I came round to the north side and walked slowly down to the south garden, still looking up at its great towers, it appeared to be looking into my soul. Maybe it was just the afternoon sun playing tricks, but it was a little unnerving. I immediately abandoned any idea of trying to sneak into the church for free, convinced that Gaudi himself was now aware of my intended 'sin' of entering without paying. I pulled back from the main site and headed across the road, back to the cool, shady side of the street and a nearby gift shop flanked by numerous postcard stands. I sought out a card of the strange unfinished church to send home to Mum and Dad. I hoped the proceeds of my purchase would in some small way contribute to the onward construction costs, and Gaudi and his church would be appeased.

It was after 4pm when I got back to my room in the little hostel. The long walk had left me tired and I decided since I was in Spain, I'd take on one of the local traditions and have a siesta for an hour or so. I had planned to visit the port area and see the coast that evening, so I would need to be wide awake for that. The sun was still high in the sky and my room was uncomfortably warm. I was only able to leave the window open for a short time because the noise from the passing traffic on the street below disturbed my rest. I also pulled in the shutters a little to black out some of the light.

I undressed to my boxer shorts, lit a cigarette and locked the door to my room. Then I lay down on the bed and, parched, took a long swig from the large bottle of water I had bought from the Spar shop on the corner. I stared at the postcards of the Gaudi church, wondering what to write. 'In Barcelona, having a great time', or 'Spain is really cool, but their churches are a bit weird', or 'I'm in Spain now after France, which was great, planning to head further south'. I didn't really know then, and still don't today, what makes for worthy prose on postcards. I've always thought the picture kind of says it all. 'Wish you were here', always sounds trite but right. I lay there thinking I should write about the blistering sun, the different culture of the Spanish, my discovery of tapas. Given the tiny space on the postcard, it would be too much to try to describe how I felt wandering around the Sagrada. How its tall towers were impressive and unnerving at the same time. How the hot sun had made me woozy and slightly ill. Nah, that would just freak Mum out. Keep it light, that's best. I dropped the postcards on the floor by the bed and drifted off into a late afternoon slumber.

It wasn't a deep sleep. The din from the street below never seemed far from my ears, although I did dream a little. It was an abstract and strange fantasy. I was in a sort of Daliesque crystal clear landscape of sand, where everyday objects took on unusual proportions and motion. A train station desk clerk became a robotic lady doll, with dark, plastic hair and deep red lipstick, but with a beard. She would point this way and that fulfilling her role as information giver, without utterance. A smiley, African stallholder floated along with me, white, feathery wings fluttering gracefully behind him in the air. In the dream I was speaking to people in Spanish. Not fluently, but confidently, using simple phrases, like ordering a beer, 'una cerveza por favor'; asking where the bus stop is, 'Dónde está la parade de autobús?'; can I have the bill, 'la cuenta por favor'. The scenes were fuzzy and blended into themselves. When I woke an hour and a half later, I felt strangely changed by the place. Everything that seemed so foreign and alien and new was becoming familiar now. I lay there, bleary-eyed, repeating Spanish words and expressions out loud, trying to work in some kind of accent. It was kind of humorous, silly in fact.

"Por favor. Por favure. Poorly favoorly..."

"Dónde está. Dondee este. Dundee East..."

"Me llamo Sam. Mee yambo Sam. Me and Fat Sams!"

My self entertaining silliness could have gone on for a few hours. I decided, though, that from now on I must make the effort to engage with the locals in the few words I had available to me in their language. It seemed right.

As the afternoon light softened, I sat up on the bed, lit another cigarette and wrote out some postcards: 'Hola, I'm in Barcelona, I went to this amazing church today built by a man called Gaudi. It's awesome and scary at the same time – but you need to pay to go in! Love you...Adiós, Sam'.

After showering I returned to the room with the small towel wrapped around my waist and noticed in the full-length mirror that my face, arms and legs had caught the sun. But I had t-shirt tan lines and most of my torso was still the pale white of a northern European. I grimaced and decided tomorrow would be a beach day, to remedy the colour mismatch.

I pulled on my shorts and grabbed a blue polo shirt from the pile of rolled-up clothes I'd placed on the small chair opposite the bed. I had a military aptitude for tidiness. Something my mother instilled in me. It served me well in small rooms like that one. One last check in the mirror. At least the tan lines were not too obvious. I sat on the bed with the small tourist map of the Ramblas area and looked for the street where the girls had told me to meet them. I memorised the route and figured it would only take about ten minutes. This would allow time to head down to the port for a look around before dinner.

Outside, the streets had again shifted into evening mode. Restaurants, bars and shops once again bustled with crowds enjoying a warm evening out in this Catalan city by the sea. Men and women stood around chatting outside bars and cafés in the balmy evening. Teenage boys scootered energetically along the roads on their Vespas; old ladies stood in doorways watching the street life, their arms folded or shoved into the front pockets of their garish aprons. It had the potency of a movie scene, ready for the main actors to turn up and play out their roles. One skinny, tanned, beautiful Spanish woman, with dark, flowing hair and bright red lipstick to match her red top and tight jeans laughed flirtatiously with a couple of guys outside one of the bars at the end of the Ramblas. She was like a young Sofia Loren. I couldn't help but smile as I passed them. They smiled back, too, so I yelled 'Hola!' and carried on down to the port.

I crossed onto the main Mirador del Colón roundabout which separates the Ramblas from the port. I looked up the tall column and uttered another 'Hola!' to Columbus, one great voyager to another, now perched forever above the port of Barcelona looking out to the seas he sailed. Everyone, it turns out, loves to travel. I continued across the road onto the Ronda del Literol, where I was able to view the iconic port cable car that cut across the skyline. I always get excited by structures like this. They seem so implausibly large and yet fragile and precarious at the same time. And the Transbordador Aeri del Port or "Port Cable Car" didn't disappoint. The cars were suspended high above the port. They glided slowly and silently, almost as if they were just an illusion. I spotted tiny faces at the windows as they traveled through the air. The view of the city must be worth seeing. I promised to find out how much it cost so I could see for myself.

Nowadays, the port area has become a thriving social hub, bustling with bars and café life, but back then, it was still just a working port, the hustle and bustle of café life still confined to the Ramblas and there were only a handful of locals out walking along the port side the night I was there.

I looked at my watch and realised I was late for my

meeting with the girls. A few minutes later, I was back on the Ramblas and then darted down the little side street to the Café Matador, where the girls had already bagged a suitable outside table.

"Hola mademoiselles," I said cheerily, showing off my newly acquired multilingual skills.

"Hey chuck, you made it," Sheryl said getting up to hug me. "We're about to order so hurry up and choose because we're starving".

Sheryl claimed to be on a 'beach diet', so was only having some albondigas and a slice of Spanish omelette. She was extremely slim, so her diet was really unnecessary in my opinion. Sandra and Collette were sharing some seafood and patatas bravas, so I went for a mix of albondigas, croquettes de jamón and shellfish empanadas. We all ordered beers and the girls recounted their 'exhausting' day shopping and sun-bathing on the beach.

"It's a bit o' a trek to the beach here, and it's not great," Sandra said, looking at the girls for confirmation.

"Nah, we reckon Benidorm will be the real deal."

"What's wrong with the beach here?" I asked, worried my chance to even out my tan were about to be dashed.

"It's really industrial and the water didn't look very clean," Sheryl said.

"We didn't even go in the water. Loads of stuff just floatin' around in it. It looked toxic."

125

"Yuk, I guess I'll be giving that a miss." I told them about my visit to the Gaudi temple and how I'd spotted many of his other constructions along my walk.

"He really didn't like straight lines or edges, did he?"

It was fun to have people to chat to after being on my own all day. As we ate, I told them about the cable cars and they all shuddered, saying they didn't look safe or particularly well maintained.

"I tell you, that's just an accident waiting to happen," said Charlotte grimly.

After dinner, we paid out our pesetas and wandered along the streets until we found a bar with some lively music. It was only around 11.30, but the dance floor inside was thumping, and we stayed dancing and laughing and drinking for a while. From time to time two or three of us would head outside for some air and Sheryl asked if I'd accompany them south to Alicante since I was going that way anyway.

"Well, when are you guys leaving?"

"Tomorrow morning, the 10.30 train direct to Alicante. It's a long journey, so we'll just sleep on the way."

"Sure, I'd love to." We made a plan to meet at the train station at 9.45am – just to be on the safe side – then went back into the bar and danced some more. Sheryl grew a little tipsy and her dance moves became more evocative. She eyed me on the dance floor and gyrated her lean sexy body toward me, beaming her big smile. I smiled back and teased her with some moves of my own and she moved closer as Bananarama's 'Venus' moved to its climax. She threw her arms around me and moved in for the kiss. I wasn't expecting this, so it was a bit awkward. But I obliged, happy and flattered that she wanted to. Then Sly Fox's 'Let's go all the way' started up and the other two girls crashed in laughing and making silly dance swoops. I looked at Sheryl and smiled, but she knew it wasn't going to go anywhere.

Later we all piled out onto the street, still happy and laughing, before I kissed them all goodnight. Kissing Sheryl last of all, I smiled bashfully.

"You're a hot kisser mister," she said slightly slurring, "but I'll settle for friends." She smiled and hugged me. "Now don't forget chuck, 9.45 at the station. Don't be late."

"Don't worry, I'll definitely be there."

I watched them go into their hotel and turned to head back to my hostel. As I walked along I quizzed myself. Why couldn't I just have gone with it. I enjoyed kissing her, but I didn't feel anything. I didn't know where to put my hands and she seemed so petite. Surely whatever life I had ahead would be easier if I could just meet a girl who made me feel something. As I wandered along the Ramblas, I reminded myself that I had just been through all of this when I was with Yvonne.

Although it was late, I noticed local guys here and there, sitting out on the street. They seemed to be waiting around for something, but who knew what? One of them approached and asked for what I assumed was a light for his cigarette. For smokers asking for a light is easy in any language: you motion with one hand making a flicking movement with your thumb towards the unlit cigarette between your lips.

I pulled a lighter from my pocket and flipped the flame on. As it lit up his face, I could see he was a handsome dark-haired boy, about my age. He offered a brilliant white smile, made even whiter by his deep bronze tan. His dark eyes flashed warmly at me and he cupped both his hands around my left hand and the lighter. He put his cigarette into my flame and took just a little longer than he should have to light it. I was nervous but exhilarated at the same time. I liked the touch of his hand on mine, I liked his lean torso, the contours of which showed through his tight white t-shirt. He looked easy and relaxed, with one hand now stuffed into the pocket of his cut-off jeans, which came to just below his knees. This allowed me to admire his athletic, tanned lower legs, which were exposed all the way to his trendy flip-flop sandals. He caressed the back of my hand before pulling back.

"Gracias," he said. "You Ingleesh?" I nodded, and replied "Scotteesh", to try to give him a bit of help in understanding.

"You have a room?" I was startled by the question, but nodded. Of course, I did. But did I want to take him there? Was I ready for this? Was it safe?

"Okay. Let's go," he said

The moment caught me off guard. I didn't know what to do, but something in me wanted to go with him, be with him, taste him.

"I'm really not allowed guests in the room," I protested weakly. But the boy just smiled and said it would be fine.

We walked along the Ramblas and turned into the street of my guest house. Fortunately, when we arrived at the entrance, no-one was around. It was late and the doors were locked, so I opened up and both of us slipped into the dark corridor and quietly up the stairs.

Safely inside the room, I turned on the small light over the sink in the corner.

"What's your name?"

"Am I Andreas, you?"

I told him my name and offered him a glass of water from the bottle I had bought. It was awkward, tense and electric. He sat on the bed and pulled me towards him. He looked into my face, moved towards me and kissed me on the lips. My head was racing, charging, thoughts tumbling over themselves. Was this right? Was it safe? Who was he? What am I doing? But I also liked the feel of his kiss, the way he touched me. It felt exciting, full on, charged. We moved closer, got more comfortable. I craned my head to the right, which allowed me to kiss him back as deeply as he was kissing me.

He gently pushed me back, stood up and removed his t-shirt. He took me by the hand, then removed my top

129

and set to kissing my slim, naked, white torso. I was hard and aching for more. We undid our jeans and slipped off the remainder of our clothes, before falling onto the bed, kissing passionately the whole time. We wrapped ourselves together, feeling our limbs intertwine until they became as one; two boys from different lands, exploring each other in the sensual, passionate, half-darkness of a hot Barcelona night. He smelled delicious, sweet, musky, foreign. I craved his soft, beautifully tanned skin, and enjoyed his taut body against mine. As we writhed around, getting deeper into each other, the dimly-lit room, the heat of the night, and the strangely disorienting headiness of the moment, were a potent mix that soon had the sweat dripping off our young bodies, like two soldiers from foreign lands engaged in an act of love, not war.

An hour or so later, we both lay silent, spent, relaxed.

"Cigarette?" Andreas asked. I lit one, and we shared it while making small-talk - if such as thing is possible between two people who knew so little of each other's tongue, other than having tasted it. We lay together, trying to understand each other, asking only the simplest of questions and working together to make sense of each other's answers.

It was that night I discovered, while there are many languages across Europe, lots of our key nouns are familiar. He was at university – *universidad* - studying agriculture - *Agriculturo* - and was in his first year, but hoped he would end up working in the nation's burgeoning tourism – *turismo* - industry. He said he would like to visit Britain.

I told him I was travelling across Europe; I wanted to go to university too; and I was very interested in other cultures. And he was welcome to come see me in Britain any time he liked. "But it's pretty cold," I warned him.

Eventually, we both drifted off to sleep; two foreigners, spooned together beneath a single sheet on a single bed in a cheap hotel in Barcelona. I slept well.

In the morning, we stirred at the same time, smiling shy and sleepy hellos - "Hola", "Hi".

He dressed without showering and kissed me again before leaving the room – we agreed it was better for him to leave first, to avoid the chance of the manager discovering our tryst. I wished him good luck with his life, while he hoped I had a great journey in Europe. And with that, he was gone. I lay back on the bed for a bit, recounting the pleasure of the night just passed. This was not my first sexual encounter, but it was my first with a foreigner in a foreign land.

I looked at my watch lying on the little chair I'd dragged to the side of the bed – 0845. I had only an hour to get cleaned up, packed and meet the girls at the station. I grabbed the towel and made for the shower with a happy spring in my step and a smile on my face. I was young, life's big adventure was only just beginning and I was discovering through experience who I was.

10. Viva España

I arrived slightly out of breath at the train station that morning and immediately spotted the girls sitting with their bags outside a café on the station concourse.

"Hey, there you are. We wondered if you were coming or not, sleepy head." Sheryl yelled upon seeing me.

I smiled back. If only she knew.

"Well, you needn't 'ave rushed. Apparently, the train's been cancelled."

"What?"

"Bleeding Spanish transport system's playing up," Sheryl explained, "but we've got to wait here for more information in about an hour."

I dropped my backpack and took a seat. No need for all that rushing after all. I ordered a cup of tea and the girls chatted about a plan-B, which was to take take a bus. For me, on an Interrail pass, that wasn't really an option I wanted, because it meant paying to travel somewhere. But the girls assured me it would be

132

extremely cheap and scolded me for being so tight, so I agreed.

We hung around for the next hour or so and talked about how wonderful it was going to be when we got to Benidorm and could start enjoying ourselves on the soft and warm sandy beaches and swimming in the balmy waters of the Mediterranean Sea. I wasn't entirely sure I'd done the right thing in agreeing to go with the girls to Benidorm. It was a bit too like a package-holiday for someone who was supposed to be exploring new cultures on a rail pass. But I resigned myself to the fact it would only be for one day. Besides, I was in love with Spain, that morning. Everything seemed so warm, inviting, alive and friendly. Even the old men hanging around the station in their little groups had a benevolence about them, smiling and waving at those who passed them by.

An hour and a half passed before the counter started offering more information, and when one of the girls returned from the queue that had formed, she brought good news. Kind of.

"Right folks, trains are back in operation, but the only one to Alicante isn't 'til 8.30 tonight," Collette said with a grimace. Our spirits sank.

"Aw, girls, what we gonna do?" This was an opportunity for me to back out. I could seize the moment, claiming it wasn't meant to be. But I did want to head further south, so I held my breath.

"Well all this beach talk's made me desperate for it,

so let's see what Barcelona has to offer," Sheryl announced.

We shared a taxi to the beach, where we would at least get to relax and spend another day in the sun, before going back to the station in the early evening.

In truth, I was quite relieved to have the unplanned opportunity of snoozing on the beach after my late night with Andreas. We took it in shifts to look after our bags on the beach and the girls treated me to lunch, a mixture of tapas from a little bar they'd spotted.

I dozed for most of the afternoon, replaying parts of the previous night's steamy encounter over in my sleepy mind, interrupted only by occasional comments from one or other of the girls about how 'buff' this guy on the beach was or how 'well fit that one over there is'. Occasionally, I would discreetly sneak a look, to see what the fuss was all about.

Eventually the afternoon sun weakened and our shadows grew longer on the sand. We took cold showers on the beach and all headed back to the train station, slightly browner – redder in Sandra's case - from our sojourn in the sun. There were lots more people milling around the station than in the morning, so it looked like it was going to be a packed journey. The train, though, would stop at Valencia along the way, so maybe people would leave there, and it wouldn't be too packed and uncomfortable all the way.

We boarded the big, dusty train, with its yellow-stained windows, and tried to find a decent space where we could all sit together. As we'd suspected it was very busy, and seats were few and far between. When the girls saw a tight squeeze of three seats together – probably the only ones on the entire train, I insisted they take them, and said I'd find one for myself. They protested in unison a little, but I assured them I would pop back to see them during the twelve-hour journey through the night if I could.

Two coaches along I spotted from the corridor one space by the window of an eight-seat compartment and claimed it immediately.

The wonderful thing about travelling alone back then was that you always had the opportunity to meet new people, fellow travellers, of all nationalities. When I took my seat in the corner of this compartment all the other occupants looked Spanish, so I smiled a greeting to the young couple sat opposite and settled in. After an hour or so, people started to move – some to stretch their legs, others to go to the toilets. The couple opposite took out fruit and napkins and quietly cut their fare into small slices. The girl lifted her napkin and offered me some slices of orange. I gladly accepted.

"I from Valencia. He from Valencia. You English?" said the pretty girl, pointing to her boyfriend (I assumed). I'd decided to get over the 'English, Scottish, British' thing and simply nodded 'Si' followed by 'gracias' for the fruit.

Mayte Sabate Lopez was a young student from Valencia, who had been visiting her family in Barcelona and was keen to know if I liked Spain. It's incredible how much we can all still communicate despite our different tongues. Expression and gesture are hugely adept ways to explain things. I pointed to my eyes to explain what I liked seeing in Barcelona, I used a wet finger to draw on the window the route of my journey so far. She smiled and seemed to enjoy our chat. The boyfriend only smiled occasionally, and never spoke. After a while, the conversation ran out and we all settling into our napping positions. I placed my head against my jacket, which in turn was placed against the window, and drifted off to the heavy clunk of the slow train moving along the old tracks towards the south of Spain into yet more new territory.

I can never really sleep on trains in a seated position. It's just a kind of semi-sleep, caught between two states of being. I'm never sure if I've actually been asleep or not. So, when we juddered to a stop in the dark of the night I awoke immediately. We sat there for about fifteen minutes before I decided to stretch my legs and go check on the girls. Before I got to their carriage, I noticed the door to the coach was open, so I leapt off and onto the gravel below and lit a cigarette. There were a few others who'd also had the same idea, so I didn't feel as if I was doing anything untoward. I looked along the train from the trackside. It seemed to go on forever at both ends. I wondered what the problem was if indeed there even was a problem. Perhaps someone had been taken ill. Maybe they had arrested a dangerous international criminal, like the ones I imagined I'd seen on the train from Calais to Paris last week. Most likely it

136

was probably just some simple reason like an engine change or fuel stop. Just as I was pondering the workings of the Spanish railway system, the entire train jolted forward slightly and I immediately threw down my cigarette and made a dash for the steps to the carriage. I was thankful for my agility as I could see some others on the track, having been equally spooked by the sudden movement, struggling to get on, now that it was inching along and picking up the pace. I stayed there in the doorway, waiting, watching to make sure everyone got on, and ready to lend a helpful hand to anyone who needed it. It's one of those things I just have to do. I couldn't have just returned to my seat unconcerned as to whether everyone had made it back on board. I can't explain it, but it's important for me to know that everyone is where they need to be and accounted for.

I made my way along to see the girls and found all three completely asleep, Sheryl and Collette snuggled together, feet on luggage, Sandra now sitting opposite them with her feet sandwiched between the hips of her two friends. I smiled and returned along the dimly lit corridor to my own compartment and its sleepy occupants.

I awoke later to find daybreak had come and gone. So too had some of my fellow passengers, including Mayte and her man. We had exchanged addresses, though, and I wondered if I would ever hear from her again – Scotland is a long way away from this world of balmy weather, beautiful sunrises and palm trees.

Soon the train shuffled into Alicante train station.

This was the end of the line. Alicant-Terminal as it's known is located just metres from the beach and the Mediterranean Sea. The streets outside the station were lined with exotic, impressive looking palm trees, a welcome sight that morning. My memory is that there were two road lanes separated by a pathway in the middle and then the sea. The girls and I stepped out and looked across at the inviting water for a few moments. It was beautiful and tempting to just drop everything a dive into it. Although still groggy from the overnight journey we decided instead to find the bus terminal and head straight for the coastal city of Benidorm. "This way," Sheryl assured us, "all the travelling will be behind us and we can just relax."

Alicante was one of the cleanest cities I had ever visited. I was amazed how organised, shiny and sparkly everything was; how well laid out and chilled (out) it was. I felt I had arrived in Utopia. There was not one single piece of litter to be seen as the four of us wandered along the glistening streets. But this was only the start. An hour and a half later we arrived in what I can only describe as 'Manhattan on the Med.' As our very comfortable coach drew around the final corner and past the mountains, the implausibly situated city of Benidorm swung into view, and quite a few people on the bus gasped.

I'd never been to New York at this point in my life, but Benidorm seemed to have more skyscrapers than Manhattan I thought, with the added beauty of miles of white sandy beach thrown in. I couldn't understand why this wasn't the capital of planet earth. Isn't this what everyone wants? I thought to myself. A city on a beach!

It was awesome for me, a small-town boy who'd barely seen one skyscraper his whole life, now suddenly entering a city made almost entirely of them. This man-made wonder was one thing, but it was nothing compared with the vast waters of the Mediterranean Sea which lapped gently at the city's feet. The towers were outdone again by mother nature, for the city's architectural skyline is dwarfed by the enormity of the Puig Campana Mountain range that cloaks the city. Offshore, sits the l'illa de Benidorm, an impressive sloping island that juts out at a sharp angle. It looks like a ship of Titanic proportions in the final moments before it is completely submerged. Yet this feature is frozen in place for eternity. I would later discover that it is also known as Peacock Island, because of the creatures that inhabit it. There are not too many beaches around the world that I seen with such a spectacular naturally occurring feature as this.

First impressions last, and while I thought the landscape of this tourist destination was stunning, the city planners had clearly not been so sympathetic in managing the construction of the city around it.

Our bus wormed its way into the heart of the city, past the endless high rise hotels and apartment blocks, and finally deposited us on a forgettable little square just off the beach. When we alighted, the first thing that hit me was a surprisingly familiar smell. Could that really be fish and chips'?

The girls didn't seem to notice this. Nor did they seem perturbed by all the 'Britishness' going on here. I'd counted the word 'Pub' above a dozen establishments as we'd come along the streets in the bus. There were signs in English everywhere, 'Ice Cream'; 'Hamburgers'; Did I even spot a 'Kiss Me Quick' hat? I really hoped not.

"Brilliant, we're here at last. Ooh, I love it," Sheryl squealed. "This is it girls, told yer Barcelona were nowt compared to this."

My heart sank. I'd travelled thousands of miles across Europe in search of new cultures and experiences, to taste new delicacies and drink new drinks, to meet new and exotic people, but instead, it was fish'n'chips, beers, and English accents everywhere. I fixed my smile and asked the girls if they fancied walking along the beach to see if there were any decent Spanish restaurants for lunch. They just wanted to get to their hotel, but I pleaded hunger and Collette agreed.

"We can check in later, let's eat first".

We walked along the well-manicured promenade, with its cutely shaped patterned tiles. There were many restaurants. To be fair, they didn't all specialise in British cuisine. I did notice a few 'pizzeria' signs. But the girls chose one of the many places which offered either Spanish or 'International' dishes. I ordered a paella, while Sheryl and Collette ordered 'salad and chips' and Sandra, who apparently wasn't hungry, nonetheless ordered sausage, egg and beans.

As we all ate in the warm shade of the terrace, the

sounds of different regional English accents permeated the air.

"There are a lot of Brits here, don't you think?"

"Oh God, yeah, they love Benidorm. Proper home from home," Sandra said.

"Mmm, but you'd think there might be some Germans, Italians, or even Spanish people on holiday, eh?" I replied.

"See what you mean," Sheryl added. "It's like Blackpool illuminations, innit."

All three burst out laughing and I could only join in. Of course, everyone had a right to be here. Why shouldn't hoards of my fellow citizens flock here for two weeks of blistering sunshine instead of Blackpool? I just wished their needs hadn't been so over catered for, that more of them demanded the 'foreignness' that should have come with this experience. Instead, they were being sold a homogenised experience, which kept them in the safety of the known, when the whole purpose of travelling, to my mind, was to experience the unknown, taste new things, experience otherness.

As we sat there eating lunch, smiling and chatting away, I quietly hoped that this city, which was at once exceptional, impressive and oddly familiar, would remain a one-off. If we're going to travel abroad we need to be willing to sample the culture of the places we visit. We need to experience the joy of eating foreign delights in a foreign land and meeting those foreign people.

The girls went to their hotel to check-in and offload their luggage, and I met them later on the beach. They were so happy and cheery when they came back with their cute beach shirts and bikinis already on. They wasted no time in expertly organising themselves in a kind of haphazard circle into which I was included. They set out their beach towels with military precision, maximising the amount of lying space they could get, handbags placed in the centre of the group to minimise the risk of theft, sandals placed to the bottom left of each towel, easier to access when they needed to walk across the hot sand. It was wonderful to watch them setting themselves up. I felt myself shift and straighten my dishevelled towel, so as not to be shown up by my little 'harem' of sun worshippers. Then, when they were all confidently perched on their towels out came the sun cream. Not just any old cream, of course, for Sheryl. Hawaiian Tropic wasn't familiar to me, but from the look of it this was serious tanning oil. Sheryl placed it to one side.

"Okay girls, ready?" Sheryl looked to Collette and Sandra and they each reached in unison for the straps of their bikini tops.

"And relax." All three at once unclipped their tops exposing their breasts to the full heat of the sun, and everyone else on the beach. I was slightly stunned, having never seen that before. Where I come from in Scotland, it's barely ever warm enough for a girl to take her jumper off let alone the whole upper deck. Add in their thonged bikinis and there really wasn't much left to the imagination. But I wasn't complaining. They were being free and 'continental' and I felt liberated just being there with them.

"Eh, luv, would you mind just putting some of this on my back?" Sheryl handed me the bottle and I clumsily set about oiling her soft flawless torso. I liked the feel of her soft skin as I worked in the oil, but that was as far as it went. I couldn't get excited about her in the same way I'd been excited about Andreas. If he were there now, if this was his back, I probably wouldn't be able to touch him without becoming aroused. I oiled her down and handed Sheryl back her Hawaiian Tropic.

The beach was packed with holidaymakers and I noticed many of the other women were also topless. Couples and groups of teenagers bathed and played in the still warm waters of the Mediterranean. Others had taken refuge from the blistering sun under the cover of the many large parasols erected in straight lines along vast areas of the long, large beach. The occasional roar of speedboats mixed with the screams and shrieks of others being splashed by incoming waves caused by the boats. As I lay in the sun, still at last, I felt happy, carefree and blessed. Chilling out alongside the girls was fun, even if it wasn't exactly my idea of a great cultural travel adventure. I'd taken in a lot of culture over the past week, so I thought of our day on the beach in Benidorm as a moment to reflect on that.

Sandra and Collette were coerced into having a go on a new kind of beach thrill called a banana boat. The long, yellow, inflatable, banana-shaped contraption was dragged across the water by a speedboat, and the trick for those sat astride it is to remain on top of it as it bumps along the waves at great speed. There was much screaming and yelping as people flew off their banana rides, though we were all impressed that Collette managed to last longest before finally succumbing to the warm waters with a clumsy splash and a muffled yelp. Later she assured us it was because of her many years' experience of horse riding. When the girls returned, Sheryl pulled me after her to head in for a dip. I love swimming: stepping into the Med for the first time was a pleasure that I have never forgotten. Once again I felt my old life wash off me, in those first moments entering the sea. I'd never felt such warm waters, such splendidly hot surroundings and such freedom. On those rare occasions I'd taken to the seas around Britain, it was always a chilly encounter, despite the sunshine, and wrapping in towels was a must afterwards. Sheryl and I swam around for a bit and then floated on our backs, baking in the sunshine.

"So, have you got a girlfriend, then?" she asked, before splashing me.

"Well, not really. Mmm, kind of. I thought I did. But it's cool. Anyways, we don't live very close to each other, so who knows?'

"I think you're not bad, in case you hadn't noticed."

"Really? Thanks. I hadn't – you know, noticed," I lied.

"Maybe you're not into girls?" She probed.

144

I wasn't having any of it. Of course, I knew what I wanted, but I was really still trying to figure it all out properly. How could I confidently tell her – someone I had only recently met - whether I was gay or not when I hadn't yet resolved everything for myself? Even though I knew I was gay, I wasn't ready for the world at large to know it, too, and it just wasn't something you could easily share in those days. If I had opened up to her at that moment, it would be all they would talk about for the rest of the day. I didn't want to be their topic. I also didn't want them to lose interest in me or become distant at hearing something confirmed that they may not like. People can be like that. They insist they're accepting and understanding of gay people, until they actually discover they have one as a friend. I had no real evidence either that coming out to friends or strangers was a successful strategy, far less so when you were on holiday. And then there was the place itself, the location. Did I really want to carry around with me for the rest of my life the knowledge that place I first came out was, Benidorm?

I looked at her and smiled.

"You're gorgeous. I mean really pretty. Any guy would be lucky to have you. And you kiss really well, too."

She stood up in the water as if carefully reviewing my description of her. I looked back at her and stood up too. Then we burst out laughing and started splashing each other crazily, shouting and laughing. She knew. And I knew she knew. But it didn't matter and it didn't need to be said. She'd meet some nice boy – the right one – one day, as would I, hopefully.

We ran back to the others and I towel dried my now tanned body and reached for the bottle of Ambre Solaire tanning cream. It wasn't as sophisticated as Sheryl's expensive Hawaiian stuff, but that was what they advertised on TV back home. So that's what I bought.

At about five o'clock the crowds on the beach started to thin out. I looked around the scene. All I registered, though, was the sea, sand and the mountains. At that moment a lifelong love affair with beaches and their warm waters started. I promised myself that every year from now on I would find a new beach, a new sea, new warm waters to explore and enjoy.

"So where are you staying Sam? Surely not here on the beach?" Sandra asked with a smile.

"Mmm, not a bad idea really. Maybe I will," I replied, laughing.

I'd already made up my mind. Hanging out with these girls had been a real treat, and a welcome break from being alone. But Benidorm wasn't really for me. It was fun to have made the journey further south and to see it with them, but I wanted to get back to exploring other places by train. I wanted to see the Mediterranean from France, I wanted to see Italy, too, and Germany. The Interrail ticket was a passport to see more new places, meet more new people, and I wanted to use it. Maybe it was just being young and impatient to chalk up the number of places visited, but I was happy to move on from Benidorm, even just after one day.

"I think I'm just going to take the bus back to Alicante and catch the night train north again. I have to get to France. You know, the Côte d'Azur is waiting."

"What?" Sheryl said, shocked. "Aren't you gonna stop 'ere for a few days? There's loads o'discos. You'll love it!"

No, I wouldn't! I liked clubbing as much as anyone else, but I wanted to see Europe, not disco dance my way across it. Although that wouldn't have been an entirely bad idea, I thought.

"I'm sorry. You guys will have a brilliant time. Look, it's been so great meeting you. I've had so much fun, you wouldn't believe it. And you three are going to rock this place. It's been a pleasure, but I'm travelling, I want to keep moving."

I'd never said that before: "I'm travelling". It sounded so new, so amazing, so different to anything I had ever done in my young life. But it felt so good.

As the sun moved behind the mountains, we packed up our stuff and the girls walked me to the square where the bus to Alicante was already waiting. I turned to those three beautiful, charming, suntanned British girls and wished them well.

"Enjoy your travels adventure boy," Collette said, smiling and hugging me.

"Say hi to the Cote thingy in France for me," Sandra added.

"Be good and have a ball, chuck?" Sheryl said. We

kissed and hugged a truly warm and heartfelt hug.

"Thanks, gorgeous, I won't forget you."

I climbed onto the bus and looked at the girls as they waved and walked off. As the bus pulled away from the square, I looked back at the girls. All three of them walked along in a line with their arms around each other. I was alone, but I wasn't lonely. They were on their journey, I was one mine. They offered friendship and I was glad of it. And I knew they would have a great time there.

* * * * *

"Another glass of wine sir? Would you like something to drink?"

The Eurostar stewardess is standing behind a trolley laden with wine, soft drinks and nibbles.

"A glass of white would be nice."

"You looked very far away," she observes, "Thinking about your holiday, perr-aps?"

"Mmm, kind of," I reply. "Merci, c'est gentil," I said when she placed an ice cold glass of wine on the table.

I have no idea where we are now. Have we already passed Paris? Who knows? Who cares? It's what I love about travelling on long train journeys. You get lost in the moments and the rhythm of the train. One can think, dream, drift, drink… I settle back again, resting my feet up on the empty seat opposite.

I take a sip of the wine. Ice cold – the only way it should be served. I often hear grim stories from friends of 'warm' bottles of wine being served on flights, usually with some unattractive, rattling discount airline. I never use them. It's not a snob thing. It's because these budget carriers have stripped all the romance of travel so far back to its bare minimum that the entire experience is bereft of any kind of charm. Thankfully, Eurostar takes a more refined approach to how one should experience travel. Even standard class on this train is luxury compared with any type of budget airline.

I think of Sheryl and her friends and wonder what they are doing now. Are they still living in Leeds? They've probably all got children the age we were when we met in Spain all those years ago. I wonder if I'll ever meet them again and if they would even remember me.

As I settle back to my thoughts, I also remember what happened later that night, when I returned to Alicante.

* * * * *

It was around 8.30pm when the coach pulled into the little square a short walk from the train station in Alicante. It was dark now and the sunny carefree fun of the beach in Benidorm suddenly seemed a long way off.

There were only a handful of us on the large bus. Having stretched out at the back, I was the last to disembark. A slight but warm, balmy wind was blowing, as I made my way across the avenue to the train station.

149

Alicante station was relatively small compared with those I'd seen in Paris and Barcelona. There were not many people around at this time of night, but the information desk was still open, so I walked over and asked when the next train was leaving for Barcelona. The old, balding Spanish clerk looked at me disdainfully, took another drag from his cigarette and uttered something in Spanish, which I really did not get. Noticing this he pulled a grubby piece of paper towards him and wrote '23.08' upon it.

"Aah, ok, thank you. Sorry, gracias señor, gracias." I had about two hours to kill.

The entrance to the station was made up of a sort of grand little cloistered portico, which meant you could wait under cover instead of inside the station proper and its concourse. Curious to see who my fellow travellers may be, I hung around in the portico area for a bit.

Eventually, a group of blonde haired boys arrived, who I identified immediately as fellow interrailers or backpackers at least. There were four of them, and they all dropped their packs onto the warm tiled floor of the portico. I watched them as they chatted and studied what looked like a tome of a timetable. I could tell from their chatter that they were not English. Their voices had a slightly harsh guttural tone. I assumed that, like Kai in Paris, they must be German. This was 1985, and although World War II was just an abstract, albeit dark, piece of history to me, I was nonetheless slightly intimidated by the thought of approaching them. They did look impressive, though. Superior, strong, perfect and beautiful. I'd only ever known one white-blonde haired guy at school, and he had an Irish surname, and to be honest he was a bit of a runt compared with these fine-looking, dignified boys.

I plucked up some courage and wandered over to say hello and ask if they spoke any English.

"A leetle," one of them replied. "We take train tonight."

"Me too," I replied with a big smile. "Can I sit with you?" The boys agreed and we sat there on the floor of the station.

I didn't say much, but the boy who spoke some English asked where I was from.

"Scotland, a place called Dundee. It's famous for jute, journalism and jam." I trotted out that phrase as a hangover from something hammered into me at school. As if to say "see, my home is famous for something."

"We from Stockholm. Swede, er, Sweden." The boy said.

"Oh, wow," I answered, "Volvo and Saab?" They laughed out loud, nodding. See, Sweden is famous for something too.

I didn't talk much after that. I just listened to them, nodding occasionally. Smiling, when I thought it appropriate. They looked casual, cool and all wore khaki shorts, which I wished I'd had. Their white t-shirts with varying motifs set off their deep tans, which gave them a more golden look despite their shockingly white hair.

They were strong, lean and more toned than I.

They opened some beers and kindly offered me a swig from one of their bottles. I gladly accepted and offered them cigarettes. Then an older guy arrived in the station and hung around for a while, before sitting down to join us in the group. He was black, dark, though I wasn't sure if he was of African descent or just 'deep Spanish'. He was wearing jeans and a denim jacket, which looked kind of uncomfortable, given the weather. He gladly accepted a sip of the beers that were going around and started to joke with us all. I didn't really get what he was saying, but I smiled and laughed anyway. We all sat in that circle, each of us lying against our backpacks, taking in the moment. Strangers at a junction.

Soon, the black guy was putting together what looked to me like a large and quite unusually long roll-up. I offered him one of my cigarettes instead, but he seemed happy with his long, stumpy roll-up.

He lit it, took a few puffs then offered it around. Each of the Swedish guys took a few puffs, and then I realised what was going on. We were being offered marijuana. We all took a toke and passed it on. When it was finished, the stranger rolled another. With the little beer I'd consumed on an empty stomach and the various tokes of the joint I'd taken, my head started to go into a sort of fudge. I felt relaxed, slightly disoriented and a bit sick. But I also felt happy, floaty and warm.

The feeling gradually became heavier. I could see the other guys smiling. Some of us started sniggering and then laughing. I was feeling uncertain, but laughing at what the guys were saying, which was odd as I couldn't understand a word.

A third joint did the rounds. I could only manage one or two tokes because by then, my head was spinning. I started to worry. What was the time? Where am I? Are we really here? Have we missed the train? The train, oh, crikey, the bloody train. I looked at my watch and it was already 10.30pm. I couldn't believe where the time had gone. The other guys were completely out of it. They were lolling around, trying to understand each other. Only the dark, denim-clad, austere-looking guy with the joints seemed to have his wits about him.

The paranoia started to hit me. It was now 10.45pm and I somehow managed to figure out through the fog that had engulfed my brain that, whatever happened, I needed to make sure I was on that train.

I decided to make my move. Getting to my feet was a struggle, after sitting around so long, but once there, I turned to the guys and said thanks for the party, and I was heading up to the platform to wait for the train. My mouth was as dry as the desert sands around Alicante and the Swedish boys seemed in no hurry to catch the train, so I heaved my backpack onto my back, shook their hands, including the guy with the joints, and stepped slowly and without certainty towards the platform.

On platform two I could see in the distance the rear end of a coach, but I couldn't tell whether it was moving or if it was just stopped there, so I wandered a little further along the platform. The weed was really taking hold. The train seemed to be backing into the station at a snail's pace. It was as if the fabric of time and space were stretching almost visibly before me. I focused on the rear end of the last coach trying to figure out whether it really was moving at all, or if I was just imagining it. I'd never seen such a slow train. I wondered if the driver might be stoned too. Is this normal in Alicante? Is everyone just so stoned that everything works in slow motion? I stood there on the platform and noticed out of the corner of my right eye, the denim-clad drug provider now standing on the main platform. He was just standing there, at the end of the track, with his hands dug into his trouser pockets, staring at me. He must've been 40 metres away, but I grew slightly nervous. My head was fuzzy and I wished I hadn't smoked his weed. I looked towards him and he appeared to have moved closer, now maybe only thirty metres away. What's going on, I wondered. Is he after something? Am I about to be mugged, knifed, or worse? Trying to appear completely calm, I walked a little further up the platform. The train was definitely coming closer. But what was I going to do? I wished I'd stayed with the other guys outside under the station portico. I looked back towards the weed guy and he was only about twenty metres away, still looking coldly, defiantly at me. I nodded and smiled briefly at him and looked again at the incoming train. Hurry up!

We were the only two people on the platform. Where was everyone else? Are we going to be the only two people on this train? Come to think of it, is he even getting on? He had no luggage at all. He couldn't be travelling on this long-distance train. I pulled myself together and started casually pacing around back and forth, ambling really, on the platform. The train was right by me now, still moving slowly back to the buffers at the end of the station. The guy had stopped now and was looking the other way. I heaved a sigh of relief. But then seconds later I turned to find him just feet away. My heart raced. Shit, something's going to happen. Certain that I might feel the cold steel of a knife in my body any second, I kept moving looking around, all the time trying to look casual to all the world – or lack of it – while inside I was tense as hell.

Suddenly out of the corner of my eye I spied few people starting to appear at the end of the platform. Then a couple more. I craned my neck past marijuana man and towards the end of the platform, as if I was looking for someone in particular. The guy also looked back and seeing the oncoming passengers, appeared to stand down.

The train came to a gentle halt. I moved forward, pulling the door open and climbing from the low slung platform onto the train. I looked back down the platform, but I couldn't see any sign of the guy. Had he gone, or was he already on board? How I hoped it was the former! Making my way along the narrow corridor, I noticed some passengers already on the train. In my fugged out mental state, I couldn't figure where they'd all come from. I thought Alicante was the starting point, but I must've been wrong. Anyway, I was too stoned to care.

I slipped into the third cabin along the corridor, sweating and breathing heavily. It was only after I had slung my backpack onto the floor beneath the window seat and collapsed into the corner seat that I noticed the three other people in the cabin. An elderly couple opposite eyed me, slightly non-plussed, with disapproving expressions. Along from me, by the door to the corridor, a middle-aged Spanish man was dozing, his head gently lolling against the corridor window. I looked around at them, relieved, but still slightly afraid. The train began to pull away from the station and I sighed in relief.

As the train snaked its way through the suburban lights and shadowed buildings of Alicante by night, I gradually slipped, stoned and exhausted, into a long, but fitful sleep, promising myself that I would never ever smoke grass again.

Through the night strange noises awoke me as the train headed northwards. Distant sounds of bells grew louder before reaching a crescendo and then passing seamlessly into oblivion, penetrating my own soporific state, briefly, before receding into the distance again. Other foreign, unfamiliar sounds came from the darkness beyond the train. Occasionally the muffled tones of foreign voices from the corridor also disturbed my drug-induced slumber, as people passed along the carriage during the night. But the long Spanish train carried me further from the hallucinogenic stupor of Alicante, the sinister marijuana dealer and my fear of being mugged or worse.

The following morning, when I came to, the cabin

was empty. For a moment I panicked, wondering where everyone had gone, dreading that I'd missed my stop and that the train had been shuffled off into a siding somewhere alien to me. But the train was still moving. I pulled myself up into the seat from my slumped slumber position and looked out the window. The sun was up. Perhaps everyone got off at Valencia or one of the other stops along the long night-time route north. I got up and stepped out into the corridor; there were at least still some other people on the train. I looked out the corridor window and could see the Mediterranean. We must be near Barcelona, I thought. I stopped a passing guard who informed me we'd passed Barcelona and the train was now on its way to its 'terminus' at the border town of Cerbère. For a moment I was thrown, confused.

"Not Portbou?"

"Non, the border to France is Cerbère," he explained.

"Ah, okay, gracias."

My mouth was parched so I grabbed the water bottle from inside my backpack. I don't think I had ever been so thirsty. I could have drunk the entire Med. I downed the water feeling it spreading, electrifying my insides as it sprang to all the parts that craved it, lubricating away the dryness. It felt good, but my mouth was furry and weird. I fished out my toothbrush and paste and started to clean my teeth. I walked along the corridor to the toilet. As usual, it was disgusting, foul-smelling and rancid, so I used what was left of my water rinsing and spitting into the shit-stained bowl of the toilet plate in front of me. I took a piss, playfully directing it towards the toothpaste spit, perhaps somehow aiming to clean it as I went, and then headed back to the cabin.

The events of the previous night played over and over in my head. "Jesus, that was scary," I said to myself. "What a state to get into." In the cold light of day, I could see that perhaps the ominous drug dealer was just a figment of my pot tainted imagination. I mean, he existed and all, but the whole spooky scenario with his stalking moves, menacing looks, and murderous intentions, were all obviously just down to the weed I'd smoked. I felt ashamed though that, for the second time in a week, I had made a misjudgement based on the colour of a man's skin. I became angry with myself for this. I wanted to understand why it had happened, and spent the next hour or so trying to figure out my ignorance. I had never really had contact with people from different races, so I hadn't prepared myself to be more accepting of this otherness. To be fair, growing up in Scotland in the 70s and 80s, I thought people from Manchester were exotic.

I felt I should have known better. In my own short life I had often felt different from everyone else in terms of my sexuality. I knew how badly homosexuals were treated by everyone in society. Even one's own family could reject you for being gay. I'd been bullied at school for 'being different', even before I realised I might be gay, so I knew what prejudice was like first hand. So, I resolved right there and then that I wouldn't be one of those people who judged others.

Eventually, the train crawled into the station at Cerbère, I grabbed my bags and prepared myself for another grilling by the Spanish customs officers. Getting out of Spain, though, was much easier than getting in. I wandered through the border point unchallenged by anyone. This could have been because the customs officers were French, not Spanish, as I had assumed they would be. I was a little confused. Why were the border checks tougher for a northern European heading into Spain, than for those going from Spain to Northern Europe? I'd heard stories about drug smugglers being caught with contraband coming into Europe from North Africa, but nothing heading the other way. However, I also realised that, given I had been completely off my face only hours earlier, and possibly still smelled of marijuana, the lack of serious checks was a very fortunate bonus indeed.

I had enjoyed Spain. Barcelona was truly a beautiful city with a vibrant pulsing heart. I was happy that this was my introduction to Spain. Benidorm had a spectacular setting, and I could even forgive the huge numbers of tower blocks. But the package holiday industry has a lot to answer for in my opinion. Even Alicante was exotic, even if a little scary in the end. I would return in the future to see more of Spain; go further south, see its capital. That would all happen years later. For now, I was looking forward to experiencing the south of France, and the fabled Côte d'Azur.

11. La Riviera

The train for Nice was already waiting on the other side of the border control station when all the passengers and I came out of the inspection halls. Once again my little three-leaf passport had been stamped with the authority to enter France, and we quietly made our way to the waiting train and boarded our respective carriages.

I like trains, and the site of the long, gleaming SNCF grey and white coaches made me feel like I was back in familiar railway territory. It was my expert opinion that the French trains were far superior and more comfortable than their Spanish equivalents. They looked modern, were cleaner, more luxurious and better looked after by those who used them. The Spanish trains I'd travelled on were those of an emerging, post dictatorship, nation, and so given more to necessity than luxury. France, however, had long since mastered the art of travel, and it was a relief to be on board an SNCF service once again. Even today, when one boards a Train à Grande Vitesse or TGV, the coach interiors are pristine and litter free. The toilets look as if they've been cleaned and refreshed after each use. They are revered. Back in 1985, the TGV had only been in existence for four years, moreover, they were still not available on any of the routes I was travelling.

The French train pulled slowly out of Cerbère and we were on our way to the Côte d'Azur. I spent most of the journey looking out of the window, ensconced in a window seat on the right-hand side of the train, and therefore able to chart our progress along the Mediterranean. On the Walkman was Simple Minds' *Don't You Forget About Me,* a great song to listen to while we wove our way along the coast past little beach towns such as Banyuls-sur-Mer, Port-Vendres and Collioure.

Often the train would plunge beneath the countryside into cool, long, dark tunnels, before emerging again a minute later into the brilliant sunshine. My fellow passengers on the opposite side of the aisle had glorious distant views of the lower reaches of the Pyrenees, while I had the sight of the Mediterranean, darting endlessly in and out of view, as if playing a sparkling game of hide and seek. We ploughed-on past Perpignan, which also brought us closer than ever to the awesome grandeur of the Pyrénées-Orientales. Sometimes I didn't know which side of the train to look out of. This was real landscape, impressive nature, beauty beyond anything I had ever seen, and all from the seat of a train, not even a First Class seat at that. After many more beautiful little towns and villages and after passing Narbonne, never far from the coastal waters of the Mediterranean, I went in search of a buffet car, where I bought a cup of 'train tea'. Back

161

in my seat again, I took out the youth hostel guide and studied the little map of Europe, to gauge exactly where I was on the journey. I was looking forward to Nice.

Later, and finally familiar with the passing scenery, and therefore slightly bored by it now, I wondered what the three nurses from Leeds were doing in Benidorm. I was sure they were having a right old party time of it. They'd probably met up with some fun guys. Perhaps I should have hung out with them longer. They were all pretty girls and up for a laugh. For a moment I wished I had stayed. This made me feel slightly lonely. So far, my first voyage through Europe had been so rewarding, but in that moment I realised that I would have liked to have had someone with me. Sitting there alone on the train, I wanted to share the experience of seeing these great views and being able to turn to that person to say 'wow, look at that?' I realised for the first time that it would be wonderful to have someone special with whom to travel, not just across Europe on this journey, but on life's journey. I'd spent so much time questioning why I couldn't just force myself to be with a girl or have a girlfriend, that I hadn't really let in the idea of one day finding a boy to spend my life with. A boyfriend. I smiled as I looked out onto the Mediterranean. One day, I thought. One day, soon.

My spirits lifted. Having recognised that one day I would have a mate, I almost immediately told myself there would be time for all that. I was still young, and on my first solo adventure. And I was content to have the freedom to move from place to place as and when I liked. This was all still so new to me and I wanted to discover and see as many new places as possible before my ticket ran out. Yes, company is good, I reasoned, but there is great adventure in travelling alone too. I returned to filling my head with ideas about what I would do in the south of France and who I might meet next on my travels.

From Narbonne, the train snaked its way through Montpellier, Nimes and Arles. I remember it was just before six in the evening when we pulled into the largest city on the Mediterranean coast, the second largest city in France – Marseilles.

I'd learned something about Marseilles in geography lessons at school. I knew it was one of the ancient cities of Europe, inhabited for almost 30,000 years. As someone who was born on the coast, I loved that it was primarily a fishing port. But the French city also had strong connections to exotic Africa with links to Morocco, Algiers and Tunisia. This also peaked my interest, because the Arab world was fascinating to me. I loved films like Lawrence of Arabia and I had read Agatha Christie's Death of the Nile and Evelyn Waugh's Brideshead Revisited, in which Lord Sebastian Flyte flees to Morocco and winds up in Tunisia. I'd always wanted to visit those places. As the train came to a stop I looked out of the window and gave serious thought to just jumping off there and then and exploring the city. However, I'd also read in the youth hostel guide that it could be a dangerous city and was not considered safe for the single traveller. This was 1985, so the scaremongering was perhaps overdone, slightly, but I was still naive and thought it best – after the incident in Alicante – to obey the advice of the guidebook. My interest in the Arab world, though, remained, and later in life, I would visit Tunisia and Morocco and, I would spend three years living in the Arabian emirate of Dubai. But that's another story.

The train stopped in Marseilles for what seemed like an age. On the platform young Algerian and Moroccan guys ran along the side of the train offering tea, 'Coka', nuts, fruit cake to the passengers. One or two even sidled along offering 'hashish'. 'Non merci' I mouthed from my window seat, thinking to myself "Been there, done that".

I went to the end of the coach and looked out the door up and down the platform. The scene was amazing. The platform was teeming, not just with passengers, but mostly African vendors with carts full of drinks, fruits, snacks, bags of dates. Hoards of little boys accosted passengers pleading with them to buy their wares. I felt as if we'd been transported to Africa itself. The station was hot and steamy, and I wouldn't have been too surprised if the stationmaster had yelled out 'Next stop Cairo'. Opposite the doorway I was standing in, I spotted a cart laden with dates, so I jumped off the train approached to the vendor, to buy some.

"Cinq, merci", the vendor said, looking me in the eye with a big grateful smile on his face. He was dressed in what looked like an extremely oversized night-shirt - but which I later learned was, in fact, a djellaba - and the flimsiest-looking tan coloured flip-flop sandals. I handed

164

him a five-franc note and made to turn back towards the train. Suddenly, I was surrounded by little urchins, all noisily yelling "Monsieur" and shoving their products at me with one hand, the other held out in hope of payment. I found it quite charming and smiled back at them shaking my head. Then I noticed one of them had an ice cold bottle of Coca-Cola in his hands and the taste buds in my mouth started to react and swell at the thought of an ice-cold drink in this heat. With my hand firmly clasping the few French coins I have, I asked how much?

"Combien?" It was one of the keywords Yvonne had taught me in Paris.

"Quatre, monsieur", the little djellaba-clad boy replied, smiling a big white toothy grin.

"Okay." I exchanged my cash for the bottle and waded through the scrum of boys back to the train, shaking my head in a polite refusal of their wares.

I had just made it back onto the train when the unmistakeable sound of the guard's whistle blew from further along the platform and another guard appeared and closed the door. I pulled down the window and leant out, smiling at the small die-hard group of young boys, who still hoped for a franc or two. I put my hands into my pockets and pulled out the small change I had left and gently offered it to them. It was seized upon as quickly as feeding piranhas after a morsel of grub. They gave a cheer and the train jolted forwards. It was just a moment in Marseilles, but it was wonderfully chaotic, noisy and alive. It was charged with the kind of atmosphere I had always imagined I would experience as a traveller and I was grateful for it. It was a glimpse of a golden age I had assumed had long since passed. Hercule Poirot would not have looked out of place, nor Indiana Jones.

I'd spent most of the journey looking out of the window and lost in my thoughts. So it was only when I was returning to my seat that I was able to survey the other passengers. I noticed for the first time that almost everyone seemed to have a sun-kissed glow to their skin. I headed for the toilets and looking in the small mirror I noticed I, too, had lost any remaining evidence of my Scottish pallor. I figured I could easily pass as Italian, Spanish or southern French at least. I'd never been this colour in my life. I never knew I could look so different. I felt for the first time like a European, instead of a pasty-faced foreign traveller from the cold north. My dark brown hair and hazel eyes, together with the deepening tan I was now sporting made me feel good, healthy and alive. I returned to my seat and enjoyed the most deliciously sweet dates I have ever eaten and washed them down with a still cold Coke. A delicious pauper's supper on a train.

It was almost 10pm when we pulled into the domed gare at Nice Ville. The sun was gone, but the air was warm and inviting. It felt a world away from the scenes at Marseilles. Nice Ville station was quiet, conservative and organised. There were no crowds hanging around the station. No vendors offering supplies to the weary traveller and no urchins begging for a franc or two.

Exiting the station I realised I had no idea of my bearings in the town, but somehow, my inbuilt radar told me the sea was straight ahead, so I started to walk in that direction. I also had nowhere to stay, so I scanned around as I was walking to see if I could spot any hotels or guest houses that looked within my budget. After the long train journey, my backpack felt heavier than usual. It was hard to believe that morning I'd been in Spain, and now I was closer to Italy, but I had to focus on finding a room.

After wandering south for five minutes I decided to take little detours down the side streets. Hotels would almost certainly be cheaper there, I figured. I wandered along past boulangeries, patisseries, travel shops, closed tabacs, with no sign of any bed and breakfast places or hostels. I returned to the main avenue, then tried a couple of other side streets. By the third, Rue Pertinax, I was beginning to think I might be spending the night in my sleeping bag on the beach, when I noticed an entrance way with a brightly lit lamp above a sign that read 'Pension Gilbert'.

I wasn't entirely sure what a 'Pension' was. Despite my relative ignorance of French, it did sound like some kind of accommodation, though perhaps it was just for old people? I stopped in the doorway and looked in to find a well-manicured lady sitting at a low desk, smoking a cigarette. It was now after 10.30, so I pushed open the heavy, glass-framed door and smiled. The lady, who must have been in her mid-fifties, looked up sharply.

167

"Oui?"

"Bonjour," I hadn't yet learned that "Bonsoir" was more appropriate for that time of day. "Je cherche pour un hotel? Sorry."

"Oui, pour combien de jours?" The lady replied.

"Sorry, do you speak English?"

"Of course, monsieur. For how long?"

"Oh, maybe five or six days." I lied. I didn't know how long I was going to stay, and anyway, it all depended on the price. And I still wasn't sure if she was offering a room in her house or whether she was going to suggest a hotel nearby.

She smiled. "I have one room left, 65 francs a night, monsieur."

I did a rapid calculation in my head and worked out that it was roughly £6 a night.

"Oui, okay, that's great."

"Parfait, I am Madame Gilbert. Welcome to the Pension Gilbert. Vous êtes tres tard, very late." She said before smiling. "You arrived late from your train?"

I figured out what she was trying to say.

"Yes, I came on a late train." Madame Gilbert opened her guestbook and asked for my passport. She noted down the details: name, passport number and date of expiry, before handing my document back. She turned and grabbed the key to room number 4 from the wooden rack behind her desk.

"Suivez moi. Follow me." She made her way up the narrow staircase. She reminded me of an actress in the way she moved: Maggie Smith, in her role as hotelier in Evil Under the Sun, another Agatha Christie story. Madame Gilbert's figure, like Maggie Smith's in the film, was slim and her long hair was neatly tightened into a ball at the back with a kind of slanted bang at the front. Her tricolour red, white and blue patterned frock hugged her body contours and made her appear efficient and slick. Her face was warm, but ageing more than her figure, probably on account of years of smoking, all that sun and perhaps a little too much of the good life. We arrived on the wide first landing.

"Voila, monsieur. I hope it is okay for you." I stepped into the room, turned and smiled.

"Merci beaucoup, Madame Gilbert, it's perfect, thank you so much. Merci encore."

"Petit déjeuner from 8am until 10am, jeune homme."

What? Brilliant - breakfast included! I closed the door after Madame Gilbert, placed my bag on the old-fashioned dark-green chair by the long window and dropped onto the single bed. The room was not so small. The bed was against the wall facing the window, perpendicular to the door. There were old wooden bedside tables on either side, and one had a small lamp with a fuchsia shade. The wallpaper, like the chair and indeed the bed covers, was green, but subtly so. I felt like I was staying in the smaller room of a grand old mansion. The wooden floor was very old but in excellent condition, and shiny clean. One could tell that cleanliness was a point of pride for Madame Gilbert. Along from the door was a heavy-looking, wooden wardrobe. On the opposite wall was a dressing table and mirror.

I undressed and threw my travel-worn clothes onto the chair, fished out my toilet bag and brushed my teeth in the small basin in the corner. I pulled back the bed covers to reveal pristine, fresh, white, tightly made sheets, which were a pleasure to lie on. That bed - a truly welcome sight after the past few days! For a moment I lay there thinking about the long journey from Alicante to the border, and then the subsequent trip along the French coast. Perhaps I should've stopped off in Barcelona. Maybe I would have seen Andreas again. And why didn't I just leap off the train in Marseilles and find a Bedouin hostelry for the night to break the journey? My eyes grew heavy, and I fell into a long, deep sleep before I'd had the opportunity to respond to my own questions or wonder more about my decision to press on to Nice.

12. Nice to see you

The next morning I woke refreshed. Realising where I was, I pulled on a t-shirt, shorts and deck-shoes and bounced downstairs to the dining room for breakfast. I was famished. This was the first place I'd stayed where breakfast was included, and any young person travelling on a budget appreciates how a free breakfast is just the trick to set you up for the day.

Madame Gilbert greeted me with a smile in the brightly decorated dining room. There were about ten tables of various sizes, but only half were occupied when I arrived.

"Bonjour Monsieur, deed you 'ave a good sleep?"

"Yes, oui, Madame Gilbert, I was very tired last night. Merci beaucoup."

"Vee 'ave croissant, toast, confiture, et per-aps pour vous un oeuf?"

"Oeuf?"

"Pah, eggs, monsieur, vee 'aff eggs, yes. You like?"

Fantastic, I'd assumed I would only be getting the bare essentials of a Continental breakfast, which didn't, as far as I was aware, usually include eggs. I tucked into the croissants while Madame Gilbert continued to fuss over me.

"And I vill breeng you a chocolate chaud."

"Do you have any tea?" Well, I thought, I am British, and that's how I've been brought up to start my day – no matter where I am.

"Oh, no, no, no," she cooed. "Yoo must 'ave chocolate, jeune homme. Like James Bond, eh? Oui. J'arrive".

I was totally confused. What did hot chocolate have to do with James Bond? Was she mad? Also, it was already a very warm morning and I could tell the day was going to be another scorcher. The last thing I wanted was a milky hot drink with cocoa. However, Madame Gilbert returned five minutes later with a soft boiled egg, some toast and a large mug of chaud chocolate. I smiled and thanked her and she threw her hands in the air - "De rien, pour James Bond uhh?"

I could tell the other guests found it amusing, and to be honest, although I was bashful at being 'adopted' by Madame Gilbert like a little lost boy, I did feel comfortable, safe and happy. How lucky I was to have stumbled across the Pension Gilbert!

After showering and unpacking, I headed out to explore Nice. I was excited to get to the beach and walked along the promenade because I'd seen many films of the city on television and it looked like the perfect place to live.

Turning right out of the pension, which I now knew was French for guest house, I headed to the end of the street and turned left onto a wider avenue that would take me to the seafront. The city couldn't have been more different from the large, skyscrapered sprawl of Benidorm I'd seen just a few days earlier. Many of the buildings were elaborately decorated and beautifully maintained. Even the modern apartment blocks seem to have been erected in sympathy with the older buildings of the belle époque. I discovered the city is called Nice la belle, Nice the beautiful, and it shows. Again, unlike Benidorm, there didn't appear to be hoards of British package holidaymakers pouring out of the hotels with beach balls, Li-Lo's and towels in hand, making a bee-line for the best spot on the sand. No 'English pub' signs and certainly no 'Kiss me quick' tourist shops.

Nice had a more sophisticated ambience. Outside the many cafés and bars I passed, people sat chatting and drinking coffee in clothing more suited to Paris fashion week than the beach. Everyone wore sunglasses, even the waiters. I felt a little out of my depth, a bit under-dressed in my denim shorts and 'Save the Waves' inscribed t-shirt. When I finally made it to the seafront, on the famous Promenade des Anglais, there were more 'cool' people, posing, as they'd say in Scotland. But they weren't posing; they were just being as chic and glamorous as the location demanded. Some people were walking their pets along the pristine promenade. Even the dogs looked super-rich. I was sure I saw at least three collars sparkle as their female owners sashayed along behind the wearers.. I wandered along the promenade taking everything in. The sun was high and hot, but I didn't mind it. Even the warm breeze floating in from the sea was relaxing and pleasant. Further along, I spotted a small tourist office and crossed the road to see if I could pick up a map of the city. The tourist advisor, like almost everyone else in Nice, was very elegantly dressed. Her beige dress and perfect tan gave her a professional air. Back home people only dressed like this for very special occasions. I thought perhaps she might be going to a wedding or something later. Her manner was very polite and well informed and she was able to suggest some places of interest that I must see since this was my first visit. I thanked her and left the air-conditioned shop, convinced the tourist officer must be a millionaire because those are the only people who can look that good all the time. I bet she's the ambassador's wife, I thought to myself, and this is how she keeps busy, while he's off handling important international affairs of state.

I was almost embarrassed to step off the promenade and down onto the beach, where the most glamorous people in the world were relaxing, but there were a lot of people there already, so I convinced myself no-one would notice this little urchin joining them. I found a suitable place in the sand, unrolled my beach towel and stripped down to my white swimming trunks. I spent five minutes massaging tanning lotion onto my exposed, northern European skin, then lay back and took a big breath. Nice was a welcome, calm retreat after the hustle, bustle and noise of Spain.

France, I decided, was a country that I would get to know very well in my life. I liked the temperament of the people, their careful attention to how things should look. Even the traffic was different here. In Spain, the roads were full of rushing drivers and the endless sounds of horns being pressed; People on motorbikes, tearing up little streets with scant regard for pedestrians, and drivers stopping wherever they wanted no matter how it may affect the other traffic around them.

But here, in Nice, the attitude of drivers was calmer. No one seemed to be in a hurry. No one had their hands permanently on their horns. The temperament of the French seemed less frantic than their Spanish neighbours. I knew that France was a wealthier nation, so perhaps this was the reason for their sangfroid. It really made a difference to how you felt walking in the streets. At the hotel in Barcelona, the manager had viewed me with suspicion and disdain and never made any effort to smile or say good morning to his guests. He was gruff. I remembered thinking "Why is he even running a guest house if it's all too much for him?"

By contrast, Madame Gilbert's welcoming smile, friendly manner and warm kindness at breakfast, was a world away.

I was young, and foreign lands were completely new to me, so I wasn't judging either place, I was simply noticing the differences in the cultures of the countries I was visiting. The Spanish were hot blooded, loud and hurried, whereas the French, at least here on the coast, were measured, genteel and slow.

Even on the beach I noticed that I had more space around me than I had in Benidorm, where it was so busy that you were almost towel to towel with complete strangers. Then I noticed one very good reason why this might be. After lying on my towel for a few moments I began to feel physically uncomfortable. I sat up, looked around and discovered that I was lying on a pebble beach. How could I have missed that? Then I saw that many of the other bathers had what looked like mats beneath their towels, which clearly softened the blow of the hard rocks beneath them. I stood up and decided to wade down to the water, and then discovered that, if lying on pebbles was uncomfortable, trying to walk barefoot across them was excruciating. It was not a dignified sight. It was a struggle to keep my balance while trying to remain nonchalant about the pebbles. Each step was an ordeal, but I persisted and made it to the water's edge. As quickly as I could I sat down in the sea to take the pressure off my feet. "Jesus, that hurt", I said to myself. I remained there for five minutes before summoning the courage to get back to my towel. What one has to remember to do is put on one's shoes, flip-flops, or whatever if one is going to move on this beach. I looked on in envy at all the clever people who had hired sun loungers and who were blissfully enjoying the beach despite these solid, burning stones of hell.

Disappointed, and aching slightly from the

experience, I left the pebbled beach soon after, vowing never to return. I longed for the crowded, tacky, lovely soft sands of Benidorm and Barcelona, and would have gladly put up with the manic driving habits of the Spanish for it.

I spent the remainder of that first afternoon in Nice, wandering along the Promenade des Anglais, studying the large hotels and other impressive buildings that adorned the waterfront. It was charming to discover that the Promenade was not in fact a French idea, but one from my own country. In the middle of the 18th century, my well-heeled ancestors escaped to Nice as a way of dodging the harsh British winter. They preferred the milder climate available in the Côte d'Azur. The story goes that when the cold weather up north also drove poorer people to the south, the rich ones put them to work building the long promenade, so they – the rich – could fully enjoy the panoramic views of the sea from a paved walkway, hence the name Promenade des Anglais. Clearly, they had an issue with the pebble beaches, too.

One of the main buildings featured on the city map I'd picked up was the Hotel Negresco. A grand, large, brilliantly white building facing the sea on the Promenade, the Negresco symbolises all that is decadent about the French Riviera. It was built at the start of the 20th century by a rich Hungarian immigrant to cater for only the wealthiest visitors, who could stay in the lap of luxury while spending their money in his casinos. It's recognised for the large pink dome located in the east corner of the hotel, apparently designed by Gustave

177

Eiffel, the French engineer who built the tower in Paris. I sat there looking at the hotel for some time. Palm trees swayed gently in front of it, while the building remained regally still. I thought it looked like a huge wedding cake covered in icing, just about to melt in the hot sun. I watched the guests and visitors come and go. Rich people, in clothes I'd surely never be wealthy enough to wear. Gold jewellery and sparkling gems dripped from the wrists and necks of sophisticated society women; middle-aged men in smart suits walked purposefully in and out of the hotel's various doors, climbing into Mercedes and Rolls Royces. These arrived so often they appeared almost commonplace. Being just nineteen and never having seen such wealth and imposing grandeur, I didn't have the nerve then to even attempt to cross the road to try to pass through its hallowed doors for a glimpse of the palatial world beyond. I felt honoured just to be able to see it from across the street. It was, I thought, strange how some buildings, by their strange or deliberate design, could command authority, a sense of foreboding, a reminder one of one's place in the world, or lack thereof in my case. I smiled to myself and made a promise that one day I, too, would walk, purposefully through those doors, and have bell boys bring in my luggage from the waiting limousine outside. That's the great thing about being young and of little means. One can always dream. Now that I'm older and better off than I was then, I have learned that humility is a better play. And although I'm travelling in a business class seat today, I didn't 'walk, purposefully' through the business class check-in area of the Eurostar terminal in London.

Later, I wandered around the Place Garibaldi and sought out the St Nicolas Orthodox Cathedral, which looked not dissimilar to Moscow's fairy tale Kremlin. Another church in another city.

It was late afternoon when I arrived back at the pension and found Madame Gilbert working busily at her reception desk.

"Aah, mon cher, deed you 'ave a wonderful day exploring our beautee-ful city?"

"Madame Gilbert, oui, it is really great." I told her about all the buildings and squares I'd seen, and mentioned how the pebble beach was a surprise to me.

"Not very comfortable at all, and how can you walk on those stones?"

She laughed out loud. "Oh my leetle James Bond, if you want to 'ave zee beach, you must do what I do – go to Cannes. Zee beach is fantastique and sablé – how you say – sandy."

"Aah, d'accord, okay, merci madame. Is it far to Cannes?"

Madame Gilbert informed me that it was only 15 minutes on the 'leettle train' from Nice or I could take a bus, so I decided I would spend the next day in Cannes.

I rested and showered before heading out for something to eat and to find some nightlife. One thing I enjoyed about travelling was having a 'siesta' between coming back from being out for the day and heading out at night. A day in the sun could leave one feeling

179

drained, so a short nap was one Continental solution I was more than happy to adopt, because it meant I could stay awake longer in the evening.

Eating out in Spain had been relatively cheap, especially given the easy pic-n-mix options of the tapas bars. Nice was a different gastronomic event altogether. For what seemed like an age, I wandered back and forth along the streets and squares down by the seafront, studying the window menus and calculating in my head the prices as I converted them from French francs to British pounds. 'Salades' were on almost every menu and they weren't cheap, but I wanted something more substantial, and affordable too. After too long looking around I could feel the hunger pangs in my stomach. It started to make little rumbling noises, so I took refuge at some tables outside a nondescript looking café-bar on one of the city's squares. Eventually, a waiter in black jeans and a fresh white shirt sauntered up with a friendly, but brisk 'Bonsoir monsieur, qu'est-ce que vous voulez?" His hair was jet black, the darkest I swear I had ever seen, he was very tanned and had the kind of skin I thought only Hollywood actors had. He could be a Hollywood star, I thought to myself. If I looked liked him, I'd be off to California in a second, hoping to be discovered. It wouldn't be so difficult, I was sure, not with those looks.

I ordered a beer from the undiscovered next big thing in movies and asked if the bar served food. Yes, but only sandwiches. I ordered a toasted ham and cheese baguette and was almost ecstatic when it came on a large plate with a healthy side-serving of salad thrown in. Perhaps they thought I looked so thin and puny that I deserved something extra. When you're young and short on cash, little moments like these are to be savoured. I'd inadvertently lucked upon a clever way to have an almost meal, without having to pay the hefty prices the more formal restaurants demanded. Again, I thought, one day, I'll come back here, wealthier, more experienced, unafraid of stepping foot inside those establishments; one day.

I sat there on the square enjoying the ice cold beer and tasty meal and watched the people of Nice come and go. Elderly ladies ambled by, walking their dogs, stopping randomly to look around them, as if they'd suddenly forgotten where they were, before turning around again and carrying on, giving their little well-manicured poodles and spaniels a gentle tug on their leash. Small groups of men stood around at various corners of the square, chatting and smoking. Didn't they have homes to go to? I thought. But the night was so balmy and warm, it was definitely better to be out than in. On the small green across from the bar on the square, people were sitting on benches, couples walked slowly by, their arms around each other, and the occasional young boy would come peddling along on his bike. Then I noticed something else. At the bottom right corner of the little park sat a couple of girls, chatting, smoking and keenly watching the cars go by. The taller of the two girls – and she was unusually tall - with large earrings, a skin-tight black t-shirt and tight little black mini-skirt, was fishing in her black leather jacket for something.

Eventually, she pulled out a small bundle and quickly handed it to her friend. All the time, they were preening themselves, adjusting their outfits, playing with their hair, swishing it this way and that. Occasionally, the really tall one would suddenly kick a leg out straight, twist it left, right, and left again, as if checking to make sure it hadn't grown anymore. In an overly affected manner, the smaller girl leapt off the little wall they were sitting on and made a really camp show of steadying herself, having descended from the great height of around 15 centimetres.

"Interesting isn't it?" I was briefly startled, having been absorbed by the little 'theatre of the absurd' I had been observing. There were two guys and a girl now sitting at the table right next to me. "We've been watching them too. Very strange duo," said the curly-haired guy sitting closest to me, in an English accent not too different from Yvonne's.

"My friends here think they're a couple of trannies," the girl said.

"What? Eh?" I didn't really get it for a second. Then I realised what she meant. Of course, that's why they were so interesting to watch. This wasn't two girlfriends just keen on looking after themselves, these were two blokes trying to pull off, well, I didn't really know what.

"They ARE," the other guy said. "I saw them the other night, trying to pull an' all, they were."

The girl laughed. I was stunned! I kept looking over at them. All this stuff they were doing was just theatre, camp, two French transvestites doing their own thing. I looked at the three English people and they burst out laughing.

After we introduced ourselves I ordered another beer. I tried to explain to them how I'd sat there totally mesmerised by their performance; how I thought they were quite odd. How I'd felt slightly sorry for the really tall, well-built girl, who, given her unfortunate frame and clunky size, must surely have found it tough to win a husband. I was almost relieved to hear they were transvestites.

Charlie, Gavin and Imogen were fellow interrailers. This was their last night in the south of France. Tomorrow they were heading up to Paris, then back to "Blighty' as Gavin called it. I had no idea back then that 'Blighty' was a synonym for Britain, but I went with it. They were all three of them sun-baked like they'd just walked across the Sahara desert. Charlie kept running his hands through his long, curly, dark hair, while he was speaking and he gesticulated a lot, too. That was fine, but the hair thing was just annoying. I wanted to yell at him "what's wrong with your hair, why don't you have it cut short?" Like something my mother doubtless would say, "it'll save you having to keep doing that thing where you're forever running your hands through it."

"You gotta go to Naples, man," he insisted. "Scary place, but amazing too, you would love the coast - Positano, Amalfi, Sorrento. So cool, man."

"How far are you going?" Imogen chipped in.

"Well, it's my first time, and money's a bit tight, but I'll definitely try to get down to Naples, it sounds great."

"I liked Istanbul the best," Imogen said. I felt embarrassed. Here I was chatting away to fellow interrailers and all I had to relate was Paris, Barcelona, Alicante and Benidorm, while they'd been to the very extremes of the Interrail experience. They'd taken the 'Midnight Express' into Turkey and managed to get out again. They'd risked Naples, 'Napoli', as Imogen called it - Italy's most frightening and dangerous city, and lived to call it 'amazing'. I didn't even know where Positano was, and Amalfi sounded like a plant. There was no way I was telling these veterans of European rail travel that I'd set foot in Benidorm. I may have been a young, naive traveller from Scotland on his first solo outing in Europe, but I wasn't totally stupid. Instead, I waxed about how exotic Portbou was on the Franco-Spanish border. I lied that I'd spent 'a few days' being lost and stoned in Marseilles – forgiving myself for relocating the events of that scary night at the train station in Alicante to the French port city. They deserved it, how dare they be so cool and worldly and make me feel like I'd done the organised-tour-bus version of the great European adventure.

"Cool, man, how did you score in Marseilles? We couldn't get anything when we stopped there."

Shit, I thought, I'm going to be rumbled any second.

"How did you like Marseilles?" Imogen piped up.

"Oh you know, it was all just a blur. Felt more like I

was in Egypt, though."

"Yeah, it has a real Arabian feel to it doesn't it?" Imogen smiled.

"Yeah, but what about the dealer?" Gavin insisted, thankfully changing the subject. Gavin, unlike Charlie, had a receding forehead and therefore couldn't play with the small amount of blonde hair he sported in the same frantic way Charlie could.

"Just a look and a wink I guess. I could tell the guy who gave us the weed was a pothead."

"You got any left?" said Gavin, looking around to make sure no-one heard.

"Sorry, all gone." I looked into disappointed faces.

It was now after 10pm and Imogen announced she was heading back to the hotel to get a decent night's sleep before the long trek back to England the next day. She pulled back her long permed hair and tied it with a bobble.

"Nice to meet you, happy travels. You guys coming?"

Gavin jumped up, "Of course darling," and threw his right arm around Imogen. Funny, I thought Charlie was the boyfriend.

"I'm gonna hang out here for a bit," Charlie said. "Keep the trannies under surveillance. See you back at the hotel". They laughed and exchanged rude mocking jests about how Charlie was a secret 'tranny fancier'.

Charlie and I had another beer, which he paid for,

thankfully. He started complaining about not wanting to go home to 'fucking miserable Britain'.

"It's that bloody Thatcher woman. She'll either end up killing us all or forcing us into hard labour. What's the bloody point of college?" It was quite strange listening to Charlie go on about the future being so bleak. I hadn't even started college yet, but I somehow knew the future was going to be brilliant. At least I believed mine would be.

"But you're at college, you don't even have to worry about work just now."

"Graduating next year man, then I've got to find a job."

I liked Charlie. He was opinionated but sincere; he had a natural authority without being oppressive. It was easy talking with him. He was like the older brother I never had.

After a while, he changed the subject by suggesting we try to find a nightclub to carry on drinking and "maybe meet some girls". We paid up, left the bar and headed across the street to where the two 'girls' were still lolling around and performing their ostentatious feminine act.

As we drew closer I could see they were far less convincing as girls close up than they had been from the soft-focus distance of the bar across the road. The tall one was far more muscular up close and didn't really seem to be trying to pass himself off as anything other than a bloke dressed up as a woman. Charlie nudged me as we came close to them, "They'll know where the fun places are."

"'Allo mademoiselles, bonsoir." Charlie was off. "Nous cherchons un disco ouvert, connaissez-vous un endroit?"

I was impressed with his confidence, which seemed to make up for the fact that even I could tell his French wasn't really up to scratch.

What followed was a lot of banter between Charlie and the 'girls'. Since my French was about as convincing as the taller transvestite's big wig, I hung around smiling inanely. I wished I knew what was going on, so I started to ask Charlie for a translation. Before I could get a response, he was pulling me along, with the girls marching in front of us. They stopped and hailed a taxi.

"Eh, where we going, Charlie? What's going on? I haven't got a lot of money on me," I pleaded, weakly. Charlie just laughed.

"Don't worry, they're taking us to a cool nightclub a few streets away, but they want to take a taxi." He explained that the club was free to get into. He also explained that most clubs on the Continent had free entry and it was best to stick to beer because wines and spirits were the most expensive.

I sat in the back with Charlie sandwiched between me and the tall 'girl'. The smaller one sat in the front chewing gum, noisy and camp, talking loudly in French to 'her' friend. Now and then she would turn round, flash me a come hither look and blow me a kiss. I smiled or grimaced nervously and looked out the window to avoid further contact. Then Charlie elbowed me and smiled.

"Charlie. Do they think we're on a date with them? Actually, are we? Are we on a date? Is that what you've told them?"

He laughed again, lit a cigarette and turned to me.

"Don't be silly, they just want a lift to the bar. Though I think Frenchy in the front might be getting ideas." He laughed again, digging me in the ribs.

Now I don't have anything against people cross-dressing, but I've never found it the least bit appealing, sexually. And as for little 'Frenchy in the front', I was truly flattered, but no amount of hairspray on his auburn wig was going to turn me on, far less the ugly ladder in the back of his/her tights I saw when we all got out of the taxi.

"Hey, Mr Eenglish man, this is it. See you lay-ter, boys," the tall one yelled. "Merci, for the taxi." With that, 'les girls' ran off inside together. Charlie and I sat at a table outside the "Tropez Tropical" disco bar and ordered a beer each from the brisk waiter. He looked at me, and we both started laughing.

"Aw, your face, man," said Charlie, pointing at me.

"Jeez, I thought we were done for there, phew!"

We talked more about travelling, or rather about Charlie's adventure, and how he felt it was nearly all over.

"I could just do this forever," he said. "Just never go back. Keep moving on to the next place."

Gavin and Imogen had their lives all mapped out, he said. They would graduate, find jobs in London and start a family. "It's not for me, though. Too many more adventures waiting out there."

I knew what he meant. Every day of my trip so far had brought new scenes and discoveries. I was learning things about myself I'd never realised before. The freedom of moving around with no set timetable, no alarm clock. Meeting new people, doing spontaneous things with them, was exhilarating. Struggling with new languages and still managing to be understood gave me the confidence and encouragement to interact more, and accepting the different and unusual in the places I had been to was character-building, mind-expanding and on occasions funny and bizarre.

We walked back along the seafront to the centre of Nice. It was late and I was slightly drunk, tired, but happy.

"Come on." Charlie jumped over the promenade railing and down onto the pebbled beach. He picked up some stones and hurtled them into the water. He was only a tad taller than I, but leaner, more defined, with strong, deeply tanned arms. As he walked along the beach his blonde hair blew in the night breeze and I remember wanting to kiss his neck.

189

We walked, then sat by the water's edge.

"Where will you go next?" he asked me.

"Oh, I'm going to base myself here for a few days and check out Cannes, Monte Carlo and a few other places around here. But I want to go to Italy next week."

"Lucky you."

He looked at me and smiled. I returned the smile. Then he suddenly leant forward and kissed me square on the lips. I was surprised, but I returned the kiss and then we were lying down on the rocky pebbles kissing more deeply and feeling each other's hardness. He pulled back for a moment.

"I'm not gay you know. I'm bi actually."

"Okay."

"A whole month of listening to those two (Gavin and Imogen) going at it, frustrating as hell."

He came at me again, taking off my t-shirt and kissing my chest, caressing my nipples with his lips and tongue. His hand undid my shorts and then he ploughed in grabbing hold of me. I let him go where he wanted to, enjoy what he wanted because I was enjoying it too. I'd never done it on a beach, under the sky at night. We both knelt facing each other on the beach (luckily no-one seemed to be around), kissing and writhing, flesh against flesh. We were hot and rising to a climax when he pushed me back onto the pebbles. Then he came up to my face and kissed me again, his lips tasting sweetly of my manhood.

Afterwards, we lay there on the beach, recovering, getting our breath back. I watched his fit strong chest heave gently as he calmed and recovered his breath.

"Thanks," he said, looking at me. "You're a sexy guy."

"You too".

I lay there looking at the stars in the dark sky. This was awesome. Such freedom, passion, liberty. I'm never going to be the same person again. If this is what life has in store, bring it on, please.

Eventually, we dressed and got back to the promenade. I told Charlie I would never have thought he was into guys.

"You too," he replied, adding that it was 'cool' to be surprised like that.

"Hey, I like girls, too," he insisted, "I just sometimes find boys more fun. Anyways, who says we have to be this or that. I just like people."

I laughed in agreement. We reached the square where we had met earlier in the evening. It was much quieter now, all the bars were closed or closing, there were no cars save the occasional taxi, and all we could hear was the gentle sound of the waves from the sea.

"Well, see you around, mister. Have a great adventure and enjoy Italy. I'm so jealous."

"Thanks, Charlie. You too – somehow I think it's all just beginning – for all of us… Be happy back in

Britain."

He leant forward and kissed me again.

I headed off towards the Pension Gilbert and Charlie went his way. When I looked back to the square he was gone. Then I noticed a familiar shape clacking across the place in heels, yelling "Taxi! Arrêtez!" It was the big transvestite we had given a lift to earlier. There was a burly man with her. They got into the cab, but as I turned to go, there was a commotion. The burly guy got out of the taxi, marched around to the other side and dragged the tranny out by the scruff of the neck and pushed her away. The guy was yelling something not very nice. He must have discovered 'she' was a 'he' and was not best pleased. The poor transvestite got to her feet as the taxi sped off, yelling something equally foul back at them.

I'd had enough adventure for one night, so I turned quickly and carried on my way to the safety of the Pension Gilbert.

13. Cannes do

I slept well and woke to more sunshine. I lay in bed thinking about my encounter with Charlie the night before. I could still smell him on my body and I liked it. I glanced out of the window and leapt out of bed feeling full of energy, up for another day of adventure in the Côte d'Azur.

After another hearty breakfast from Madame Gilbert, I packed a towel and headed to the station to catch a train to Cannes. I didn't shower because I wanted to keep the scent of Charlie on me until I swam in the Mediterranean Sea on the beach at Cannes. Anyways, I was always told that too much showering can wash away your body's natural minerals. At least that's my excuse.

The train wasn't busy and the 40-minute journey to Cannes passed quickly. Along the route, which uses the Marseilles-Ventimiglia line, we stopped for a few moments at Antibes. I liked the name of the station, so I promised that whatever Cannes was like, I would spend tomorrow checking out Antibes. Cannes is, of course, a world-famous city, but I had begun to realise that one should visit other lesser known points on the map, too.

Today, though, it was Cannes, and I had high expectations. In my ignorance, I even wondered if the famous annual film festival might be in full swing and that perhaps I would arrive in a city heaving with Hollywood stars.

When I came out of the station at Cannes I knew immediately which direction to head in for the beach. My radar was now finely-tuned to finding my way around the coastal cities of the Med, although it did strike me as kind of natural for a seaside town to have the exit to its train station facing towards the sea. The hot sun radiated off the pavement, so I took refuge on the shady side of the street. The beach here lies only a short four or five blocks from the station, even closer than in Nice, so the walk, even in the shade, was mercifully brief.

A few minutes later I emerged onto the Promenade de la Croisette, a beautiful palm-tree lined avenue with the sparkling, gently lapping azure waters of the Med on one side and a seemingly endless line of grand white villas on the other. I crossed the road and stood under a palm tree taking in the view. It was pristine, perfect and intimidating. The impressive avenue of almost perfectly aligned, palm trees stood to attention, like a garrison of soldiers protecting the white palaces behind them from attack by Med foes or pirates. How did they get them all to behave so well and grow so uniformly? There were palm trees in Alicante and Barcelona, and they added to the ambience there, too. But they were less orderly, less arranged. Here in Nice the French seemed to have ordered them to stand to attention like infantry, saluting the presence of royalty, the rich, the revered. Vive la revolution, eh?

Complementing the obedient battalion of palm trees, were beautifully laid pavements, as if laid by artisan masons rather than council labourers. The roads were flawless surfaces clearly designed to carry only the world's most expensive cars. Even the lines on the roads looked as if they had been freshly painted that morning. If I thought Nice was rich and authoritative, Cannes was positively regal. It commanded respect and turned its nose up at poverty.

I was relieved that today I had decided to wear khaki shorts and a plain white t-shirt with my flip-flops. I felt at least now that I looked a bit more neutral, and not immediately like a tourist. I could even be one of them. People swished past me like extras from *Dallas* – unnaturally fit, coiffured and televisual. Two very pretty French girls came towards me, both in white t-shirts, one with white shorts and sandals, the other in white flannel trousers. Chatting and smiling easily with each other, they'd surely just stepped off some catwalk nearby.

Crossing the road, a guy I guessed to be in his late twenties put his hand up to signal his presence to unseen friends. His sky blue polo-shirt and white linen shorts gave the impression of a playboy lifestyle. His black hair flopped confidently as he walked towards his party.

How did they do it? I thought. They must all wake at some ungodly hour and spend the entire morning preparing their 'look' for the day, before emerging to intimidate all we poor, lesser mortals into making more of an effort next time.

Now the smell of Charlie on my unwashed body felt a bit clammy. These beautiful people of the Med have probably had three showers by midday, I thought.

The only let down in my attire, I decided, was the cheap white-rimmed sunglasses I'd bought in Boots before I left Dundee. Everyone else seemed to have expensive dark-rimmed shades that screamed "'I'm uber-cool, don't even talk to me unless you're a millionaire." Still, I was here. I was young. And I was going to enjoy it!

Thankfully, I'd bought some water and a can of Coke from the little Spar shop at the end of the street from Madame Gilbert's hostel in Nice. I didn't even want to guess how much such luxuries would set one back in Cannes. For all its pretension, though, Cannes had the chill-out factor. Beautiful as everything was, it all appeared effortless, easy, comme il faut. There was no manic noise, no hooting of horns like in Barcelona; no lawless gangs of young lads eyeing up potential targets from whom to steal wallets and handbags. Everything in Cannes felt as if it had always been this way – chic, calm and easy.

When I got to the pathway alongside the beach, I was pleased to see Madame Gilbert was true to her word and Cannes had even got one over Nice on the beach stakes. There were no awkward, uncomfortable pebbles here, only warm, soft, golden sand stretching all the way along the shore. I took a spot directly in front of one of the nicest hotels – the Carlton - and unrolled my beach towel. I was slightly embarrassed by the towel, because, although almost brand new – I'd bought it in Paris with Yvonne – it was composed of red, grey and black lines with the letters VIP at the head end and 'Reserved' writ large down one side. It was ironic though. I bet none of those millionaires had one like this – reserved especially for them.

I stripped to my white swimming trunks and lay on the towel. Closing my eyes and feeling the warm September sun wash over my skin, I thought again about why the coastal resorts I'd been to so far were so different. Barcelona was a port town, therefore an industrial place, so I kind of understood its frenetic noisy nature. But Benidorm and Alicante were mainly tourist destinations and yet they had none of the calm, slow easy pace that Cannes offered. It occurred to me this was a difference of culture and money. The Spanish were much more talkative, they lived life on the streets of their towns and cities. I remembered passing through French towns on my various train rides and noticing that they always seemed to be deserted by comparison. I was processing in my head the two different peoples of the countries I'd visited so far, trying to understand them and finding their similarities too. As a Scot seeing these countries for the first time, I liked what I saw. Why couldn't our coastlines be adorned with five-star locations like this? Why did we have to think twice about wearing sunglasses on a sunny day in Dundee for fear of being beaten up, when here in Europe people look at you oddly if you don't cover your eyes in the sun? The answer was easy of course. It was the weather. There I was, almost asleep under the hot Mediterranean sun in mid-September, while back in Scotland it was already time for duffle coats and umbrellas. I loved Scotland, but the draw of a hot southern climate was irresistible.

I turned over on the towel to get some sun on my back and took out the little guide to Cannes that Madame Gilbert had thrust into my hands when I set off on my day trip. It was in French, so I was definitely going to struggle to glean any knowledge, but by concentrating hard I was able to make some sense of the words.

Cannes could trace its origins all the way back to the second century when it was first recorded as being a port settlement for fishermen. Later it became a Roman outpost and it has strong connections to religion with monasteries of one sort or another emerging throughout the ages.

Again the mention of 'Les Anglais'. The British were never far off. The guide explained the British and Spanish tried to take control of the region in the 1800s, but the French were having none of it and stood their ground. However, the British persisted and their love affair with the balmy climes of the Mediterranean heralded the birth of the area's association with wealth and aristocracy. It was also popular with Americans who started coming in numbers after the first world war.

I discovered the Cannes Film Festival started in 1946, an initiative to associate Cannes with the glitzy show-business world. So that's why all those people I saw when I arrived looked like film stars.

I wished I had transport of some kind. I would have loved to have taken a motorbike and headed up into the mountains around Cannes. It would have been great to have checked out the hidden village retreats, the endlessly winding roads and the panoramic viewpoints, which, according to the little guidebook, offered marvellous views of the Riviera and its scattering of coastal towns.

But money was tight. Instead, I put the book down and lay there, thinking about what it must have been like all those centuries ago, when this chic city was in its early days.

It was like being in history. You could feel the weight of past ages all around, much preserved and repaired now; transformed, but present nonetheless. The sun was hot and pleasant and lulled me into a half sleep. In my half-dreaming state, I seemed to travel through time to the future, knowing that I would visit this place again. Déjà vu? Does it always have to be a past memory? It was like a borrowed emotion from the future the universe was allowing me to experience now, right there in 1985 on that beach in Cannes. The sun can play with your head! I came out of my half dream, sat up and lit a cigarette. Looking around at the other sun worshippers on the beach, I wondered who they were? Where they'd come from? Where they'd go next? Two infants playing together ran back and forth from the water's edge filling their little castle-shaped buckets with wet sand and running back to mum and dad where they upturned their instant constructions to great squeals of delight. Dad stuck little French flags in the castle towers as they again ran to the water's edge and refilled their buckets. They seemed so carefree and happy. For an instant I wished I had children, too, to build sand castles with. I walked over to the water and waded into the fresh sea. I swam out as far as I could, before turning onto my back so I was just floating there. No-one was near. Everything was strangely quiet, serene. I was aware of only the sound of the water and my breathing. It was meditative, relaxing, tranquil. Again, I committed myself to creating many more moments like this in future. I would work hard and always remember to take a moment to stop and appreciate the life I had.

I made my way back to the shore, feeling renewed in Mind, body and spirit. My head was clear and alert, my outlook somehow renewed. The smell of Charlie had gone from my body. But I felt good, better than I ever had. I was young, bronzed, fit and full of hope. Ideas about my future began to take shape in my mind. Not fully formed ones, but a sense of understanding what I wanted from this life.

I stayed on the beach in Cannes until the heat of the sun began to dissipate. The other tourists and sun worshippers began to pack up and leave the beach. I read a little more, dozed and smoked more cigarettes. For half an hour I toyed with the sand. Bliss. I stared at my feet as I dug them into the warm grains, dragging my toes gently in an arc in front of me. I picked up handfuls of sand, inspected the tiny fragments that made up this strangely tactile material. It struck me how strange sand was, this perfectly powdery substance, made up of minute particles of solid rock. It must take tens of millions of years of being chipped away at by the oceans and seas to reach this stage. It occurred to me the sand on Cannes beach had probably been there for millions of years, before even the Pyramids were built and this sand would most likely remain there long after we have all annihilated each other.

In the 1980s, we were still in the era of the 'Cold War', so we expected that at any moment, someone, somewhere – probably in America or the USSR, as Russia was called then - would push a button and nuke us all.

These threats to our existence became more pronounced when I caught sight of a headline in an English language newspaper on a newsagent's rack on my way back to the station. Russia was expelling 25 British expatriates in a tit-for-tat retaliation over similar moves by the British government. It wasn't a safe time in global politics, but it was also a million miles away from the journey I was on. I wasn't going to let the Russians, or any other government spoil my adventure in Europe. Though it did make me think that they could be anywhere; even here on the Côte d'Azur, on the very train I was now on, heading back to Nice in the evening sunshine. I looked around at the few other passengers on the train. Thankfully, no-one looked like a Russian agent, and there would definitely be no British agents on this little train, because, as everyone knows, MI6 double-0 agents are glamorous, tuxedo-wearing schmoozers who go around in Aston Martins.

It was after seven-thirty when I arrived back at Madame Gilbert's.

"Ah, mon petit James Bond, 'ow was your veeseet to Cannes? Did you see all ze glamorous people?"

"Madame Gilbert! Yes. It was fantastic. C'est une très belle ville."

"Ah, bien sûr. And tonight, you enjoy Nice."

"Oui, I hope so. But first, une douche, je pense."

While drying off, I caught sight of my body in the long, rather camp, free-standing mirror in my room. The sun had transformed the colour of my skin to a deep tan like I'd never seen before. Standing there, naked, I was almost shocked at the difference between the white of my buttocks and the deep bronzed colour of the rest of my body, the sharp tan line created by my little swimming trunks. I hardly recognised my own face. My hair had grown longer and when I smiled, my teeth appeared brilliantly white. It was like looking at a new me. How long would I stay this colour?

That evening I took my camera and wandered around Nice on a photo mission. I wanted to capture all the night-time scenes and sites so I could remember this place when I returned to Scotland. I surreptitiously took shots of groups outside cafés and restaurants; I captured the big white grand villas on the seafront, then headed along the promenades trying for artistic shots of the beachfront and avenues. Street signs caught my eye, palm trees and exotic plants that adorned the seafront.

Later, hungry, I sought out the bar from the night before and ordered the same sandwich again, knowing it would come with a large side salad. Charlie and his friends would probably be in Paris by now. I wanted them here though. How good it would have been to chat with them about my day in Cannes.

As I munched my way through supper, I remembered the three nurses I had met in Barcelona. I thought of Yvonne and Suzi – Paris seemed a lifetime ago already - and where they might be now. Jeff, the guy I met in the MIJE in the capital, floated through my mind. The image of his almost naked body from that first time we met in the dorm at the MIJE, was still crystal clear. I sat at the table looking down the street to the seafront, and the endless stretch of the Mediterranean. I inhaled the warm sea air. For the second time, I felt that at some point I would like to meet someone and build some kind of a life with them. Whoever that would be, whenever it would happen, I knew we were going to have adventures together, go places, see things, do things. I'd bring them here to romantic Nice and Cannes, and we'd explore the entire coast together. We would make love anytime we wanted, have great jobs and build a home. My life had only really just started, but I could almost taste all the possibilities of the life to come. I acknowledged it and it felt good.

But first I had to complete the rest of this journey and there were still more places to discover, more people to meet along the way. Of all the folks I had met on the journey so far, Jeff was the one I most wanted to talk to about my travels. I was certain he'd be full of excellent ideas about what I should do next, where to visit, what to see. I felt slightly fraudulent about my journey, like I didn't really know anything about the places I had visited, or indeed whether I was missing some vital stops along the way. I did have a rough plan, but having someone like Jeff around would, I imagined, help in deciding what particular places would be worth visiting most. But I was travelling alone, so it was all down to me. I examined the tiny map of Europe in the youth hostel guide that I had taken out with me that evening and resolved to continue east. I wondered if my money would last long enough to get to Greece. Should I do Germany, Austria, Switzerland? They'd be cold and I was enjoying the warmth of my coastal tour too much. So I decided Monaco was definitely the next place to explore.

I'd been fascinated by Monte Carlo for years. Growing up I'd watched the world's most glamorous and thrilling Grand Prix on television, and wondered at the awesome energy of the race and the spectacular setting. It oozed the kind of aspiration you couldn't even dream of back where I came from. As a thirteen-year-old, I would stay up late on Sunday nights, after Mum and Dad had gone to bed, so I could watch 'The Monte Carlo

Show' on ITV. It was a bizarre spectacle, with an improbably good-looking host who had a strange female, muppet-like side-kick called 'Plume' in the shape of a feather Boa, who would tease and joke with him in between the acts. The acts, as far as I can remember, consisted of singers, comedians and magic acts. I recall Shirley Bassey headlining once, singing one of her 'Bond' themes, but I wasn't familiar with many of the other singers, who may well have been famous elsewhere in Europe, but not known in Britain. I always remember, though, being impressed by the theatre itself. The Monte Carlo Sporting Club was a large circular structure with a roof that rotated so half of the auditorium was open to the warm, balmy night air of the Côte d'Azur. I'd always wanted to see that and now was my chance. I remember thinking, there in Nice, how strange it was that I was on the verge of visiting a building I had seen as an adolescent. How did I make that happen? I wondered if this was what life might turn out to be like – you just wish deeply enough to do, be or see something and the universe conspires to make it happen. One day the opportunity suddenly and unexpectedly presents itself before you, even if you forgot that you desired it at some point. I didn't know what 'Cosmic Ordering' was back then, this idea that the universe provides and you can ask it for whatever you want, but maybe we're all naturally tapping the Cosmos subconsciously with our dreams and desires.

And after having experienced the glamour of Monte Carlo, I planned to take the long train trip to Venice. One summer, while I was a 16-year-old schoolboy, my girlfriend had given me *Brideshead Revisited* by Evelyn Waugh to read. In this tale of power and privilege of the English aristocracy in the 1920s, the Brideshead family invariably spend time in Venice, which I'm sure must have been the Monte Carlo of the 1920s, full of mystery and glamour in an equally exotic setting.

Yet again, places and characters I had only read about in books or seen on TV were now within touching distance.

Later that night I packed my little day bag in preparation for the short trip to Monte Carlo. I turned in fairly early, ten o'clock, as I had no idea how often the trains between Nice and Monaco ran, and I wanted to make sure of enough time to explore Europe's glitziest destination.

14. Monaco or bust

Sunlight streamed in sideways through the bedroom window of the room at Madame Gilbert's. "Today I'm off to Monte Carlo!" I said to my reflection in the mirror, as I brushed my teeth.

Downstairs at breakfast, I noticed new faces. I nodded 'bonjour' as I passed. An English couple, who'd arrived two days earlier, asked where I was planning to spend the day.

"I'm taking the train to Monte Carlo. I want to see all the millionaires in their natural habitat," I replied, jokingly.

"Oh it's very rich and chic," said the lady. "Take your own water and sandwiches, though. It's very expensive."

"You won't like the beach," her husband warned. "It's not very exciting and they make you pay a ransom for a sun-bed."

"Really? Thanks for letting me know."

"You'll enjoy it though, the casino's quite a building," he added. "Don't gamble all your holiday money, though, eh?" He chuckled.

"Monte Carlo or bust, eh?" I replied, winking at them as I finished the hot chocolate. I was too considerate of Mme Gilbert's generous motherliness towards me to refuse her persistent efforts to give me energy and sustenance for the day. I figured she probably knew better than I what was best for me.

The train ride from France to the principality of Monaco was short but spectacular. Expensive-looking properties dotted the hilltops as the train weaved its way along the main Marseilles-Ventimiglia railway line. I lost count of the number of private swimming pools I glimpsed in the gardens of these lavish residences. The train darted into tunnels hewn into the landscape, shielding us from the heat of the day, the cool darkness a brief respite. A second or two later we'd emerge again into the brilliant sunshine of the Côte d'Azur. The sea to the right looked vast and endless, stretching off to the horizon line where it blended in a haze with the blue sky. I kept my white-rimmed sunglasses over my eyes in the tunnel to reduce the sudden blast of light when we came out of the other end.

Half an hour later I was wandering around the elevated hillside streets of the world's richest principality. The hilltops and mountain terrain are covered in a forest of expensive tower blocks. Each seemed to have spacious, hotel-style foyers with exuberantly large reception desks, manned by very official looking guards. Scattered between the myriad tall towers were low-level, walled residences, with opulent, sturdy gates. I had learned as a child, reading the books of 20th century Scottish writer, Lewis Grassic-Gibbon, that buildings mostly use stone hewn from local quarries. In Aberdeen, for example, cold grey granite is evident in much of the city's Victorian architecture. But here, by the balmy shores of the Mediterranean, the bright limestone was warm, clean and bright, and where there wasn't limestone, white plaster made the grand palaces and houses of old into huge, ornate confections. They were bright, fairy-tale constructions baked by the sunshine for sure every day of the year.

Occasionally, I caught sight of a vehicle leaving this or that house, the open gates providing me with a fleeting glimpse of the lavish world beyond. Pristine and perfectly manicured driveways wound their way to houses so large that each must surely be a palace. From my outside vantage point, I looked upon perfect lawns and carefully planted exotic trees. An abundance of palms, pines and cypresses complemented by dazzling floral arrangements of carefully planned colours – red bougainvillea draped lazily out of huge pots and along limestone brick walls, fiery orange red hot pokers shot like fountains out of beds along the driveways, white and red roses commanded grand doorways, while blue delphiniums promised calm.

I'd seen, or rather noticed, my first palm trees in Spain, first in Barcelona and then arriving in Alicante. I had never seen them, or perhaps just never noticed them, back home in Scotland. But here, in Monaco, they were two a penny, commonplace, yet no less exotic.

I was impressed by these beautiful gardens. They cheered the soul. Every colour you could imagine had been invited to reside in these wealthy, ordered, exclusive homes. Who lives there? I thought. What do they do? How can they afford such grandeur? Hollywood actors, noblemen of Europe, famous writers, politicians? Maybe even rock stars? Although I discounted the latter because this was probably too ordered and luxurious for rebellious rockers.

Glimpsing what lay beyond the majestic streets of Monte Carlo it was not difficult to feel poor and insignificant. So far I'd thrown myself into the mystery of all the new places I'd seen, but here, in one of the richest city-states in the world, I felt like an urchin, an outsider, a lowly traveller, not even a real tourist. I was just a young, working-class boy from a cold country passing through the gated, closely guarded suburb of a balmy paradise that I couldn't afford to be part of. I wasn't alone, though. There were plenty of other tourists also nosing a glimpse of the high life.

I allowed my built-in natural compass to lead me down the meandering mountain streets until I eventually emerged onto what looked like a heavenly park. A sign by the expertly crafted railings read 'Allées des Boulingrins'. I wandered along the pathway flanked by yet more tall palm trees. Unlike the grand gardens of the private residences further up the mountain, this park was open to all, yet no less pristine or colourful than those exclusive mansions with their huge gates and guards.

Gradually, the line of palms revealed a huge building at the far end of the park. I'd never seen anything like it. It may as well have been the Taj Mahal. I crossed the road to the perfectly mown, round lawn and stood before the majestic building, a ruffian stumbling upon the king's castle in a fairy tale. Was it for real? Two turrets nestled in a grand repose either side of the main entrance. Statues of graceful mythical creatures stood guard either side of the ornate iron and glass canopy where the words Casino Monte Carlo were written in gold. I looked around and noticed every car parked in the street outside the casino was worth a king's ransom. Porches, Rolls-Royces, Ferraris, Lamborghinis, Aston Martins… and more vintage models and makes I couldn't name, that I'd never seen before, and have never seen since.

I was in paradise. This is where I want to live. I want to drive all these cars. I want to walk into that casino and look at all the people, talk to them, ask them how they got where they are now. Then it hit me! I recognised this place. I'd been here before. How could I not have known? James Bond himself had parked his car here, walked up those steps and charmed his way around evil villains and beautiful women all in the name of saving the world from destruction by psychotic madmen. It was strange being in a place I'd seen countless times in films, and all of a sudden, I felt like I belonged there after all. Unlike like James Bond, though, I was in a scruffy black t-shirt, skimpy white shorts and there was no way the grey-capped gendarmes in their black and yellow striped trousers were going to let me wander into that palace of the rich and famous. So I loitered, taking photos, admiring the statues and ogling the world-class cars on the street.

Down at the marina I marvelled at the luxury yachts and gin palaces moored along the pontoons. All the world's money must be here for the summer, I thought. It never seemed to end. I never thought there could be so much wealth in the world. When I finally made it to the beach, Monte Carlo's exclusivity slapped me over the head. A beach guard demanded 70 francs.

"What for?" I asked, smiling uncomprehendingly. Feigning surprise and ignorance can sometimes work to your advantage.

"Monsieur, the beach here is not free. If you want to sunbathe in Monte Carlo, you must pay."

"Really? It's free everywhere else."

"But this is not anywhere else, this is Monte Carlo." He paused and looked towards the beach. "This is your first time here?"

"Yes, I came all the way from Nice this morning, just to try the beach and to swim monsieur."

"Mmm. Okay, c'est pas grave. Here, you can go down and enjoy the plage, the beach, just for today." The guard took his little machine, tore off a ticket thrust it into my hands, and put a finger to his mouth "Shh".

I smiled. "Hey sir, merci beaucoup. Thank you so much. That's very kind."

The guard smiled and gave a friendly laugh. "Don't

worry. Enjoy our beach. It is one of the finest you will ever see. Welcome to Monte Carlo."

I had to smile back. Here I was in one of the most glamorous and exclusive cities in the world and I had just been given a gift – access. I sauntered down onto the beach, unpacked my knapsack and laid out my towel. The guard was right. Even the sand in Monaco was like no other beach. Every beach I knew was made of very fine tiny grains of sand that got between your toes and stayed there, or they were pebble beaches like in Nice. But here in the oasis of Monaco, the sand was less powdery, it didn't stick to you. Rather, it was cleaner, stronger and rolled off your skin gently and obediently. The sand was like tiny little rocks, smaller than peas, but larger than typical sandy beaches. Millionaire sand for millionaire people. It was the best beach experience so far and it was about to get even better.

I swam in the sea to cool down and made my way out to a little diving pontoon anchored (about 90 metres) offshore. I climbed onto the deck and looked back to the spectacular view of this mountain meeting the sea city of luxury skyscrapers, lush flora and shiny money that rolls all the way down to the Med.

You never know if you start a rush or whether other people just had the same thought as you did, but not long after I'd swum out to the pontoon, other beachgoers started paddling out. I shifted over as young boys pulled themselves up onto the platform, smiling as they said 'salut' and 'hello' in their different languages. Two pretty girls with deep suntans and long blonde hair also made

213

the swim. When they arrived at the pontoon we helped them clamber aboard. There were no steps, so the trick was to wait until the water bobbed higher and then winch yourself up.

One boy around my age nudged me. "You are Eenglish?"

"Yes, Scottish. You?" He shook his longish bob of light brown hair and smiled.

"Francais. French. Scotland man. Whisky, eh? Haha." I nodded back at him, smiling. I was tempted to say "France man, champagne, snails and frogs' legs", but I just laughed along with him. By now there were nine or ten of us on the pontoon and we all took turns jumping off into the warm sea. The French boy put his hand out to help me back up onto the platform and a sort of informal competition ensued to see how professionally we could each dive off the pontoon. We did backflips, somersaults, twist dives and belly flops. When someone performed a particularly clever dive with a little splash, we all applauded with enthusiastic sportsmanship.

The French guy introduced himself as Henri. He was from the Loire, which I had heard of, but had never been to.

"You speak French?"

"Non, un peu, peut-être."

"It's good, you look Italian though, not like a white Eenglish man." He smiled and I felt his slim suntanned arm nudge mine to compare the colour of our tans.

214

"See, you are like French. You are dark, haha." His green eyes were clear and bright and I was grateful that I had someone to speak to.

"Are you on holiday?" I asked.

"Oui, with my papa. We are staying here in Monte Carlo."

"What about your mother?"

"They are finis, how you say, er, divorcés..."

"Oh, divorced. I see, quel dommage. Desolé."

"Yes, divorced. Oh, you have great French."

He dived off the platform again, his slim tanned torso was tight and beautiful to watch. When he'd placed his arm alongside mine, I felt a rush of warmth and attraction to Henri.

The two young girls left after about 20 minutes and a few of the other boys also raced each other back to the beach. I lay down on the deck, my head over the edge and my arms lopping in the water. Henri paddled around the pontoon, coming back to me eventually with each turn. One time he rested with his arms holding onto the pontoon astride my arms. He made more idle chat, smiling and spitting sea water out of his mouth. I told him I was travelling around a few countries by train and I loved France and wanted to see more of it. He told me his father insisted he travel with him and his little sister to Monaco. His mother was home in the Loire working with her new husband. Occasionally he would come round from another circuit of the pontoon and stop, stare

215

at me intently for a few moments; then he would flash another lovely wide smile of perfectly white teeth.

"Come in the water. We can race," he said.

"Sure." I dived off and we headed around the far side of the pontoon from the beach. We set off into the Med racing each other as we swam through the water like two blades of steel. I knew I could cut fast through the water if I got my breath right. It's always in the breathing. Eventually, Henri called a truce and we headed back to the pontoon, still racing each other a little.

When we reached the back side of the pontoon, we were out of sight of everyone on shore. He stopped, turned around and planted a breathless kiss on my lips. I kissed him back, as we both held onto the pontoon. We smiled at each other, coupled our bodies together, and kissed again. Longer this time. The adrenalin was incredible. A stolen moment with a beautiful stranger, both our youthful, tanned, wet bodies glistening in the hot sun. His salty breath was delicious and exciting to taste. He let go of the pontoon, put his hand under the water and pulled at my trunks. He went under the water and pulled them clear off my feet, and resurfaced to place them around my neck. Then he took his own trunks off and did the same. He pulled me towards him. All the time I kept hold of the pontoon, excited, afraid, aroused. No-one else was near the platform as we made out together in the warm sea, kissing, touching and feeling each other. He placed his lips on my neck and pulled on me beneath the water. I returned the action until we both reached the point where it was all too much. I felt this warm rush below as his hand worked on me and mine on him. We came at the same time, the momentary warmth filling the water between us as we each writhed in a kind of stifled ecstasy. The hot sun was our only witness as we both hung there, by the pontoon, floating and spent on the sea.

"Thank you," I said, smiling into his face. He beamed back.

"Merci, Scottish man. You are très sexy."

"Et toi, aussi."

We kissed again and he said he must get back to his sister on the beach.

I watched as he pulled on his swimming trunks, still catching my breath. I pulled him back for one last kiss.

"Merci, Henri. You taste very nice." We smiled, and he was off, cutting through the water again back to the shore.

After a moment I pulled on my trunks, swam out to sea again and turned onto my back to gaze upon the azure sky. I felt like a timeless being. What an experience! We could have been two lithe youths in ancient Greece. Two Persian boys, young cadets in some Alexandrian army. Did that really just happen? I asked myself. I'd never done anything like that before. So public and private at the same time, so risky and spontaneous. I felt free, liberated and happy.

It was like a dream. I revelled in the ecstasy of what had just taken place. I had suddenly turned a corner in my life; it had changed me forever. Those beautiful, innocent moments of passion with another boy convinced me beyond doubt that I was no longer on the fence, sexually. Right there and then, lying on my back in the sea, looking up into the blue sky and the universe beyond, I knew that I would never marry, never have children and never settle down to a 'normal' suburban life. It was like a great weight lifted off my shoulders. The gay guys I had met on this journey across Europe were just like me, I was just like them and I knew there must be many more. To taste those moments is to live, truly, beautifully, innocently. It was natural.

From now on I was going to accept that I was wonderfully, confidently, happily, unapologetically gay.

I swam back to the pontoon, and stood tall and proud on the deck.. Looking towards the beach and the whole of Monte Carlo, I shook the water from my hair and beamed a smile at the world. I knew who I was and that world, back on the shore, was a world I was going to grow up in, progress in, savour and live in as a gay man. I didn't feel like an outsider anymore. This world was mine and I was going to enjoy it. And this world was going to have to get used to acceptance, because I wasn't going to hide or worry any more.

I moved to the edge of the deck, turned my back to shore and dived a confident, graceful, almost splash free backflip into the warm, friendly waters of the Med. I didn't know if Henri was watching. It didn't matter.

Once back on shore, I flopped onto my towel and let

the sun dry my body. I noticed Henri about four metres to the right of me. His father was packing up their beach kit and he was ordering his offspring around. Now and again Henri would glance over at me, a furtive look, smiling covertly. When they headed off, they had to pass by me, Henri lagged behind his sister as his father led the way. As they marched by, Henri looked straight into my eyes. He kept walking and said nothing, but as he went by, a small piece of folded paper fell onto my towel. My right hand moved over and grasped the folded note. I didn't look at it immediately. Instead, I lay there, motionless, giving my spent, wet body over to the warmth of the dying afternoon sun.

I fished out the Walkman from my bag and lay on the sand bronzing myself to Spandau Ballet's *Gold*. Annie Lennox and the Eurythmics seemed to be aware of my earlier encounter with Henri as they sang *Sweet Dreams* into my ears. Who was I to disagree?

Later, the beach thinned out. A beautiful moment at the end of a surprisingly lovely day. People gathered their towels, suncreams, parasols, bags, paraphernalia and began to make their way back to their houses, apartments and hotels. But, when you have no timetable, no commitment, nowhere you have to be, the gradual space of an empty beach is a pleasure to behold.

I lay there until the warmth of the sun was almost totally gone. Then, I pulled on my t-shirt and began to pack my own stuff away. The unique sand of the Monte Carlo beach fell easily away from between my toes, my sandals, towel and bag. I spotted the scrunched-up note

Henri had dropped earlier. 'Je t'aime, I will be here tomorrow. Come. Henri x'. I smiled and decided I would return, for I too, wanted to see him again.

It turned chilly on the beach, but once I was walking through the streets, back towards the train station high up the hillside, it became warm and muggy again.

I passed by many restaurants I couldn't afford to eat in. Even if I could, I wasn't exactly dressed for these smart places in my grubby t-shirt and Marc Christian shorts.

I arrived at the train station just as the regional service to Nice was pulling in. I smelled of the sea and I could still taste Henri's pleasant saliva in my mouth. Once on the train, I sniffed my fingers and I could still smell his sweet, sugary odour, my mouth still tasted of him. I closed my eyes and half-dreamed the moment again when he pulled me towards him in the sea, wrapping his legs around me and kissing me in the unbridled, free and passionate way only young people do. I pulled on my Walkman headphones and got lost in Bronski Beat's *Smalltown Boy* as I looked out to the dimming sky and darkening waters of the Mediterranean.

When I arrived back at Madame Gilbert's, she was sitting in the lounge, smoking and watching the evening news.

"Ooh, monsieur Sam, you look so 'appy and bronzé. You 'ave a good time in Mon-aa-co?"

"Aah, Madame Gilbert, bien sur. It was très bien.

Mais, je suis fatigué maintenant. What is the news?"

"Pfff, rien, nothing. It's just the mad world. But you, my boy, you look so full of everything that is good. I think your day, it was better than the world, non?"

I smiled, but gave no reply.

Upstairs, I closed the door to the shared shower room and shed my skimpy beach clothes. In the long, wall-mounted mirror I surveyed the colour of my skin. The only parts of the old me that remained were the bits covered by my Speedos. My hair had grown longer. I looked nothing like the pale Scottish lad who'd set out weeks before. Everything had changed: My physical appearance, my thoughts, my attitudes. I was even becoming much more confident in my French.

I was like a salamander, shedding its old skin for new. But far from being skin deep, the changes I was feeling inside were opening up all kinds of possibilities.

I replayed the passionate moment with Henri over and over in my head. I tingled recalling his slim figure pressing against me in the water; the moment he pulled me towards him to kiss me; his tongue in my mouth as we kissed; his body wrapped around mine as we writhed in the sea. It was heaven and still I could taste him.

My thoughts then turned to the rest of my day trip. I wanted to learn about those people in Monte Carlo. Who were they? How did they make their money? Had they ever heard of Scotland? Did Sean Connery live in Monaco? If so, I was sure he would definitely have mentioned Scotland to the other rich people of Monaco. They probably all flew up there regularly, staying in lush Highland castles and the like.

I wondered how young people like me could afford to live in places like Monte Carlo.

It seemed the further east I travelled along the Mediterranean, the more exotic the lands were. If this was what Monaco was like, what was I going to find in Italy? My head was full of questions. That day the world became a much bigger place. When I got back to my room, I climbed into bed and replayed the whole day once more over in my head, visualising in my mind's eye all I had seen – and done. Spent, again, I fell into a long, deep sleep, having had no supper.

The next morning, the weather had clouded over for the first time on my voyage. I decided to take my clothes to the launderette for a wash and was lugging my rucksack down the winding stairs of the pension when Madame Gilbert marched down the hallway.

"Huh, are you leefing us, young man?

"Mais non, Madame Gilbert. My clothes, I need to wash them. I'm going to the launderette."

Madame Gilbert protested, insisting she would be happy to do my washing, but I resisted. I was "a big boy now" and I wanted to see if I could work my way around a French launderette. Anyway, it was only around the corner.

While shorts, underwear, and t-shirts whirred in the

industrial-looking washing machine I thought of Henri again. I was sure he hadn't gone to the beach in this kind of weather. No-one does when there's no sun. Or maybe he was there now, after all. A lone figure on an empty beach, hoping I might arrive at any minute.

I distracted myself from becoming maudlin by studying my guide book and settled on Venice as the place I was going go to in Italy. I sat in the drab launderette staring at the washing machine trying to imagine Venice. According to the guide book, bridges seemed to be the best things to see for free so I'd seek out the Bridge of Sighs and the Rialto Bridge to start with and take it from there. I wondered what it would be like wandering around a city full of water. But as I stared at all the water swishing around in the washing machine, all I could think of was Henri. I paced around the launderette trying to convince myself that he would not be upset or angry with me. His father would have organised something else for them to do that day, I was sure.

The thoughts exhausted me. Eventually, I pushed all ideas of him out of my head. I sat and stared at my washing going round and round. Every so often my large beach towel came into view in the washing machine glass. Its red, white and black stripes meshing in with the foamy suds of the washing powder. I'd lumped all my washing in together, to save my dwindling finances. Other travellers in the launderette seemed to be doing the same. It was comforting to know I was following the established budgeting rules involved in backpacking.

I thought about how little money I had left and decided to rework my plans. I had intended to spend a day in Venice and then head down to Rome. But I decided it would now be better to spend two days in the floating city, then head back to Nice, where Madame Gilbert would eventually adopt me, and welcome me to a life in the Côte d'Azur, where I would spend the rest of my days enjoying the easy life, maybe with someone like Henri. He just wouldn't stay out of my head.

I returned to the pension and informed Madame Gilbert I'd be leaving the next day for Italy. I didn't discuss my plan to return because there was no telling what might happen on the journey and I wanted to be free to change my plans.

"Oh dommage," exclaimed Madame Gilbert. "Okay, young Eenglish man, eet 'as been un plaisir to 'ave you in my hotel." She always called it her hotel. "I 'ope you veel come back to see me one day, soon, huh? Do not forget your maman in Nice, eh?"

"Of course, Madame Gilbert, merci beaucoup for all your kindness. I may be back sooner than you think."

"At what time ees your train demain? I will make breakfast and some sondweesh for you, hmm?"

"Oh thank you, Madame Gilbert." What a dear she was.

When I headed out into the warm Nice air, the clouds were thinning and the sunshine was returning. It felt like home away from home now. The shop signs, the phone boxes on the streets, the cars and people, all seemed benignly familiar. As I took the ten minute walk to the station I realised I'd fallen in love with the French Riviera. It had caught me in its grip and anchored me in Nice, a base for travel to nearby places. Even as I looked up the train times for Venice I knew I'd return here many times.

Madame Gilbert was suitably sombre and teary on the final morning when I came down to breakfast. My train was at 11am, so I scoffed a hearty breakfast of scrambled eggs on toast, Madame Gilbert's special treat for me since I was leaving, and a large mug of hot chocolate, of course.

I settled my bill and Madame Gilbert hugged me as if I was her only son heading out into the world.

"Take care in Italy, sweet boy," she sniffled. "Zay can be unpredictable, huh? Do not show them your money, eh? Be safe." She pushed a small brown bag into my hands. "Some-sing for your long voyage. Bon courage."

I smiled, picked up my rucksack, gave Madame Gilbert a kiss on her right cheek, thanked her for being my 'maman de Nice', and bid her au revoir.

* * * * *

Most of the passengers in my carriage on the Eurostar have drifted into afternoon slumber. I need to stretch my legs and slide out of my comfy window seat. The carriage is silent now. The young female executive has gone. She must have got off at Charles de Gaulle Airport for her Paris connection. I pass through the sliding doors into the corridor and wander down through the next cabin to the restaurant car. People are standing around at the high bar tops, chatting, joking, drinking. I stand around for a moment taking in the scene, before ambling back down the train to the sleepy quiet of my carriage.

The sun is still shining across the landscape, but it's weaker now. Evening is coming. We're deep into France – 'La profonde' as they call it. Gently rolling hills flank the distant horizon, which tells me we must be close to the Loire Valley. It's all familiar to me now, but no less impressive. The crew are about to liven up the somnolent calm of the business class cars with an early evening aperitif and snacks.

"Good evening sir, would you like an aperitif?"

"Oui, vin blanc s'il vous plaît."

A dozy businessman, French, I suspect, a few rows away orders 'un café' and a cognac. He pours the latter into the former. Always a good idea. We smile in a brief acknowledgement of a shared guilty pleasure. I'm a fan of blending my brandy in this way, too. I look out the window to the setting sun and think not of the Loire or brandy, but of Venice in 1985.

* * * * *

15. Slow train to Venice

The train to Venice was very long. As we snaked our way along the Mediterranean coastline, I looked out the window back and forth along the full exterior. It seemed to go on forever in both directions. I was excited but slightly nervous about heading to Italy. I didn't know the language at all and couldn't get my head around the few words and phrases in my guidebook. Although 'prego' seemed to be a word that could be used for most things. It's important to make sure one knows how to say please and thank you in another language, so I made sure I had 'per favore' and 'grazie' instilled in my head.

On this journey, I could stretch out with plenty of space around me. From the voices I could overhear, no-one seemed to be English, so I was on my own.

Soon we were approaching the Franco-Italian border and slowed to a halt at a customs station. A large sign read Ventimiglia. The French guards strutted through the train ordering everyone to have their passports ready on the long concrete runway that passed for a platform. I saw others picking up their baggage, so I grabbed my rucksack too. We all climbed down the steep steps of the train and lined up in front of the small customs building, for processing for admission to Italy. Everyone looked slightly nervous. It reminded me of the customs going into Spain weeks earlier. Perhaps the officers here will be friendlier, I thought to myself. But it didn't look hopeful.

A band of three surly, unshaven customs officials passed along the line, checking for obvious criminals, spies or terrorists. The shortest guard was led along by a large Alsatian dog, which sniffed keenly at peoples' bags. Although the dog showed scant interest in anyone, in particular, the guards stopped by two young couples, prodded their long batons at their luggage and asked them where they were from. I heard one of the guys utter a few rapid words in a nervous voice, but I picked out 'España' in his jumbled reply..

Having witnessed this brief, humourless interrogation, everyone else in the line was now silent. I tried to keep looking straight ahead to avoid eye contact, but it was useless. It was one of those moments where, no matter how much you want to do one thing, your body compels you to do the opposite. I was curious about them, and I had nothing to be nervous about, I thought. They were fascinating, almost unreal, like actors from some old war movie. Did people really still behave like this? Was it just an act, perhaps an exercise in intimidation? Or were they looking for the known face of a devious spy, dangerous terrorist or drug smuggler?

Just then it occurred to me my rucksack may still have a whiff remaining from the joints I had smoked in

Alicante station. At least enough to send the security dog into a frenzy. My heart beat a little faster as the thoughts once again raced through my mind. Had I checked my bag for any remnants of the night in Alicante? Had a stray joint somehow become lodged in the deepest recesses of my bag? Were my clothes tainted with the odour of marijuana? My chest became heavy as the three stooges got closer. The line nudged forward, so I took advantage of the moment to make a casual action of picking up my pack and slinging it on my back as I moved forward. To my mind this masked the fact I was ensuring it was no longer at ground level for the sniffer dog to get up close and personal with. Panic was slowly rising in me. I thanked the stars that I'd washed most of my clothes the day before. The guards and sniffer dog were almost upon me now. Still prodding baggage, they moved along the line. Then the dog was nosing closer. My mouth felt extremely dry. In my left hand was the bag containing the food Madame Gilbert had prepared for me. The dog lifted its nose and sniffed. The guards stopped. I felt the baton of the tallest guard lifting the bag in my hand. I looked him squarely in the eye and held it out.

"Sandwiches," I muttered through my dry mouth. Why hadn't I learned the Italian word for a sandwich?

"Here. Look," I offered.

"English?"

"Yes. No. Scottish. Scotland."

The tall guard took the bag and opened it. He looked

inside, took out an apple and handed the bag back. He held up the apple and wagged a finger at me. So, fruit is not allowed. Okay. I can live with that. I nodded, saying sorry in English.

They moved on down the line. Relief poured over me like sweat, but I made sure to keep my breathing steady in case they noticed the change in my stance and returned. Thankfully, Madame Gilbert's sandwiches had deflected potential interest in my rucksack, even though I knew there was nothing incriminating in there. With each step towards the passport desk in the customs hall, my breathing returned to normal and saliva began to flow in my mouth again.

It took an hour and a half for everyone to be processed through the customs hall. On the other side of the customs hall our Italian inter-city train was waiting, and, once everyone was back onboard, the train heaved into motion.

I remembered *Midnight Express*, a film where the main character is arrested at a Turkish airport for attempting to smuggle hashish out of the country, and spends years languishing in the brutal cesspit of a Turkish prison. I resolved there and then that, whatever happened in my life, I would never try to smuggle drugs across country borders.

Feeling better, I opened my lunch bag to find Madame Gilbert's baguette, a KitKat and a small bottle of red wine. I savoured the delicious taste of that sandwich and, having pushed in the cork, swigged the wine. It may have been that the security guards had heightened my sense of the value of freedom and liberty, but that cheese and ham baguette and cheap wine sure tasted great on that train that day.

The journey was a long nine and a half hours, but it was a direct service straight to Venice, with countless tunnels as we crossed spectacular low lying mountain ranges and endless rolling fields and hills of the Italian countryside on the route up to Milan.

Once again I was in a country unknown to me. What would it be like? How would I understand the people? Would I find a decent place to sleep? Would I be safe?

I consulted my International Youth Hostel Guidebook, but there seemed relatively little in the way of accommodation for backpackers in Italy. I resolved on taking my chances when I arrived. Anyway, it was still balmy and warm. I reckoned I could just kip on the floor of the train station if need be. I've seen many fellow backpackers sound asleep on the shiny tiled floors of train stations, using their backpacks as pillows, which also provides security from opportunist thieves.

It was dark by as passed by Verona and headed on the last leg down to Venice. I was sleepy and bored after such a long journey. The train slowed a long way ahead of our terminus and I was strangely disoriented when we drew near Venice's Santa Lucia station at around 9.30pm. I felt the difference in the terrain below our train as we left the mainland for the long pontoon to Venice island. I looked out to total blackness, broken only by the occasional glimmer of light flickering off the waters of the Laguna Veneta. The train edged slowly, trepidatious, along the tracks of the pontoon, as if shifting its weight carefully on the bridge connecting the mainland to the island.

16. Venezia

The station was chaotic. People scurried back and forth; station guards yelled animatedly. I imagined they were telling people to hurry up as this or that train prepared to leave. Near the main exit I noticed, over on the far left platform, the impressive, shiny, dark livery of the Venice-Simplon Orient Express. It stopped me in my tracks. I had only seen pictures of this palace on wheels or witnessed its grandeur in films like *Murder on the Orient Express*, so seeing it just feet away from me was breathtaking. Majestic, regal, and improbably clean and shiny. The pristine, dark royal blue exterior of the coaches emanated a gravitas that yelled unapologetically 'only the very rich may board'. Indeed, through the carriage windows, I saw well-dressed people reclining in luxurious chairs, as waiters fussed over them, filling their flutes with the finest champagne. They looked like film stars, industry barons and royalty, all the characters you'd expect on a train of such legendary status. I wondered if a murderer was lurking among them, ready to strike as the grand train meandered its way across Europe through the dark night. I stood taking in the opulence of the world's most luxurious train, considering how fortunate it was that it happened to be waiting in Venice, just as I arrived. "One day I will earn enough money to take a trip on that train,", I promised myself.

Eventually, somewhat humbled, I made my way down the broad steps of the station entrance and onto the wide Venetian quayside, where a number of large river taxis waited to carry new arrivals to the centre of the floating city. Because I'd stopped to take in the splendour of the Orient Express, I'd missed the first few, which was fine as it also meant that I didn't have to queue up with the hoards. I was able to walk directly onboard one of the boats with the last stragglers and we were soon cruising our way through the Veneta towards the Piazza San Marco. It was airy, a little on the breezy side, out on the open water and I felt a brief shiver for the first time in weeks. But the chill had gone once we were back out of the open water and in the warm enclosure of Venice's most famous square.

What to do now? I wandered around taking in the imposing floodlit facade of the San Marco church, the famous Basilica di San Marco. It was around 10.45 by now, and the square was still busy. It was a stark contrast to Nice, where most people would by now be heading home for the evening, or indeed already in bed. The cafés bordering the square were full of Italians and tourists, all noisily chatting and gesticulating. I loved it. It felt alive, buzzy, exciting. There was an energy in the air. It was my kind of energy, an enthusiasm for life itself. In France, people sat chatting quietly and calmly to each other, occasionally shrugging their shoulders in resignation or nodding agreement. Here, in the bustling cafés of the Piazza San Marco, conversation was a far more dramatic and colourful activity. Grown men gesticulated wildly with their arms as they hammered home a point they firmly believed was true or pressed the fingertips of a hand together before waving it at their friend as if asking for proof to support their point of view. Voices raised in exuberant interchanges, not in anger, but rather enthusiasm for being alive and engaged in the great conversation of life.

I wandered past the rows of seats outside the many cafés, people watching again. Italian people appeared to be more genetically beautiful than any other nation I could think of. Everyone seemed to be blessed with the same glossy jet black hair, men and women alike. One slim, tanned and smartly-dressed young woman tossed her hair seductively as she spoke rapidly to an equally attractive boyfriend. Either could have easily graced the cover of Vogue in my opinion. The boyfriend flashed a blinding smile of white teeth as he replied to her. As I passed by, each of them made a micro-glance towards me, as if checking me out, assessing my potential and then disregarding me as any kind of threat or opportunity. All this in the briefest moment. I wondered if this was how we all judge others. Is it possible to decide in a flash of a second whether someone is a potential object of desire? I'd read that it takes us five seconds to assess each other visually, but I think the Italians have distilled this to a fraction of a second, a micro glance.

A few tables along, four elderly gentlemen sat gathered around a game of dominoes. They studied their respective counters carefully, taking occasional sips of coffee. One looked furtively at his three friends as he slurped on his drink, taking a long sigh as he replaced his cup. Two tables back in, four elderly women – the domino group's wives, I surmised – sat idly watching their husbands and the world in general. Young and old alike were gathered here together, enjoying the late September air. It all looked very enticing, like a grand European drawing room. You never saw this kind of scene back home. In Scotland, it is almost a crime against humanity for parents and children to be seen socialising in the same establishment. Even then, in 1985, my father's local pub had a separate entrance to what was known as a 'snug' bar, still the preserve of male drinkers. This scene before me now looked a far more socially inclusive way to live. Or perhaps it was simply because the Piazza San Marco in Venice is one of those places in the world that draws both locals and tourists of all ages together, to linger for hours in a place of religious importance and historic interest, where you can be part of the world and also watch it pass by at the same time. If you sit here long enough you'll probably see everyone in the world pass by at some point.

Inclusive or not, I felt incongruous in my shorts, travel-weary t-shirt and backpack, compared with these smart-casual café customers, so I gingerly wandered out on the main square. I hovered outside one of the bars, under cover of the colonnade, my plan being to ask someone if there was a youth hostel or cheap guest house nearby.

A waiter spoke to me, briskly, in Italian. It was my first real encounter with the Italian language and I was utterly lost. Nothing that came from the waiter's mouth sounded even vaguely familiar. Having struggled to improve my French over the past few weeks, I was now firmly back to square one. Even in Spain, I'd managed to figure out what was what or find a Spaniard who spoke a little English to help. Here, now, in the Piazza San Marco, it was time to face the prospect of trying to communicate with people in their own language once again.

The waiter yelled 'Inglesi' to a colleagues, while gesturing towards me. For five minutes the waiters marched back and forth, ferrying espressos, cappuccinos, small cakes on plates and, decadent little glasses of liqueur. Deciding perhaps I stood a better chance of help if I was a customer, I took a seat at the nearest table and waited for service. I didn't even know Italian for 'half a lager', but eavesdropping on other customers and listening-in to waiters barking orders back and forth to the barman pays dividends. Eventually, one of the older waiters reluctantly approached my table with a curt nod. He had an impatient air, but I impressed him when I said loudly and clearly, "una birra, per favore", flashing a triumphant, white smile. Then he nodded and smiled, gave another bow of the head and repeated my words to his colleague behind the bar, before scurrying off to another table.

The waiters buzzed here and there, serving their

customers. I sipped my beer and soaked up the balmy evening and these new surroundings. I had no idea how long the bar had been established, but it gave the impression of having been around for centuries. Perhaps they'd been serving drinks here since the Piazza was created.

Some of the customers had that look too. They were like immortal actors, rolled out extras providing the backdrop. The ageless hum of the locals.

Under the colonnade large lamps hung, atmospheric stage lights, illuminating the walkways around the Piazza. The focal point was the tower of St Mark's, tall, proud and quiet against the starry sky. Couples ambled across the square. The sound of moored gondolas and riverboats bumping and grinding against each other provided a background for the chatter on the square.

"Mi scusi – I'm looking for a student hotel. Can you help?" I held out the youth hostel guidebook to the old waiter. He inspected the page where I'd found a list of cheap student hostels. I couldn't figure out where they were as there was no correspondent map that made any sense. And I was so sleepy… The Italian waiter studied the book for a few minutes. He walked over to the bar and shared the pages with the barman, who glanced over at me before studying the book again and then muttered something to the waiter while shaking his head. It didn't look hopeful.

Eventually, the old waiter returned and handed the guidebook back.

"Ehh, dunno," he said, shrugging his shoulders. I looked back at him. "

You speak English?" I asked a couple of times, but he just smiled and scuttled off to serve some new customers out in the square.

I settled up and left the café, deciding to take one of the small passageways behind the colonnade, to search for a hostel. The colonnade was lined with glamorous shops with names I'd never heard of and strange new words skilfully etched into the discreet windows: Versace, Armani, Gucci. My sheltered Scottish upbringing had never introduced me to these names. I reached an eerily quiet street, with few people, no boats drifting along the river-way and it was less well lit. Old buildings loomed over the canal reflecting in the gently bobbing water. Glimmers of light trickled from occasional doorways and foyers beyond small closed gates. None appeared to lead to hostels, so I crossed a bridge and weaved my way deeper into the back annals of the city on the sea.

The deeper I penetrated the city's back streets, the quieter it grew..

Now and then I'd turn a corner to find a few guys lingering by the steps of a bridge, or by the entrance to a bar, already closed. Didn't they have homes to go to? A faded sign on the corner of a building indicated I was on the Rio Terre Assassina, a narrow, winding street, where the buildings on either side seemed about to fall onto each other. As I looked up I saw arched windows, some framed by ornate, decorative stone. Islands of exposed brickwork on the walls of these otherwise plastered, close-quartered buildings suggested times were not easy. When the plaster fell off no-one seemed to repair it.

I turned another corner. On the steps of another tenement block, sat a trio of youths. Some eyed me, suspiciously. I tried not to eye them back.

Deeper into the labyrinth, I came across another tiny street bridge, where yet more guys were gathered. I took a big breath and decided to approach them. I used the pretence of asking for a light for my cigarette and then tried to make them understand I was looking for a hotel or guest house.

The tallest, slimmest guy looked at his friends, then me, and smiled.

"Aah, signor, PENSIONE, PENSIONE!"

"Yeah, that's right, si, si, Pensione." I couldn't believe it. That's the exact word they use in France! I'd spent days at Madame Gilbert's Pension in Nice, and here I am in Venice and it's the same word! I beamed back, laughing at the strangeness of it all – why hadn't the waiters at the bar just said "pensione"? How did I not even think of trying to use the French word? I stood before these four Italian guys with my arms in the air saying: "Si, pensione. Où? Where?"

One of them beckoned to me to follow, so we set off along a series of new passageways and over little bridges, in search of a room for me. Occasionally, he would look at me and we'd smile. His long jet black hair and tanned skin made his teeth look super white.

Italians, I decided, were even more handsome than the Spanish or French. They seemed more confident, too. I remembered the friends I knew at school, the Mordentes, Capaldis and Anconas, but they didn't look like these guys. Back in Scotland, my Italian school friends had Scottish accents and pale skin, although their parents, the first generation of Italians to move there, still had traces of their exotic accents.

"Eenglish?" he asked.

"Si, Scottish", I replied.

He smiled again and shook his head. I offered him a cigarette, which to my mind had pretty much become the international symbol of peace whenever I encountered strangers and needed their help.

"Mi Sam," I said to him as we walked along.

"Aah, si. Sam," he repeated pointing at me. Then, turning his hand to his chest, "Francesco."

"Great. Francesco." I repeated, returning the gesture by pointing back at him. I extended my hand and he shook it vigorously, but playfully.

After five minutes of winding our way through the close-knit streets of Venice, he stopped outside a building that had seen better days. The red plaster finish was riddled with spots where it had eroded and fallen away leaving the sublayer of brickwork exposed to the elements. Stepping back, Francesco shouted up at a window on the first floor. His voice was loud and I was embarrassed he might wake the entire street with his yelling. Soon enough, though, a woman appeared over the lip of the first-floor window sill and yelled back. He shrugged his shoulders and moved to squat on the step of the large green double-doors.

A moment later the left section of the door creaked open and the woman beckoned me in.

"Grazie, Francesco, grazie."

He waved as he sauntered off down the street, while the woman ushered me in through the door. Her jet black hair revealed a few strands of grey along the temples. I guessed she must be in her forties, perhaps older. She gave a perfunctory smile as she fished in the pocket of her green apron, eventually producing a key.

"English? One room, numero tre. Nommer three," she said. You pay now," she insisted.

"Si, grazie. Okay, how much? Quanto?"

I fumbled with the lira notes, showing her eight thousand, nine thousand, ten thousand. When I reached twelve thousand, she held out her hand uttering 'si, si'. I calculated it was just under five pounds (twelve pounds in today's money). Well worth it to have a place to rest after the long journey.

The room was small and sparsely furnished. The bed was to the left as you entered through the door. There was a small white porcelain sink on the wall and a little wooden table beneath the window. A small, floral shade hung from the light fitting on the disproportionately high ceiling. In the dim light, I undressed and brushed my teeth before collapsing into a long travel-weary sleep on the uncomfortable, wood-framed bed.

It was after nine in the morning when I awoke. I jumped into the communal shower along the corridor and headed out to explore Venice. Unlike Madame Gilbert's wonderful hostel in Nice, the guest house here in Venice offered no breakfast hospitality. I found an average priced café. The counter had what looked like croissants, labelled cornetti and pain au chocolat was saccottino al cioccolato. Back home, a cornetto was a famous ice cream cone. Had the ice cream company realised they'd have named their product in error? I also ordered a coffee, the first drink of all Italians, with lots of milk and sugar. I asked the old lady behind the counter to put my coffee into a paper cup as I wanted to have my breakfast on the Canale della Guidecca in front of the Piazza San Marco.

The city was different in the full light of day, but still buzzing with traders and tourists. The occasional group party of tourists gathered in a huddle as their guide stopped to explain this or that particular building of note.

I thought about tagging along, an uninvited addition to the group, but decided against it in case I was spotted by some eagle-eyed tour guide, who'd then make a scene trying to fleece some cash out of me, and rightly so. The shops on the streets near the Piazza San Marco were all open. I looked trying to calculate the prices for wallets, clothes and other items. They all seemed incredibly expensive.

At the Grand Canal, the full splendour of Venice was revealed. In the bright sunlight, the water glistened and sparkled while the ancient buildings, towers and domes sat proud and regal in the haze. I watched the near-mythical gondolas, water buses and speedboats come and go.

I stared across the water to the Isola di San Giorgio Maggiore, where the impressive rust coloured monastery and its attendant buildings floated in regal age-defying splendour. I guessed it must be around 500 or so years old and wondered how they built such a structure in those days, without modern machinery or transportation. It must have taken decades and cost a king's ransom. Sighing, I realised Venice must have cost many kings' ransoms as the opulence and grandeur exuded from every building.

I wanted to speed across the canal for a closer look, but my budget dictated the distant view was all I could afford for now.

Instead, I finished my pauper's breakfast and walked back to take in the famous landmark red-stone tower that dominates the main piazza, the Campanile di San Marco. The most famous landmark in the city, I thought it grand but slightly austere and overpowering. It looked out of place sitting right next to St Mark's Basilica – which I immediately thought of as Venice's Taj Mahal. By comparison with the bell tower, the Basilica, with its ornate domes, opulent gold crested peaks and spires, the grand arched portals and detailed design was breathtaking. I spent an hour outside, taking photographs, inspecting the celestial looking mosaics depicting the life of Christ. Mum would love this, I thought, as I inched my way along the building's facade. We were raised as Roman Catholics, so she'd doubtless be inspired that I was appreciating the history of our family religion and not just beach-bumming the entire time.

It was late afternoon by the time I had finished inspecting every inch of the Piazza San Marco and its imposing architecture. Then I headed along the Riva degli Schiavoni, a promenade that heads east along the canal from the Piazza San Marco. The promenade was bustling with market stalls, selling olives and oils, cheeses and meats. Hunger pangs erupted from my stomach as the smells wafted past. I noticed many of the stalls had tiny little taster plates and seized on this as a way to enjoy a free snack. To cover my embarrassment at not being able to buy any of the foods, I'd fall in with a group standing at this or that stall, and, along with them taste samples of the vendors' products. Members of the groups would then purchase some of the products. After ten minutes I'd eaten a hearty lunch of olives, cheese, dried meats and delicious Italian rough cuts of bread dipped in an assortment of delicious olive oils. One stall offered tiny cups of white wine for tasting. The group bought two bottles, and after washing down my lunch with a mouthful of wine I casually but resolutely wandered away from them and disappeared into the city.

A large crowd had gathered on a bridge over one of the tributaries leading to the main canal and I went to see what the fuss was about. I didn't know what we were looking at, but fortunately, a small party of American tourists were also looking up the canal.

"Look, Lindsay, it's the famous Bridge of Sighs." I'm not sure whether they commented it was "quaint" or anything, but I was pleased for once that the habit of making loud proclamations, for which Americans are so often maligned, had paid off in my favour. I hadn't realised it was so close to the main piazza, and I was glad to have stumbled upon it. I'd read about the legends and stories of the Ponte dei Sospiri. I imagined the criminals of old heaving their last sighs as they were ferried by gondola to the cells of the adjacent prison. Another legend says the lovers who kiss on a gondola as they pass under the Bridge of Sighs will be forever blessed with an unbreakable love. I made a mental note that if ever I fell in love, I would bring my lover to Venice and carry out this legendary deed.

The afternoon sun was losing its intensity as I walked back through the tiny streets to my room. I felt that I had done Venice, as far as possible on a backpacker's budget. Perhaps I should take the train to Rome after all, stopping off along the way.

Back at the hostel, the landlady was waiting with a pensive brow. As I passed through the open door to the hallway she started talking to me in a slightly apologetic

246

and pleading voice.

"Scusate, scusate signor. Scusate."

"Sorry, I don't understand." After about five minutes of trying to comprehend what the signora was saying and making my own gestures I managed to fathom she was saying that she couldn't let me have the room any longer and I had to leave.

"Problemo?"

"Non, eh, si, mi famiglia..."

Ten minutes later I was again on the streets of Venice, with nowhere to stay. The landlady's family squabble seemed to have necessitated the requisitioning of my room. A neighbour joined the conversation to help explain the reasons for evicting me. At least she refunded some of the upfront cash I had paid her the night before.

I sat in a café on the Piazza St Marco, wondering about had happened. Cupping my hands around a sugared, chocolatey cappuccino I weighed things up. France I loved, because it felt so, well, French. It was becoming familiar, yet foreign at the same time and steeped in history and decadence. Spain had been great. Barcelona was deliciously heavy with heat, dust and had an edginess to it that mesmerised me. Benidorm and Alicante appeared to have succumbed to the package holiday industry. Honestly, I'd never seen so many fish and chip shops in one place as I had in Benidorm. Monte Carlo was the first playground of the really rich and famous I'd encountered. The opulence, finely coiffured public spaces and the sheer smell of money and wealth was so heavily scented James Bond himself appeared to lurk around every corner. And it wasn't just wealthy Brits that Monte Carlo drew to its luxurious apartments and hotels, overpriced restaurants and pristine beaches. The rich worldwide lined up for a place in the millionaire sunspot of Monaco.

I'd only spent one night in Italy and I wasn't sure I wanted to risk being turfed out of another hostel on some whim of a family dispute. I thought about the plan of catching a train to Rome, visiting the coastal towns on the Mediterranean and finding unknown villages to explore. I dug out my bumbag from the rucksack and inspected my travellers' cheques. I was running out of money and wasn't sure how much longer it would last. After an hour, I resolved instead to head back to France. I liked Nice and Madame Gilbert's cosy – and affordable - pension. Finishing my cappuccino, I reckoned I could still catch a train tonight, be back in Nice by tomorrow morning and the journey would also save the cost of a night's hostel accommodation. The more I thought, the more determined I became on this plan.

The river taxi was particularly fast tonight. It was as if the world was conspiring to help my back up plan. It stopped just once on the route from the Piazza to the station.

I lopped up the wide steps and jogged over to the ticket office. There were some people ahead of me in the queue. A good sign, I figured, as this meant there must be a train heading somewhere tonight. While the couple directly ahead of me arranged their travel documents with the station clerk, I fished out my little Interrail travel booklet for them to stamp. Standing there, travel documents and passport in hand, I realised how great it was to be able to be so mobile at such short notice. Youth and its unbound sense of freedom allow for such instant and clear decision making.

There was indeed a train leaving for Marseilles, which would stop at Nice among many other places along the route. The station clerk took the Interrail booklet and inspected it closely and carefully, noting all the previous stamps. Eventually, he picked up his stamp tool and added the words 'Venezia, Italia'.

I had an hour to spare, so I I bought some crisps, a cheese sandwich and a small bottle of Valpolicella.

The train wasn't anywhere near as crowded as the trains in Spain had been. I boarded at coach four and wandered along the carriage corridors until I reached coach nine, where my cabin was situated. I had discovered a long time ago, when I was much younger, that a great way to check out the other passengers on a train is to board at an earlier point and then amble through the train, slowly. You never really know who you're going to meet.

I wasn't expecting to meet anyone I knew on this train, so far away from home. But I was able to get a passing glance at what Italian people wore when they travelled, who they were travelling with and how they spoke. I decided that Italians were the most mysterious and exotic I had yet encountered. There were elderly women who for some reason seemed to keep their heads bowed. If they spoke, they only did so in whispers to each other. Was it a profound respect for the peace of other travellers, or a lifetime of being seen and not heard? I couldn't know. I made my way past them. Scattered through the coaches, businessmen with briefcases and overnight bags sat alone. One, in his late forties, with greying hair, expertly and neatly greased into place, took drags on his cigarette as he wearily studied some thick document. He looked bored with it, as if he'd suffered years of silently doing a job that meant little to him, the dreary drudgery of selling some product he had little personal connection to or interest in. But how could he have any alternative ambition at his age? What else could he do in life, but work, whatever it may entail, to give him the income required in order to keep a roof over his family's head, put bread on his table and heat in his home? It reminded me of the dull job I'd left only a month ago. If I hadn't decided to get out, this man could have been me in about 30 years time.

Another man, slightly younger, tanned, slim and confident looking, also studied his papers closely. His aura conveyed less weariness, more youthfully self-assured confidence. Flipping a page of his document, his face suggested whatever the pages were advising on how to achieve success in his mission, he knew better and was going to follow his own method of achieving the same result. I decided this was a modern Italian. Unlike his older counterpart further down the train, his vibrant jet black hair was cut short and close and smart. No Brylcream for this ambitious young entrepreneur. His smooth skin and beguiling smile would doubtless charm many secretaries into giving him access to the people in power. While the first man reminded me not to get trapped in a job I would loathe, this gentleman made me realise that some kind of occupation is important. One needs to be useful.

He dragged on his cigarette – everyone seemed to smoke in Italy – and suddenly turned his gaze towards me. Our eyes met briefly, then he cut away again, back to his papers. Perhaps he just saw another tourist visiting Italy. A generic representation of a new generation of people slightly younger than him, for whom the world was a place to explore.

I wondered what Madame Gilbert would have to say about them. She'd point out that they were most certainly spies. "Look at zhem. Zhey could be Russians, Non?" I imagined her voice whispering into my ear. "Zhey are supposed to look like ziz, you know. C'est vrai. I read about it in Le Figaro. Who can say?"

Everyone was calm, ready for a long night's journey. Back then, before mobile devices, laptops and tablets, people respected the peace and quiet of their fellow passengers. All these modern devices are an essential part of my life now, and I couldn't be without them. But I take great care not to inflict my telephone conversations on anyone around me when I'm traveling. I'm also too embarrassed to carry on such conversations when others can eavesdrop on them. The mobile phone has revolutionised our lives, but, with the great leap forward in personal mobile technology, some personal space has also been sacrificed.

The hushed voices on the Venice-Nice overnight express petered out as the train edged out of Venice Station. I still hadn't reached my carriage, ambling as I was through the train. I wondered if I looked to them like the embodiment of the modern traveller. The bright rucksack on my back, with the lumber support across my waist and the electric blue sleeping bag, rolled up and firmly strapped to the bottom of it. Elderly travellers took more interest in me than the other passengers did. I must've looked like an alien invader, a strange new product of a modern age that they were yet to understand.

I'm convinced that there must have been some young Italians of a similar age as I was then, embarking on similar journeys of discovery. However, most of backpackers I encountered were British, northern European or American. Perhaps, given the socio-economics of Spain and Italy back then, not every young person had the wherewithal (or permission) to head off for a month in Europe. And why would they want to anyway? The British are among the most seasoned travellers in the world. We've always gone out to see what the rest of the world is like. Perhaps it's because we're an island race. More likely because our climate is so wet. I wondered if I'd ever leave home if I was lucky enough to be a southern European.

Unlike the open carriages I'd passed through further down, coach 912 was comprised of a long corridor with private cabins of six tan coloured leather seats. I pulled open the door, unfastened my rucksack and threw myself into the forward facing window seat.

The cabin was large and the seats surprisingly sumptuous for my 19-year-old frame. I sat staring out of the window for about ten minutes. I could see the darkness of the water interspersed with rippling light from the shore and then we were back on the mainland and it was increasingly difficult to see anything.

There was a light switch above the door to the cabin, with a turnable nob next to it. I worked out that this dimmed the cabin lights to the point of darkness. Cool. I then discovered that each of the large, bulbous, leathery seats pulled out towards the midsection of the cabin effectively creating three beds. So I tweaked the levers to create a window bed out of the two window seats. I unpacked the pillows and white sheets that were carefully stored in the overhead rack and pulled the curtains closed. This was travelling in style. I thought for a moment that I may be in the wrong coach, but I double checked my ticket and this was definitely the right place. It was a welcome break after being turfed out of the hostel in Venice I was so happy that I was going to get a fairly decent night's sleep in an almost flat bed, that I didn't even wonder what the first class cabins on the train might be like.

The cabin was warm. I lay on top of the sheets in just my shorts, reading through my travel guide. Strangely, after the surreal beauty and strange water based experience of Venice, it somehow felt like I was heading home, even though only a few days ago the Côte d'Azur was just as new to my young eyes. Perhaps Venice would have lent itself to me in a similar way, had the senora not evicted me. Madame Gilbert at the pension in Nice would never turf out her 'James Bond', I was sure. I looked forward to being fussed over by her again, forcing hot chocolate on me at breakfast time and making sure I knew where I was going each time I set off from her guest house.

My thoughts were interrupted by squeals and raised voices coming from further down the corridor. I threw on my t-shirt, pulled open the door and popped my head out looking right. A small group of slim, Italian boys were making boisterous noises and laughing loudly together. They seemed on a mission, searching for something, or someone. They would converse in hushed tones and then let out loud squeals of excited laughter. As suddenly as they appeared, they all filed out back to whence they came. Their voices now dimmed by the increasing distance between us. I lingered in the doorway to my cabin for a bit. I smoked a cigarette and practised a moody, scowl in case they came back. I miss being able to smoke on trains – and planes – I don't care what anyone says, it adds a romantic patina to one's journey. There's something about a smoky haze on a train and back then, no-one seemed to complain about it.

The group of Italian boys all smoked too. That's what made me want one myself. Just as I was about to turn in

I heard the connecting door at the end of the carriage open once again and prepared myself for them to come screeching down the corridor. Instead, two girls, I guessed to be about 20 years-old came limping towards me, struggling with their backpacks, handbags and sleeping bags. The first was a rather attractive girl whose vibrant yellow blonde shoulder-length hair swung jovially as she wrestled with her luggage. Behind her, a tall brunette with a sculpted look and athletic body had no such problem and appeared to be patiently waiting as her blonde friend struggled ahead of her.

"Hi," I said, moving into the cabin and out of the way.

"Oh God, are you English?"

"Yes, well, actually, Scottish, but..."

"Oh great. Lucy, we're going in here. Look you're my brother alright? Anyone asks. Shit, just get us away from these bloody sex mad dogs."

"Of course," I said, "Come in, actually I have..."

"Hi, I'm Lucy, thanks, thank you, so much...can we just shut the door, quickly and turn out the lights?"

I ushered both girls into the couchette, pulled the door closed and dimmed the lights.

"Let me take that," I pulled the rucksack off the blonde girl's back and tossed it up onto the rack, Lucy did the same with her own bags. "Quick, both of you sit there with your legs up off the floor." They obeyed as I pulled out all the other seats to make additional beds, yanked down the other blankets and told them to get under them. I took the "bed" by the door, tore off my top and just as the guys came noisily down the corridor I opened the door...

"Oi, shhhhhhhh, famiglia. Huh?" I wasn't even sure that this was Italian or that they would understand what I was saying, but I had learned that in some circumstances, the moment itself, together with the tone of what is being said, leaves people in no doubt that they are being told to shut up and be quiet. The gang of youths all stopped, glanced in briefly and gestured apologies, before quietly sloping off. I closed the door and squinted out towards the corridor from an awkward corner of the curtains. They had gone.

"Oh my God," said the bouncy blonde, she seemed to like the God word, "that was bloody cool, what's your name? I'm Sally. Thanks for helping us. Those guys are feral. Typical bloody Italians. Girls aren't allowed to travel alone in Italy, so they think it's the only chance of any nookie they're gonna get."

"I'm Sam," I said chuckling, "Glad I could help you out. You're English then?"

"Yes. We've been travelling around Italy, but you won't believe how much hassle we've had with blokes every bleeding place we go."

I took out the cheap bottle of wine I'd bought in Venice, pulled out the cork, and we talked.

Having only done France, Spain and Italy on my

travels, I said I felt I hadn't chalked up enough countries on the 'backpackometer' and thought I was letting the side down, but Lucy was having none of it.

"Oh God," she uttered (again), "That sounds so much better than what we've been doing. We flew out to Rome and had this great idea we'd travel around the entire Mediterranean coast discovering the small villages and towns off the beaten track. It's been lovely, but we've also had to deal with desperate country boys stalking us like women were a dying breed. I'm completely over it."

I laughed, "It must be great to be hot property, no?" Sally pushed her blanket away from her body, and confidently crossed her long, slim legs. Her tight blue and white striped tank top revealed slender tanned arms and a flat stomach. She was assured, graceful and vulnerable; the kind of girl I liked. I could see why they both attracted so much attention.

"So where are you planning on going next?" I asked.

Sally took a long glug of wine from the bottle, "Where are YOU going?"

I thought for a moment. "Well, I know a rather exclusive little hotel, just minutes from the beach in Nice. The landlady insists on calling me Bond, James Bond."

They looked at each other and nodded.

"Well, that's settled," said Sally. "We'll be your Bond girls..."

We chatted for another half hour or so before fatigue

257

and the wine got to us and we surrendered ourselves to the gentle rumbling of the Venice-Marseilles express.

* * * * *

"Ladies & gentlemen, we will shortly be arriving at Tours, this is a disembarkation stop only," the Eurostar manager repeats in English and French.

I look out the train window to see only three or four people disembark. Half an hour and we'll be pulling into Poitiers. I'm looking forward to dropping my bag and heading out to the restaurant to see everyone.

I message Michelle from my iPhone. "Just pulling into Tours. See you soon. Sx"

* * * * *

17. Return to Nice

The girls and I were groggy and dirty after our journey from Venice. I led the way to Madame Gilbert's little pension.

"Oh, oh, il est retourné, tu es ici. Bienvenu, welcome. Ooh, my little James Bond." Madame Gilbert made quite a motherly fuss over me before turning to the girls.

"Ca va Madame? Madame Gilbert, these are my friends. They need a room and I told them about your fantastic hotel."

"Aw, c'est gentil, but eet is no good. I only have one room free. But leesten. It has deux lits, two beds. One double and one single. Why not the three of you stay in thees room?"

I looked at the girls and they happily agreed. When you're travelling in Europe on a budget and need a room, you don't waste time being prudish about the nature of your accommodation. The bathroom facilities were in the corridor anyway, so the three of us piled upstairs behind Madame Gilbert.

We took turns to shower and dress, and headed out to the beach. After the overnight train trip, today had to be a chill-out exercise, to recharge our batteries and enjoy the hot, restful calm of the Med once again.

I got to know more about these two English girls. They had been friends since school and this was their first expedition to Europe by train. They had been on package tours before, of course, to Spain's Costa Brava and to Corfu.

"This is much better, though," said Lucy. "You really get to experience the countries better by train."

"We were thinking of heading to Monte Carlo tomorrow for the day. Want to come?"

"Well, I've already been. You should go, though, it's really expensive but worth seeing how the other half lives, eh?"

I had other plans. I wanted to head into the hills around Nice. I had read about the town of St Paul de Vence, an old fortified hilltop town about 40 minutes away. It has amazing views of the surrounding landscape, which I was told was covered with colourful flowers, olive trees and vine groves.

The girls lay back on their towels and soaked up the late September sun. I went into the warm Mediterranean waters for a swim. It was great being on my own adventure, but I greatly enjoyed their company. No, I craved it. At 19, I was still young enough to be able to easily make a party, a group, team up with strangers. A handy side benefit to having company at the beach was that, once again, I didn't have to watch my belongings from the water.

I swam lengths, spending energy, making myself breathless from the swim, the endorphins coursing through my body, the hot sun beating down on my back and shoulders, now bronzed beyond any colour they had ever been. I liked it. I felt invincible, youthful, joyous and happy.

I was like a fish in the warm waters of the Côte d'Azur. Perfectly at home, slicing through the gentle sea, arm after arm. With one head turn I saw infinity, where the azure sky appeared to meet the sea; with the other, I saw where the shingle beach ducked down into the sea, the whole scene flanked by the gleaming white buildings of the promenade. This must be the most perfect place in the world.

Nice was lethargic, lazy, reposed, at leisure. Everything and everyone moved in slow motion, the hot sun acting like a slow-mo on energy levels. Tourists baked on towels and loungers. Everyone seemed content, enjoying their rest, their 'vacances', the two weeks of the year they would frolic carelessly with nature.

After fifteen minutes swimming parallel with the beach, exhausted, I stopped for breath. Treading water, I faced the beach and watched the girls sunbathing. Gorgeous, beautiful, graceful creatures and I was sharing a room with them.

'What's wrong with you?' A voice in my head asked.

'Why don't you just make a play for one or both of them?' Perhaps that's what they were hoping for. 'Do they even like me that way?' How could they know that I was by now almost certain that I was gay? Almost certain but still trying to figure out my identity. Perhaps they could tell? Was their women's intuition allowing them to read the unspoken signals I was giving out? I wanted to be excited about them, by them. I found myself wanting to want their bodies. But it was no use, I just couldn't feel it. I let out a sigh, knowing that this was not the life I was going to live. Here, face to face with two lovely English girls I should have been flirting, cajoling, chasing and getting horny, but no matter how much I wanted it, it just couldn't be and I knew I could never live a lie. Taking a girl as a cover to help hide my true nature would be to destroy the life of an innocent. I could never do that. And I never have. Enough thinking of this, I told myself. I took a big breath and dived down again into the cloudy sea.

Later, at the pension, we took turns to shower. Although we shared a room, we still had modesty. The girls got changed in the bathroom, I returned wrapped in my towel, sat on my bed while I dried fully. I was always told not to rush dressing after a shower or bath. The body needs time to cool down, the skin should be fully dry before one starts dressing. Years later, in London, I would become a regular at the luxury gym that occupies the old arches beneath Cannon Street Station. I'd shiver in disdain as the other guys in the changing room rushed to dress after their showers, the wetness of their bodies seeping into their shirts, through their socks.

I've always thought it looked most uncomfortable.

Once dry, I pulled on my underwear, the girls discreetly talking to each other and looking away from me. There's something about the way we Brits always seem to get it, without needing to be told. By turning away of their own accord, the girls were trying to prevent me from feeling any awkwardness or shyness. But I wasn't shy. Strangely, I didn't care that they saw me changing. Once I had my underwear on I threw off the towel and leapt up. "Decent again," I joked, as I stood there in the tiniest pair of briefs I owned.

They both laughed. Sally exclaimed "Jeez, look at your tan line. You are so black." They laughed about my underwear, which was more like a thong. "Chuck me your camera, we need a memento of this..."

I resisted, but the girls started rifling through my rucksack and pulled out the camera.

"Now pose, hot shot," Sally said, as she pointed the little camera at me. I tried to flex my torso, hoping that any kind of muscle would make the effort to show up.

These were the days before digital cameras, before selfies, before camera phones. It would be weeks, possibly months before I could see the photos. Too late to edit them if they were unflattering. The spool of camera film would sit at home until I got around to posting it off to the processors. Then more time would pass before they were developed and sent back.

It's a world away from how we do it nowadays. We

can instantly view, review, edit, delete or keep a photo. I love this instant ability to see if an image has worked. I take most of my pictures with my mobile phone now. And while there was a certain something about having to wait weeks to see your photos in the old days, I'm not sure I would want to go back to the old ways.

I pulled on the now faded Pepe shorts (they used to be jeans, but I'd cut them down after they'd started to soften) and a t-shirt and we all headed out into the warm evening air.

We wandered along the Avenue des Anglais, taking in the vista of the Mediterranean. Cars and mopeds sped up and down the long beachside road, while hordes of other tourists and locals meandered along the promenade. Once again the resplendent facade of the Negresco stood out. We looked into the upmarket restaurants at all the well turned out grown-ups, ordering their suppers, tasting their wine, chatting to each other. Waiters glided around them, tending their needs.

We found a little café just off the seafront, agreeing the prices were just about within our budget. We grabbed a table on the pavement outside, ordered three omelettes and three beers.

Over the next few days I trekked up to St Paul de Vence, alone, and spent a hot afternoon wandering around this Provencal hilltop town. It was like you could see forever. I spent more than an hour sitting at a viewpoint alone, almost meditative, taking in this beautiful place, wondering what the world had in store for me next.

We spent a couple more days together at the beach in Cannes. Like all young travellers, we'd got to know each other quite well in that short time, but it seemed like longer. When you're young, time is more elastic. However, it was getting close to the moment for me to start making my way north. Time to leave this beautiful place and take the train up to Paris, then on to London and finally home to Scotland.

"It all seems so far away and unreal," I said to them as we sat in a café waiting for our dinner to arrive. "It' would be great to just keep going, but my money's getting low."

"Well, maybe you could get a bar job here," Lucy suggested, helpfully. I smiled, knowing I'd never succeed on the tiny amount of French I understood.

"We have another week, so we're going to train it over to Barcelona and see all that wonderful Gaudi architecture," Sally said.

"It's great, when you get to the Sagrada Familia, let me know if it follows you around. You'll understand what I mean later." I also warned them to be mindful of pickpockets, especially on the Ramblas.

"What will you do when you get home?"

"Dunno. Try to find a job. Save more money to go travelling again. Maybe I'll travel across America next," I fantasized. "I just want to see the world".

"I'd love to go to India," Lucy declared. " I hear it's

incredibly cheap once you're there. I mean ridiculously cheap. You can live for a month on twenty pounds."

"Yeah, but the Deli-belly's a bit of a turnoff, eh?" I told them about my friend Simon, who had been in India staying at an ashram for six months. He had written home informing everyone that he'd lost half his body weight during his time there, having caught amoebic dysentery.

"But it'd be great to visit, just to see all the temples and the plantations in the mountains," I agreed.

Later, we strolled along the promenade one last time. We promised to keep in touch, to write often, to send our holiday photos to each other once they were developed. It was a warm and balmy evening and we all agreed we were going to miss the carefree life of an Interrailer.

Sally offered a philosophical solution to the poverty of teenagers and students. "We should all be given a million pounds at the start of our adult lives and it has to last us. That way we can go see the world, then buy a flat and start our working lives once all the travel is done."

"I'm up for that," Lucy chipped in.

"Aye, aye," I added, raising my arm. "Motion carried."

On our way back to the hotel, Lucy bought a cheap bottle of red wine from a little store. We crept up the stairs of the Pension Gilbert, our motherly hostess nowhere to be seen. Lucy prised open the wine grabbed the sink glasses and poured us all a farewell drink.

"C'était un plaisir de te connaître, compagnon de voyage, Sam," Sally said. I had a rough idea what she was saying.

"Merci mademoiselles. Et le même à vous."

18. Journey home

As usual, Madame Gilbert was fussing and running around serving breakfast to her guests. But today she appeared to be slightly more vexed than usual, holding back sniffles as she tended to us all at breakfast.

The three of us sat at our usual table, furthest from the window. Madame Gilbert poured coffee for Sally and Lucy, then disappeared briefly into the kitchen, before returning with a large mug of hot chocolate for me. She didn't look at me, but hurried out of the room once more, before returning a minute later with a tray full of eggs, enough for three.

"Ah am veery sad zat yew are leafing my hotel today, mon petit chéri." She gently ruffled my hair with her left hand as she placed the freshly boiled eggs before us, with a plateful of toasted croissants in the centre of the table.

"Ahm sorry, I don't know if yew vil get ze croissants in ze egg, but I thought yew would like seez."

I looked up at Madame Gilbert and smiled, then I rose and gave her a hug. She sniffled once more, smiled and planted a kiss on each cheek.

"Oh it is so silly of me, eat before it gets froid," then she rushed out of the room.

"Aw, you'll always have a mother in France," Sally said. I blushed as I tucked into my egg and croissants. I was so happy to feel safe, cared for and loved so far from home. Mum would have been very pleased to know that people like Madame Gilbert were looking after her son on his European adventure.

When we settled our bill at the tiny counter in the tight hallway of the Pension Gilbert, our landlady bade the girls goodbye with polite hugs and kisses. And as I picked up my rucksack and thanked our hostess once more she threw her arms around me.

"Beautiful boy, yew must veeseet us again very soon, oui, yes? We love to 'ave people like you 'ere, eet is always our plaisir. Oh, bon voyage. Be careful huh? Oh, and 'eer is a little snack for your long voyage. The train food es 'orrible" She thrust a neatly packed parcel of sandwiches into my hands.

"Madame, merci beaucoup, you have looked after me, us, like a mother. I will never forget you. Je ne t'oublierai jamais."

I left and joined the girls on the street. Madame Gilbert stood in the doorway of the Pension Gilbert and waved us off.

"Au revoir, au revoir."

We waved back, echoing her goodbye and marched

off feeling happy and sad. That was the last time I ever saw Madame Gilbert. I often wonder what happened to her. The Pension Gilbert, as far as I know, no longer exists.

We had hours to kill before our trains, so Sally, Lucy and I meandered down to the seafront laden with our backpacks and bags for one last look at the French Riviera.

The three of us sat on a bench looking out at the sea.

"Season's changing," Sally said. "The clouds are coming, so it's a good job we're going south to Spain. And it's good you're heading home, just as the weather's changing."

"Wish I could come with you, though," I moaned.

"Well, we love you for saving us in Venice. Don't know what we would have done without that wonderful night in your couchette. Mr James Bond," said Sally.

That last afternoon we ambled around the streets, looking in shop windows at things we couldn't afford, watching les Nicoises go about their business, pointing out things we'd not noticed before in a last gasp attempt to nail our experience of Nice. Then, in the late afternoon, we made our way to the Gare, where our trains would spirit us apart to our next destinations.

When you're young you don't mind spending hours waiting around in towns and train stations. You find things to talk about, joke about, laugh about. The stations themselves are points of interest and destinations in their own way. They are points of separation, for romantic goodbyes, where families wave off loved ones, or indeed welcome them back after being away on their travels. And, of course, they are also places where spies furtively linger, perhaps waiting to meet a contact with a package that will end the Cold War.

I envied that Lucy and Sally were bound for Spain. I'd only briefly tasted the wonder of that amazing country and I wanted more, but money forbade that possibility. Just then I really wished for Sally's idea about a million pounds for the young.

My overnight train to Paris was first to arrive, and as it pulled slowly into the station, I jumped up, dusted myself down and wiped my face with my hands. I was more tanned than I'd ever been in my life. This was the end of the sun-seeking on my journey. Lucy and Sally leapt up too for a group hug and I kissed each of them on the cheek.

"You lucky girls, Spain is gonna be great. Remember what I said, though, about being careful with your valuables."

"Oh shut up, we'll be fine," Sally chirped. "It's been great hanging out with you."

Lucy smiled at me. "And thanks again for saving us from the Italian guys on the train. And for Madame Gilbert, we are definitely gonna go back and visit her."

We had one last long hug and then we all walked towards the long train. I threw my rucksack in the doorway of one of the carriages and turned to the girls.

"Thanks for being such great travel friends. I'll write to you later when you're back in England. Just don't forget this Scottish guy. I love this whole travel thing."

I squeezed passed them and made an exaggerated wave to the city. "Goodbye Nice." Then to the sky. "Au revoir hot weather", then in the direction of Cannes, really stretching now "and sandy beaches."

We all laughed and fell about, revelling in the moment. I climbed the steps of the carriage as the train shunted forward. The girls jumped and waved as we left Nice station. Sally started to run along mimicking a left behind sweetheart, blowing kisses and laughing. I waved back until they disappeared from view in the warm evening dusk.

The sun was setting and the Mediterranean was turning dark as I wandered through the carriages of the train. I found a set of four empty seats I could claim for myself. I settled in, removed my shoes and put my feet up on the opposite seats. Shortly afterwards the guard arrived to check my ticket. After he had stamped it, he asked if I would like a bed for the night. I knew the routine now and protested I couldn't afford it.

"Pas grave. Vien, il n'y a pas beaucoup de personnes."

I picked up my bag and shoes and followed him through the train to the couchettes. Thirty-five francs was all I could give him. He smiled and wished me a "bonne soirée".

The little cabin was like a suite. Four beds all to myself. I sat down, turned down the lights, lit a cigarette. I took out my Walkman and played a tape. It was halfway through Simple Minds' *Glittering Prize*. After this, as if cued up by a DJ for the moment Grace Jones' *La Vie en Rose* trickled into my ears. I stared out of the window knowing these were the last glimpses I would get of the Mediterranean. Who knows when I'll see this again, I thought. Eventually, the little coastal towns and villages became beacons of light above the now black mass of the sea. We ploughed through countless tunnels until the coast disappeared. No more beach.

I made up a bed in the couchette and settled in for the long overnight journey to Paris.

I was awoken by a shunt. Bleary-eyed, I reached over to the window and pulled back the curtain from the right side.

The lights of the station were cold and garish. There were only a few people coming and going. A couple did their coats up before lifting their suitcases and walking along the platform towards the sub level exit. I couldn't see a sign for the name of this town. I didn't care. The warmth of the Mediterranean country was far off now. I pulled the sheets over me, feeling cold for the first time in weeks.

As the great train hauled itself north towards Paris, I drifted in and out of consciousness. Now and then a distant bell would grow louder, before subduing back into the night. I dreamed of the sea, the warm sun, the sand between my toes.

A loud knock on the carriage door woke me. I turned with a start, then remembered where I was. I pulled on the window curtain to find that the sinuous train was weaving its way through the blue-tinted dawn and into the sprawl of suburban Paris.

The morning air was cool and chilly as we all disembarked onto the platform at the Gare D'Austerlitz. I remember thinking how utterly different this was to the lazy heat I'd left behind the previous evening and yet this was still the same country; this was still France. It was early October, so why should it be warm?

The city rush hour was in full swing, but, still wrapped in the odour of the Mediterranean, I couldn't muster the energy to join it. Instead, I headed for a little coffee and pastry stand just outside the station. On a nearby bench, I tossed my rucksack and other bags onto the ground and enjoyed my coffee and croissant.

I must've looked strangely out of place. Still in my Pepe cut-offs and t-shirt, beneath a jacket I'd fished out from the bottom of my rucksack.

I spent half an hour on that bench, smoking and observing the people as they came and went. Every now and then a fresh stream of commuters emerged from the station fanning out in all directions. Metropolitan Paris was handsome, good looking, smart. But the seasons had shifted since I was last here a few weeks ago. In the hot days of early September, Paris went about its business in bright summer wear, white shirts, light trousers, brightly coloured skirts; now Paris wore coats, jackets and autumn scarves.

Some of the people I watched eyed me back, briefly, as they marched to their offices, perhaps envying my fresh sun-tanned face, knowing I must have just returned from warmer climes. I felt European. For the first time, I had a sense of myself beyond the small Scottish world I had been raised in. I was a part of this great vast Continent, by official membership and also as a young traveller discovering new cultures.

The hair on my legs bristled in the cool morning air. I gathered my bags and took refuge in the subterranean warmth of the Paris Metro system. It was a shame to be crossing Paris underground, but I had no idea how to cross the city from Austerlitz to Gare du Nord by bus.

The counter assistant at the SNCF desk in Gare du Nord advised me that the next train to Boulogne-sur-Mer wasn't for another five hours.

"Cinq heures?" I said to the middle-aged clerk. "Okay, monsieur, merci." I offered him my Interrail book which he duly stamped.

I left the station and killed time in the surrounding streets. Despite the cooler weather, the many cafés and restaurants were still busy as customers sat sipping coffees and cognacs. I thought again of Yvonne, having first wandered around the streets of Paris with her only a few weeks ago. I wondered where she was now. Had she enjoyed her travels, too? How did she think of me, now

275

that she must know that I was not the boy for her?

I caught sight of my reflection in the windows of a closed down shop on a street leading down from the Gare du Nord. I stopped and looked back at it. Standing in my denim shorts, sneakers, big jacket and backpack I asked myself: "Who are you? You look different. Taller maybe? Wiser? Perhaps. Or maybe just travelled." I chortled at the mirror image of myself and carried on back to the station.

After an endless wait on the leathery, polished concrete concourse of the station, worn smooth by the shoe soles of millions of travellers over the years, it was time to board the train to Boulogne and the ferry to England and then the final train back to Scotland.

I didn't want to go. Thoughts of turning around and heading back south to the coast rebelled in my head. Why was I going home? What was waiting for me there apart from family? I loved them all of course, but at nineteen I knew that change was coming. It was time to grow up. I had to make something of my life.

Scotland, militant as it was in the mid-1980s, was starved of jobs, opportunities seemed thin on the ground and there was no way I was going back to a numbing existence as a clerk in a place like the Post Office. I needed to make some choices. What would I do in this world? How would I earn, and live? What about university?

Riding through northern France, I sat in the little six-seat compartment and stared out of the window at the green fields, trying to figure out what I wanted to do. I've always fancied myself as a writer. But where does one start? There were just the two of us in the cabin. An older, bearded man, with receding grey hair, sat diametrically opposite, hunched in the corridor seat. He remained buried in his private papers for most of the journey as if trying to figure out some unfathomable, cryptic puzzle. I vaguely observed a figure enter the cabin without taking my eyes off the passing countryside.

"Hello again. Remember me?"

I looked up to find the same journalist I had met on the train to Paris a month ago. What were the chances?

"Oh, hey, hi. Yes, of course. Wow, how are you? What are you doing here?"

"Well, I had to get my interview. Do you remember?"

"Yes, erm, the guy who found the Titanic, right?"

She laughed, "Well remembered. Yes, Jean-Louis Michel."

"Well, it must've been a long interview if you've been gone all this time."

"Ha, ha, very funny. No, I went to do some research and interviewed some of his colleagues. But Michel was still in the US, so I had to come home and then came back out a couple of days ago. But I got it."

"Is it good? Did he tell you everything? How dangerous was it?"

"Well, they never tell you everything, do they?" She winked.

I listened as she told me all about the interview, her questions and his answers, the photos she was shown of the doomed ship at the bottom of the ocean.

"You look different," she said after a while. "Very tanned, wiser perhaps. Did you have a great adventure?"

I blushed at her compliments. Then told her about Paris, Portbou, Barcelona and robbery incident. I was too ashamed to mention the freakish night after imbibing marijuana in Alicante. I went on about how I fell in love with the Côte d'Azur and that I only spent one day in Venice. I told her about Monte Carlo, where all the richest people in the world must surely live, but how the wealth of Monaco had left me feeling very insignificant.

She laughed and commented on the various places I'd visited; smiled as I mentioned the fellow travellers I'd met, and delighted at my description of Madame Gilbert in Nice.

"So what's next?" She asked.

"Well, home first. But I've decided. I'm going to be a journalist, too."

She beamed a smile and sat back in her seat. "Well, that's fantastic. Excellent choice, young man."

* * * * *

The voice of the Eurostar train manager over the

278

onboard tannoy system pulls me back to the present.

"Mesdames et messieurs, dans quelques instants nous arrivons à Poitiers. Poitiers Futuroscope la prochaîne gare..."

Along with some of the other passengers, I gather my belongings. I unplug my iPad, having not watched any of the TV programmes I had loaded for this journey. It doesn't matter. As we wait for the train to enter the station, I savour more thoughts of that long ago journey and how it shaped my life.

How different the world was then and in some ways how similar. For a moment I wish I could be back there, young, free, without a care in the world. Then I wonder about the young traveller I had seen boarding the train at St Pancras International in London, who had prompted my memories. I hope he'll have an equally adventurous time on his travels.

The evening air is warm and balmy, the sun still high in the sky. As I exit the station, there leaning casually against the door of her BMW convertible is my friend, Michelle, gorgeous, glamorous and tanned. She lets out a scream and throws open her arms.

"Hey, darling. Welcome. Great to see you. Everyone's at the restaurant. It's going to be a fab evening. So much to tell you. How was your journey? Relaxing?"

"Yes, lovely. I dreamed I was young again."

"Oh, really? I love those dreams. Now, you get in the front. We have another passenger. Now, where is he?

Oh, there he is. James, sweetie, hello. Look at you."

She hugs the handsome, young backpacker who'd been the prompt for my reminiscences throughout the journey.

"Okay, get in the back James, I'll put your rucksack in the boot.

By the way, this is Sam, he's a TV journalist from London. He knows your mum and dad."

James smiles and holds up his hand to hail me, but says nothing.

Michelle jumps into the driving seat and we speed off up the long hill to the west of Poitiers Gare before taking the N10 south.

"James is spending the weekend with his parents, then he's off Interrailing around Europe of all things," Michelle yells, as we coast through the French countryside in the warm evening sun.

"Lucky thing! You're going to have an absolute ball, young man. I'm so jealous! Aren't you so jealous of him, Sam?"

I look round at him, then turn back to the road ahead and smile.

"Europe by train, eh? Yep, I can guarantee you're going to have a really great adventure."

The End

I just wanted to say a thank you for
reading Changing Trains.
I really hope you enjoyed Sam's journey.
It's very close to my heart.

Now, no pressure, but reviews (any kind) are
super important, because they help
keep my work visible.

If you're happy to add a review, it would help
me more than you know.
Here's a link to the Amazon review page:
https://www.amazon.co.uk/dp/B0791L458N#customerReviews

I also love hearing from my readers,
so please do feel free to come say hi.
You can follow me on social media and
via the website below.
Look forward to hearing from you.

www.mjohnson.uk
Twitter: @MJKennington
Facebook: Mark johnson – Writer
Instagram: Mark Johnson – Author